The Smoking Gun

The Smoking Gun

A.P. Rogers

Matador
Unit E2 Airfield Business Park,
Harrison Road, Market Harborough,
Leicestershire. LE16 7UL
Tel: 0116 2792299
Email: books@troubador.co.uk
Web: www.troubador.co.uk/matador
Twitter: @matadorbooks

ISBN 978 1803132 426

British Library Cataloguing in Publication Data.
A catalogue record for this book is available from the British Library.

Printed and bound in Great Britain by 4edge Limited
Typeset in 11pt Adobe Garamond Pro by Troubador Publishing Ltd, Leicester, UK

Matador is an imprint of Troubador Publishing Ltd

For Gwen

I'm reminded of your wit at the time of that first documentary.

At the media launch the journalist predictably asked me what I'd be if not in the Police. Lost for an answer I said I'd like to be a writer.

When you saw it in print, you laughed and said it was a spelling mistake. It should've read 'waiter'!

Bless you Mum.

CONTENTS

1
COCK UP

"It was the biggest cock up in the annals of Police history." The Deputy Chief of the Force declared as he leant back in what was an obviously comfortable green leather executive style chair, but it gave him little comfort as he sat uneasily opposite Detective Inspector Bob Trebor to whom he was trying to sell a scenario. Trebor faced the second in command of the force who was dressed in full uniform, badges of rank ever prominent on his shoulders, together with a plastic embossed badge on his right chest indicating his name and rank declaring to anyone reading, how important he was.

What a wanker Bob thought, as he let the deputy commit himself to more *'bollocks'* as Bob knew he was listening to, and knowing that 'annals' are history.

To assist you, the reader, where ever you see italics in this account, it's me talking to you, and giving you the 'inside track' on the story, so now I'll put you in the picture. My CID team and I have been raided and arrested on some spurious allegation of corruption seemingly made by a pickpocket who none of us at the material time, had knowingly met. What we think we know is that a bent detective, in every sense of the word, by the name

1

of Dennison, has enabled another pickpocket entirely separately, to make allegations of corruption against us. I suspect the officer did this to cover his own corrupt activity of the past. The. upshot of this is that we as a team are threatening to sue the Force for unlawful arrest, false imprisonment and malicious persecution if not prosecution. It's rattled a few cages as I'm sure you would imagine and is why I find myself, not at my instigation, in front of the deputy chief, a man by the name of Boles. He's trying to effectively buy me off, from continuing with our complaints of corrupt practices of those investigating us, and the threat of litigation, thereby preventing a massive 'shitstorm' for himself and of course those flunkies who carried out his bidding. Being such a pompous prick, what he naively doesn't realise is that this is the age of the micro cassette recorder. So I'm covertly recording his bid to have me over, two hours worth of his lies at slow speed, in my inside double breasted jacket pocket, and you can't tell or see a thing! You'd never know I had it on me. Not bad; before I have to make an excuse to leave like those News of the World reporters, to change the tape over. The quality of recording is superb, well I don't want to be mistaken in what he says! A senior officer by the name of John Stalker late of Greater Manchester Police reasoned it was permissible, and more importantly, legal, when he was challenged by his own chief about his 'shoot to kill' investigation in Northern Ireland. It would seem it succeeded in him not being 'fitted up' on major criminal enquiry into his actions. Who am I to challenge a senior police officer and his methodology? To help with setting the scene of how we got to this point, I'd advise you to read my first weighty tome called 'The Fit Up – A Noble Cause', if for no other reason than to boost the funds of our litigation costs! To continue;

Boles commenced ingratiating himself with Bob as if they were both 'old sweats', and more bizarrely were old pals and seasoned detectives having a chat over old times. However, Bob had done his homework, as you would expect him to do. It turns out Boles had risen through the ranks, purely in uniform. Nothing wrong with that you might say, and one would wholeheartedly agree with you. In his case however, after his two years probation, which of course everyone has to complete, he took his first promotion exam as quick as he could, and went straight into research and planning, then professional standards, then race relations, then community policing and so the list of 'plum' office jobs continued. Finally he got a degree in jurisprudence, the study of law, which of course, his force at the time paid for, and eventually ended up in a position where he could tell everybody else how to get their hands dirty without ever having done so himself. Bob speculated to himself *probably Boles ended up as officer in charge of paper clips*! On paper these 'uniform carriers' promoted academic theories on efficient policing which looked quite persuasive. One glaring problem, they fell down on pragmatism, and practical application, so consequently were the curse of the poor coppers who were actually doing the job. In short Bob didn't rate him.

"Hello young man, right it's a bit like, *'dearly beloved we are gathered together'* isn't it. It's up to you to start this one, I think, but before you do, let me say this, I have drawn no papers as a result. Whatever I say will be based on memory and gut reaction. Okay?"

I doubt it, but my point made, failing to plan is planning to fail. Had no papers on it, utter bollocks. And an unconvincing liar!

"If we at any stage, we want to make it formal, you know, he said, I said, then we have a different meeting at a different time. If you want to just talk about the principles, a bit of gut reaction. I'm perfectly happy to do that with you today. So you can mull that over, what sort of meeting is it? I am being asked as I see it, to establish the ground rules, if that's the right word, for a meeting between Detective Chief Superintendent Branch, and yourself and the others who feel bit pissed off as a result of the enquiry. But if there were anywhere in the system the tail ends of legality, I couldn't allow Mr. Branch to talk to you. I mean, do you speak for the others as well? I assume they know you've asked to see me, Mr. Branch is perfectly prepared to see all of you. Has been all the way along, let there be no doubt about that. The situation that arose at the end, at the end of formal hostilities, I was also prepared to see the officers concerned. So I've declared my hand, because had I been in your shoes I'd have been pissed off and you'd have heard a lot from me, whatever rank, P.C., D.C., you know Inspector, I'd say you would've heard a lot from me if I'd been in their shoes."

"But sir, I hear what you say, and I think understand what you are driving at. I appreciate your concern… but I didn't ask to have this meeting albeit you may feel the need. I was told that I must see you today, so this is not at my instigation." Bob asserted.

Boles sensing Bob wasn't going to roll over that easily said, "Well, really it doesn't matter who asked who."

Yes it fucking does!

"I just hope we can make some progress and put this to bed. I mean it was a public complaint so that bit's inevitable, but how it was investigated could have been better I think," in a vague hope of distancing himself from any culpability albeit he couldn't avoid the fact that he was ultimately the head of discipline. In essence what he says goes, but he needed to put some space between him and the 'cock up'.

You have to remember he thinks he's cleverer than everyone else and by virtue of his senior rank, has a better grasp of the English language. Twat!

Now it was Bob's turn, " Sir when we were raided and arrested, none of us could believe nor did we accept what was going on. I was told that I, as with other members of the Pickpocket Squad should remain at our desks, not to touch anything, not to talk to anyone, and not to use the telephone. And if I was to leave my office I had to be accompanied by an investigating officer. At one point my phone kept ringing and was answered by Acting Detective Chief Inspector Secrett, and C/I Spooner the officers who'd arrested me. Eventually Secrett ripped the phone line out of the wall."

Boles butted in saying, " You weren't arrested, this was an unannounced visit by my officers which I am entitled to order as Deputy Chief and head of discipline."

Give me another example of it then. Nope, didn't think so. Tosser! He must think I came in with the milk!

"There was sufficient information — in which the word 'corruption' may not have been used, but certainly what amounted to corruption — put before me and was certainly put before those investigating on my behalf, and they acted on it at my request. McMurray made a scattered complaint about people on the Dip Squad. You know, no names, but people on the squad are on the make or something or doing something else — some phrase, some catch-all phrase, okay? — which was included in the complaint."

Bobs turn, "If that's the case sir, your suggestion would be that Secrett and Spooner didn't arrest me for what, in anyone's view was a very serious criminal offence. So with all due respect sir, (*Not*, Bob thought), I was arrested, and detained in custody for something like six hours, as were my team. I assume a statement must have been taken from McMurray before the raid surely? And I guess you'd have seen it before sanctioning the raid — or 'visit' as you describe it. Surely the easiest thing, sir, would be to show us the statement as to what he said, and when. Because I was under the assumption that I was arrested along with my team, and we'd be taken to Paddington Green nick for processing. But all that happened after various documents, case files, photographs and registers were seized, we were just told to get on with our work! We were completely bewildered as to what happened. Then nobody dealing with our alleged activity spoke to us for months. The next day I was removed as head of the squad."

Boles containing his agitation at Bob's forthright attitude, said, " You were not removed. You were transferred from the squad, which I am entitled to do, or anybody else is entitled to do."

Bob suggested, "Can you enlighten me on what it was that prompted this arbitrary course of action sir? Perhaps a way forward would be for my squad, who have all been affected by the arrest and incarceration, to have a meeting with you, sir, in order their grievances could be aired?"

Boles shook his head, "No I couldn't allow that meeting to take place. Professionally I couldn't allow that to take place. I mean, don't people realise that if McMurray turns up here and says to us that he wants to make a complaint, and if we don't take it, then he'll go to CIB2 at the Yard to report us as well. Then we look at what he says, and say he's a lying bastard, he's a villain, he is this he is that and he's dangerous, but he is a villain and he has complained and the threat to give it to CIB2. If we had 'cuffed that', then we would've been done for certain. I mean you, can't determine to ignore a public complaint on the grounds of a complainants criminal record. Prostitutes can complain of rape; so too can convicted pickpockets make allegations."

What the fuck, I've heard it all now. The man's a Neanderthal! You didn't have a statement from him beforehand did you, lying shit. You thought your officers would get all they needed once they'd turned over the office!

Bob pushed Boles commitment to his fabrication further. "So on that basis, it was McMurray who made the complaint and nothing specific, I want to understand what necessitated the excessive raid on us, sir? I mean, we have similar allegations of corruption on a regular basis. It's part of the game plan of many of the defendants. In many cases they'll use to smear the arresting officers with a dubious reputation to sway the jury. And of course their their allegation is treated as sub-judice until the trial is over. Why this one sir?"

Right I've got him, I'll drop the next bomb in a moment. I thought he might go down the route of 'mea culpa', but no, he was sticking to his position that he was right to see us all nicked really, and with a large portion of victimhood on his part, what else could he do. He doesn't look so comfortable now. By the way, sub-judice means it won't be investigated until after any trial. Lord Byron said something like, 'watch the mouth, it reveals what the eyes try to hide'. He's got plenty to hide. Watch this!

Boles moved uncomfortably in his chair as the late afternoon sunshine prompted beads of perspiration on his forehead. He was unhappy with Trebor's continued challenge to his justification for the raid. "Now listen, D/I Trebor. I invited you here today in the anticipation that my intervention might take the sting out of this impasse. I realise, of course, that you and your officers may have misgivings about the events, but I do think you should reconsider yours and those who work for you, their positions.

Oh lovely, now a veiled threat, as to our well-being and future progress in the job. Don't push it or I will make your lives a misery. Irrespective of whether you've done nothing wrong, I cannot afford to let you win this argument. The gloves are off!

"I understand what working detectives get up to. You know, you've got a team of thief takers who are all going out nicking villains and covering themselves in glory," Boles said.

Bob interjected, "No, sir, that's not the case." Boles quizzical expression showed to Bob that here was a senior officer clearly had never been in charge of a squad. Obviously he had no idea how to lead. "Sir, my squad has been successful in quelling the scourge of pickpockets and knife pint robbers precisely because all the officers of my team are not the same. A blend gives you the best chance of success. Yes sure, there are active thief takers, but then there are officers who are good at paperwork, others who are good at intelligence gathering, building the more complex cases, putting files together —and one officer I can think of, pivotal to the squads success, minds the 'shop' while the others are out working. And most importantly for the best possible team spirit, those who work on the team are part of the selection process on new attachments to the squad, and who want to be on the team. It ensures each member is comfortable working with the others."

This one will hurt!

"Sir, you mentioned McMurray as being the author of the complaint against us. But that's not correct, is it, sir. He's a professional pickpocket arrested by Detective Sergeant Dennison as I understand it, and made a complaint. As a matter of fact he was known to a number of us. He'd passed through our hands, so to speak, some time ago when on information we had received we had a warrant to search his home address long before, if DS Dennison is to be believed, he'd allegedly committed an attempt theft and had assaulted the officer in a bid to escape."

Boles tried to look unfazed but the look of shock in his eyes realised that Bob had taken the meeting to clear the air, to a whole different level. "In fact sir, we know the original allegation of corruption against me and my team was made by a man called Sutton. He did so, long before McMurray had even been arrested or his home address search by us. I understand that following allegations he made to Detective Chief Superintendent Branch and D/I Secrett while in Pentonville prison he made a broad allegation of the squad being on the take, me in particular. I resent those allegations most strongly as I had never had any dealings with him, save looking through the wicket gate at him, at Snow Hill police station when he was asleep. The only reason I took a look at him was because my officer who had arrested him for attempt theft had doubts that Sutton was giving correct personal details; he believed him to be another pickpocket. He was wrong in that belief but absolutely right in doubting his details, as we subsequently learnt. A second statement was taken from Sutton, again at Pentonville, when he was shown photographs of the squad by Mr. Secrett, which were seized at the time of the raid and arrest. They were photos from a social gathering we'd had months before. He identified an officer who was clean shaven, but at the material time the officer had a full beard. He then went on to identify me, but I'd never met him. On the strength of that, we were arrested. There's more to this than we are being told, sir".

Bob realised Boles was about to call time. In his mind was Tom Petty and the Heartbreakers singing, '*You can stand me up at the gates of hell but I, I wont back down.*' Boles arrogant attitude had got to him.

And with that, Boles had enough of me pushing him too far. The meeting to 'clear the air' was terminated with more smoke and mirrors than he ever envisaged. I think I was right about his stance. He talks a good battle but never engaged. He walked the walk, talked the talk but he didn't think the thought. I don't take to being threatened by anyone, I can't abide bullies, and I don't give a fuck how important he thinks he is. Those that have done their best at a fit up on our squad have just booked themselves a very rough ride!

2
RETRIBUTION

"Turn your drawers out, will you, Detective Inspector Walker," said the dour looking Scotsman from the 'rubber heel' squad — so called because rubber is quieter than leather and 'Blakey's' on their shoes as they silently stalk their prey — known as CIB2, the investigation branch called in to root out corrupt or bent coppers. They'd been called in by Deputy Chief Constable Boles, whose responsibility covered the policing of transport infrastructure including those charged with policing the London Underground system. Walker nervously rummaged in his right trouser pocket, thoughts racing through his mind of prevarication, but surmising that delay to Detective Superintendent Lyle — standing menacingly, together with his side kick, or 'bag carrier', one Detective Sergeant Tate, beside the drawer pack under his desk — would do no good. He knew the contents of his top drawer, and realised some of them would cause him a problem.

"Is there anything I can help you with guv? Anything in particular you are looking for? I mean, I don't really understand why you're here," He said nervously in a soft Geordie tone. The investigating officers displayed their displeasure and annoyance at Walker's refusal — as they saw it — to co-operate with their instruction.

"Just open the fucking drawers," boomed the Glaswegian, upon which Walker, who had aged in the last couple of years of his service, produced a small key on a key fob declaring his allegiance to Newcastle United football club. Snatched from his clammy right hand, Tate synchronised the locks and tumblers, pushing the key home, whereupon the one full turn to the right unlocked the entire pack of three drawers. He gravitated to the deep bottom drawer first of all. He pulled it from the body of the pack revealing a pile of loose papers, discarded statements, crime reports, and the well hidden half empty bottle of 'Teachers' together with two shorts glasses, one suspects courtesy of the latest garage give away, buried under the correspondence. Now, while regulations stated that officers were not allowed to drink on duty, it would be quite out of character to find a Detective Inspector without a bottle in his possession. It's usually for 'visitors' to have a nip in extending the hand of friendship where a degree of reciprocation, perhaps on some joint enquiry or in celebrating a good result on a job, was necessary.

Tate pushed on with his ferreting, choosing to ignore the alcohol, preferring to focus on the seemingly discarded paperwork and crime reports as he loaded them into a newly opened property bag.

"Why are these crime reports which all appear to relate to dippings on the Underground, in this drawer?" asked Tate of a visibly perspiring Walker, who had resigned himself to being in deep shit, although his natural instinct — as with any detective of his calibre or service — was never to plead guilty to anything, the lead in this being taken from the villains they've nicked, who will say black is white if it means they have chance of getting away with whatever offence they've been arrested for!

"I've no idea how they got in there. Obviously it's a mistake; I think they should be in the crime folders over there on the shelf," Walker retorted, in that he was as mystified as Tate was, in the hope he'd not spotted crime reports were duplicates of those in the folders, but with some 'minor' alterations on the list of property stolen.

The Detective Sergeant continued by sealing the contents of the bottom drawer making a great play of signing across the seal, where-by the contents couldn't be interfered with unless Tate or someone else reopened the bag.

On closing the bottom drawer Tate focused in on the contents of the second drawer being drawn to about a dozen different purses and wallets. As he scrutinised them further he could see a number of them still had credit cards and other means of identification inside, as to who the owners may be.

"Okay, I give in, tell me why you've got a do-it-yourself property store in your drawer? What kind of mistake is this then Inspector?" enquired an unimpressed Superintendent Lyle.

Walker sensing things were only going to go from bad to worse, decided the best policy was to remain mute as the two officers revelled in the thought they'd got their man — albeit after shaky start by fellow officers working along with those of CIB2, which had started some twenty four hours earlier in the offices of the Central London Pickpocket Squad. There was every possibility the two enquiries would cross-pollenate in the fullness of time, but at this point they had been directed to do this subsequent raid — or unannounced visit — to lend a degree of independence from that of the earlier raid. Tate, not troubling to examine the property too closely, knowing it would be thoroughly examined at a later point back at their offices, simply loaded them into another property bag, folded over the self-adhesive serialised seal, and signed across it.

Next came the coup de grace. Walker resigning himself to being well and truly potted by the two unsavoury characters, whom he regarded as having doubtful parentage. The top drawer!

Tate's eyes lit up with alarm, coming out on stalks like in a Tom and Jerry cartoon, as he saw a revolver, together with four loose bullets scattered around the drawer lining. He carefully lifted the weapon, breaking it to ensure no discharge could occur accidentally. Satisfied the revolver was safe, and that all six chambers were empty, he scooped up the bullets together with the gun dropping them into another newly opened property bag. He smirked at a grinning Lyle.

"And once more Mr. Walker, I find myself wondering if you have an explanation this time,for possessing what looks like a Section One firearm — as classified under the Firearms Act 1968 — together with ammunition, on police premises and not secure in the property store, where at first sight both should be?" Lyles supercilious tone showed he was tiring of Walkers lack of explanation to anything. He recognised he was playing the Superintendent at his own game. He had been cautioned that he didn't have to say anything, but whatever he said would be quoted in any subsequent internal hearing or court case, and so for Walker, silence was golden, despite being told by Lyle that it was his duty to answer his questions.

Is it fuck. Once you're cautioned, that's it. You have the same rights as any villain, so duty to answer flies out the window. By the way, a Section One firearm requires a firearms certificate under the Firearms Act 1968 to possess such a weapon. If it's his own then that's different, but I don't believe Walker has such authority. Well well!

The raid drew to a close. Walker fearing the worse, assumed he was now going to be carted off to Rochester Row nick to be processed and interviewed. To his astonishment and overwhelming relief, Lyle said, "Walker you are to carry on in your post, I'm satisfied I have everything I need for further enquiries. You are instructed not to engage in any major enquiries, and confine your duties to office work. Any more than that and you will be suspended from duty forthwith. Do I make myself clear? I'll tell you, if it had been left to me, I would be suspending you from duty now, but those instructing me have decided at this point in time not to pursue that course." Walker gulped, taking in the 'gypsies warning'. He didn't know if he should say anything in response, but the shock of the directive rendered him unable to say anything even if he'd wanted to.

*

May I take this opportunity to introduce myself, I'm Detective Inspector Bob Trebor. I used to be the youngest CID boss on promotion, in the country, not any longer I'm now 32 years. Don't let my boyish charm and good looks mislead you! I reckon

I'm a good guv'nor, and I get respect from those working for me. Those I work for see me in the main as an asset, albeit some of my number working for me, have curious peccadilloes which I won't go into now. It doesn't make them nasty people! Until a couple weeks ago I ran the very successful Central London Pickpocket Squad. 'Successful?' I hear you ask. Well yes, very. We broke all previous records of arrests and convictions for the hideous offences around pickpocketing, whether that be theft, or knife point robbery, armed robbery or serious assault — or conspiracies to engage in one or a combination of all of them. However, as with Newton's law for every action there is, as seemed to be the case with our success, an equal and opposite reaction. This could be termed briefly as a high level of complaints against the police, to be expected, invariably levelled by the protagonists or by someone they had recruited to do their bidding. But, far worse in my book, was that emanating from fellow officers, if I can use such a term, who, through their own jealousy, fear of discovery of their own past dishonesty, call it what you will, were hell bent on making mischief for the squad, or better still cast doubt on the officers integrity, that might then lead to criminal or disciplinary sanction. What shits! As if the job isn't hard enough as it is, to then have treacherous bastards within your midst taking pot shots at you. Now I won't deny we have a 'talent' when it comes to arresting the low life, but then it's nothing less than they deserve. And if we don't do it, who will? It keeps a lid on their thieving activities.

So I currently find myself posted to Divisional CID, running several squads engaged in all sorts of crime up to and including murder, whilst a number of my officers from the Dip Squad — to use the colloquialism — and I face an internal investigation for corruption. But as is the fashion now, we are not suspended. My take on that, is that those investigating think they are saving money by not suspending us, or are so confident they've already got their man they believe only a complete idiot would get involved in more corrupt activity, so why not keep him or her at work rather than give him extended 'gardening leave' through suspension from duty? In fact the only officer who is suspended, Detective Sergeant Hunt, is suspected of having killed one of my officers by allegedly pushing him down a set of escalators, causing fatal injuries. What a mess, you may think. But already I'm beginning to shine some light on the dark forces operating against me and my team! Not for the first time, all is not as it seems. News of my demise is exaggerated, I'd say. But as Mandy Rice Davis observed, then I would say that!

*

Tommy Francis, a South London thug from the Walworth Road, strode purposefully towards the Wellington pub opposite Waterloo Station. He looked older than his thirty five years, probably due to many years training in the Thomas a Beckett boxing club, in the Old Kent Road. He swaggered his broad six foot frame, accentuated by his dark blue Crombie overcoat, to the middle doors of the pub, brushing past two young pretenders just leaving the establishment. Once inside, he removed and shook out the now glistening coat, no longer needed to protect its owner from the light drizzle outside. As *The Good, the Bad and the Ugly* theme played on the 'Rock-Ola' juke box, Tommy ignored who he thought was yesterday's man, a local thief infamous for being involved in the great train robbery, one Buster Edwards, now a pitiful drunk and flower seller with a stall under the railway bridge opposite the pub. It was early evening, a time when Edwards sought solace in several large gin and tonics, invariably sponsored by whoever was the latest mug to be regaled with Busters tales of derring-do.

Tommy didn't need to say 'excuse me' as he went towards the quieter end of the bar to the left; many of the inhabitants of the expansive pub knew him and his reputation. It was like the Red Sea parting as a human corridor opened before him, and closing equally as quick once he had passed. The subject of his interest was another of his crew Roger Clementine, who went by the nickname of 'Darling' and another, a hanger-on who was always useful for fencing gear — in other words, handling and disposing of stolen property — Trevor Sutton. This was the name he gave to Police if he was stopped or arrested although his real name was Jones. The name Sutton came from his belief that his mum was born there.

"Alright darlin, do you want a rinse?" Tommy asked Roger as he nodded to the presence of Sutton in their company. Roger, sensing it would be churlish to refuse, although his response was more 'industrial' in origin, asked for a top up to his lager. Sutton hoped he would be included and asked for another pint of bitter. Once served, all three moved away from the bar to a row of bench seats beyond the vacant pool table. Tommy then outlined the need for this urgent meet on a 'job' he was running. It involved a bit of debt collecting from a face who owed thirty 'large'— or thousand — to Tommy's pal from East Lane market and had been a bit slow in weighing in with the outstanding amount. Hence, Tommy's assistance requested to be more physical to resolve this difficult situation.

"As I told you before, that wanker Moody owes. Now he's got to pay. This Thursday I know he going to be in Ladbrokes in Walworth Road, doing his dough on the dogs at Catford. He's let it be known, he's got a red hot tip on a rank outsider and reckons he's going to clean up. He's laid off a lot of side bets so he doesn't show out for the big one. Darlin what we're going to do is, you and me pitch up about five and wait for him to come out, hopefully happy he's had a touch. He'll need to be 'cos he owes big as it is. We're going to tail him off past Carter Street nick to the flats at the back. You know, where the garages are. He always parks his motor there. We'll invite him to join us for a chat in the end garage, and I've got the keys for that. I'll be tooled up just to give it a bit more muscle. And if he wants proof I'll let one off just to prove we mean business. With any luck I won't need to do any more to ensure the debts paid pronto. That's it. Any questions."

"No Tom. We'll sort out on the day where you and me meet yeah?."

Tommy agreed with Roger. Sutton, being the windy bastard that he was, realised that he wasn't involved in the arrangements and was relieved. A couple more drinks, which Sutton bought, and the three left the Wellington in different directions.

Jones was the shit who, in later times thought he'd try and get out of his trial with Conroy when he gave a false surname of Sutton. I got called to Snow Hill nick to do a wicket gate identification as Conroy thought he was another white dip, but it wasn't him. On the strength of the false name, which he'd used before, and someone who I assume couldn't be arsed to be diligent when doing the bail enquiry, he was given bail again, and then never turned up to answer his bail at the nick or at court! Unbelievable but true!

*

Manzies pie and mash shop, on the Walworth Road, just a few doors from Carter Street nick was doing a roaring trade in the early Friday evening, as the late afternoon sun gave way to a unseasonably, warm night air. Young Trevor and his best mate Tommy were comparing their latest Ben Sherman shirts they'd 'relieved' from the ownership of the stall-holder in East Lane market. He knew not to challenge these two skinheads, whose gang in later times would see notoriety as part of the 'Bushwackers' a violent group of football thugs at Millwall Football Club. They talked about their forthcoming remand coming up at Camberwell Green magistrates Court on Monday, the other side of the weekend. But before then was Saturday and Sunday which would see the pair of them renewing their association with the Locarno, latterly the 'Cats Whiskers' night club at Streatham or their usual haunt, the 'Croydon Suite', a much smaller club near the Whitgift Centre in Croydon.

*

"No I cant make it, mate," said Darling on the phone to Trevor, lining up that afternoons hoisting a colloquialism for shoplifting, at Woolworths. The two of them, Sutton and Clementine, together with Tommy, had made regular trips to the Elephant and Castle shopping centre, and while Roger kept lookout, the other two would set about thieving as much Lego in gift boxes as they could carry out of the store. The toys were easy to shift — there was always someone wanting something for their little kid — and Woolworths, with their revamped self-service shelves, meant the gang did precisely that. They just didn't see a reason to settle the financial side of things. But this Saturday their luck had run out. Without Roger acting lookout, they were captured by a new addition to the store, an officious-looking store detective who handcuffed them to each other and march them to the managers' office to await the arrival of the 'Old Bill.'

And so it was, that Tommy and Trevor added to their compendium of petty convictions, warranting a period in Borstal. They were released only when they had accepted their responsibility for their crime and had behaved without incident. Likewise, Roger had been actively acquiring his own 'form' but not the great Lego scam, for which he was grateful to Tommy for not grassing him up, albeit Trevor didn't possess the same loyalty, and saw no reason not 'grass' if it would get him off the hook. But he wasn't going to go against Tommy's code.

*

Cascade forward, Trevor sat silently on a barstool at the far end of the long bar in the Wellington, deep in thought as he caressed with both hands the pint of bitter from which he'd taken a couple of sips disposing of the small head. He'd phoned his 'friendly' CID officer who he had used as a conduit to dispose of stolen property — in particular, many purses and wallets he'd dipped from unsuspecting tourists, usually on the Underground system of central London. That said, he wasn't averse to doing the bus stop queues around the Elephant and Castle or down the Walworth Road. The weather had turned decidedly autumnal which enabled Sutton to use his best aid to his thieving enterprise; a large caped overcoat, like that worn by that fictional character Sherlock Holmes. It meant his hands and forearms were hidden from sight until he pounced, when they'd emerge from the slits either side of the cape, like a praying mantis, would relieve the victim of their purse or wallet before returning under cover with the stolen property. He did have the deerstalker hat to go with the coat, but wouldn't use it as well unless he was operating his modus at the Marylebone Road bus stops or the Underground near Baker Street.

Detective Inspector John Walker pulled open the left hand door leading to the saloon bar of the pub. *'Every breath you take, every move you make, I'll be watching you'.* menacingly threatened the latest selection from the juke box within. John saw the reason for his attendance at the 'Wellington' to the left. He casually nodded towards him, making his way past the latest fools to part with their money to Buster the flower seller. He sauntered across to Trevor pulling up a stool to his right.

"Hello Trev, how you doing? What've you got for me then? You said you needed to talk urgent. What's the problem? Your mates been thieving again?"

Sutton lost no time in whinging to Walker about being nicked by Bob Trebors' Dip Squad, and how he thought the guys who had arrested him had taken some of his money, before he got charged at the nick. He didn't actually want to make an official complaint, he understood the concept of 'taxing' which he'd known from previous years, when the coppers nicked money off him. What he couldn't understand was why he had just been nicked straight, without any room for negotiation. He did though have some wallets to give to Walker and something which he needed to get rid of.

It's difficult to know which way round this was working. Walker was of the opinion that he had cultivated Sutton as an informant, especially as he bought the beers for the officer. Although in his usual sloppy way he operated, he hadn't quite got round to registering him as such. This presented Walker with all sorts of problems not least his ability to meet Sutton if he was on bail without it drawing attention as to whether there was a corrupt motive requiring an investigation by Professional Standards Department or CIB2. Of course he'd have trouble paying him for useful information unless he paid him out of his own pocket. This would ordinarily mean he couldn't claim he expenditure back, but that mere trifle didn't seem to present a problem to Walker, he just laid of the expense to something else such as a meal. Sutton on the other hand was happy that he'd 'mugged' off the trusting CID officer with a few free drinks, and conned him into believing the wallets or purses he passed across to John in the 'Happy Shopper' carrier bag had been stolen by his mates. Not wishing to be seen as handling stolen goods he suggested Walker take care of getting them back to their rightful owners. Needless to say there was no cash in them because

Sutton had liberated it, although he'd deny ever doing so, just identification of the owners through correspondence or cash cards within. Walker, 'the old sweat', was then dumb enough to hand them into the lost property office on Waterloo station, as if he'd found them. What a prick! The reality was Sutton was the thief, he just got great satisfaction in using a dumb arsed copper to dispose of what he didn't need.

3
HOLA!

Detective Constable John Conroy had been examining the daily deluge of 'Theft Person'— or dipping — crime reports arriving at the Dip Squad office over the past couple of weeks as the sun made a tentative invasion through the Georgian windows at the front of the nick. The reports of thefts from the person across just the Underground network had been totalling anything up to twenty a day. Given that some would be simply be losses, perhaps in the street, but blamed on being jostled when boarding a train to satisfy the losers insurance claim, this was nothing really out of the ordinary. Among those reports might be two or three robberies usually by black suspects mentioned by the victims, sometimes pulling knives to enforce their aim, where it seemed the offence had started off as a theft. When the prey then objected or put up resistance the failed dipping would go up a notch to a knifepoint robbery to achieve the object of relieving the victim of their property. John, always looking for trends in the crimes, phoned the Crime Squads operating out of Gatwick and Heathrow nicks. Armed with their information and believing he'd found a pattern in the crimes he knocked on the guv'nor's door. Looking through the porthole window to the guv'nor's office, seeing D/I Trebor savouring a third mug of coffee, he entered carrying a sheaf of yellow carbon copies of the crimes.

Bob Trebor singing along to Tears for Fears rendition of 'Everybody wants to rule the world' on his newly acquired Sony Walkman cassette player, looked up from a prosecution file, to see a casually dressed Conroy entering. He watched him carefully sidestepping the four-foot tropical fish tank on a substantial metal angle iron frame that enabled Bob to be mesmerised by his latest fishy acquisitions as he sat at his desk. Bob had been given the tank by one of the detectives attached to Divisional CID who had gone upmarket in his own house to a larger, more sophisticated model. The officer in question was just chatting with Bob over a tea one day when Bob decided there was no reason why he couldn't have the tank in his room at the nick. So, without question, and giving the officer permission to use one of the CID cars, it was quickly delivered to Bobs office. Within a day or so, it was filled with many and various plants and fish! A few 'jobsworths' tried adopting a high moral ground and musing whether he was allowed to keep livestock, as they called it, on police premises. Bobs reaction to these challenges was to start a rumour that he was contemplating acquiring couple of guinea pigs and naming them after two of the senior officers! That gave them a distraction to think about, and a kind of acceptance that fish were alright but anything more would be too much. '*Twats*', he thought.

"Guv, the fish are looking good, no dead ones I see, Guv I've been doing a bit of digging on the crime reports over the last couple of weeks. On each one of these there's a vague description of suspects who seemed to be near the victims when their property was nicked. I know it's not much but they describe sort of middle-aged men, fairly smartly dressed and looking like Spanish or Italian or of Mediterranean appearance. I've been on to the crime squads at the airports and they reckon they've had similar crimes and suspects reported to them. They've had a couple of results: three nicked at Heathrow in the terminals were Chilean nationals with nicked or forged Spanish passports, and two more at Gatwick who were a Colombian husband and wife team with bent Italian identity cards. Is it okay if me, Hazel and Farmer follow this up?"

Bob still with headphones on, told Conroy to repeat what he'd just said, carefully placing phones and Walkman in his 'In tray'.

"Yes, John. Go out to the airports and get their info. It's about the right time of the year. The Chileans usually get here about now just in time for Wimbledon. Do you remember we had a spike in crime reports last year? Oh no of course not, you weren't with us last year, were you. Yes well spotted, keep me posted," said Bob as he resumed his focus on the file in front of him.

Conroy, happy with his praise and permission, tapped on the front glass of the aquarium on his exit, sending the residents into panicked retreat, prompting a one word bollocking from Bob, for such an attack on his latest acquisitions.

I'll tell you what, those fish have wonderfully calming effect you know — at least, that's what I tell the bosses if they're troubled by the tanks presence. Typical of that clumsy paddy to tap the glass, making them dart all over the place. But I forgive his funny ways because he's a good digger of information, just what you want from a keen detective, and he's certainly that, so little indiscretions can be forgiven. Mind you, he thinks he's having me over on blagging a couple of hours overtime for going to 'Awaits Callers', in the Criminal Records Office at the 'Yard' in the dead of night, to view microfiches of villains he thinks might be of interest. The office, in an effort to reduce their paper mountain had microfilmed all the forms we submit to them whether at the time of arrest or at the conclusion of a case. It makes it easier to view a villains entire history on one piece of fiche. But because this is a new system, they jealously guard them. They don't mind you attending their reception on the fourth floor at the 'Yard' to view them, , but if you actually wanted to take one away it has to be signed for together with the reason for its removal before release. So they'd created a kind of audit trail.

Bob was completely absorbed by watching his latest acquisitions to the aquarium — a couple of dozen neon tetras — shoaling from one end of the tank to the other, as Europe declared *the final countdown* on his Walkman. His mind drifted back to a chance meeting he had at Inner London Crown Court with an officer who in his opinion was 'bent.' Not in the usual sense of the word, he strongly believed he had been on the take from various dips in the past as well as in his mind, being bent in the homosexual vein as well, and someone who he would give a wide berth to at anytime. He thought about Greg Dennison's comments to him although he hadn't given much weight to them at the time. But the words coursed through his mind time and again. Bob's idea was to treat the veiled threat with the contempt it deserved.

*

"Hello sir, how are you?" enquired Detective Sergeant Dennison in a tone not dissimilar to that of Larry Grayson, Bob thought, as he waited outside Court 2, to give evidence in a guilty plea for yet another dip trial.

"I'm fine thanks Sergeant, what demands your presence here in this fine edifice dedicated to seeking the truth? I assume you've come here to do just that, surely? Have you got a trial here?"

"No sir, I'm just fixing a trial date in the list office." His patronising voice irritated Bob as he moved in beside him, and said in a low voice, "You know all that business with your squad wasn't aimed at you. You do know that don't you? But there will be more, there always is sir." Dennison sauntered off, happy he'd delivered his message to Bob. Bob thought *'he minces like his arse is chewing a toffee'*, prompting his response to tell him to go forth and multiply but he resisted the urge, not wanting to give him any issue to complain about, as he continued to wait outside the courtroom.

Bob dismissed the words from Dennison as shit stirring, as quickly as they entered his mind, from a person whom he felt, delighted in creating mystery and misinformation, and someone he suspected was probably hiding something himself. His musing was interrupted by the shrill of his new office Trimphone. He answered in his usual belligerent tone, irritated with his new addition and fleetingly wondering why he couldn't have his old phone back. The news from Pete Farmer was music to Bobs ears. Apparently, no sooner had he left the office with Paul Hazel and John Conroy and travelled two stops on the Bakerloo line down to Oxford Circus, than they dropped straight on top of a three handed team of little middle-aged Mediterranean looking men, thieving right in front of them. Paul outlined to Bob the attempted theft from an elderly man who, whilst they hadn't got his name, they had another man who saw everything the thieves were doing, and was willing to give witness statement. Bob said he'd meet up with them at Bow Street nick to see what they had, in about an hour, but it looks like they'd arrested one of the many groups of South American 'dips' that John had spoken of earlier. With that he congratulated them, replacing the receiver, before his continuing with countersigning the deluge of crime reports ever present in his 'In' tray.

*

"My one's got a Spanish passport in the name Ramon Bartez, but the photo doesn't look right. It's peeling away from the page and the stamp printed on it doesn't marry up with the bit of the stamp on the rest of the page" said Farmer as the three prisoners sat quietly looking bemused on the long bench in the Charge room at Bow Street. He was in the process of booking them in with Sergeant Satchell, newly promoted into his role.

John said, "Look at this, there's no passport on him but he's got an Italian I/D card in the name Franco Vilabos. It's got to be bent; the stamp is missing from the photo but it's been riveted on the card to keep in place. He's got about five hundred quid in tenners and twenties. What about yours Paul?"

"He's got Chilean passport in the name Manuel Sanchez. It might be right, but two problems: one, it doesn't really look like him and two, he's got letters on him talking about someone called Juan Salazar. Either the passports bent or he's nicked the letters, maybe. He's got about two hundred notes (meaning pounds) on him again in twenties, and they're all sequential. He must have nicked off someone as they came away from the hole in the wall cash machine," said Paul, sifting through the rest of his prisoners property.

Sergeant Satchell said, "Look, lads, it looks like you're going to be a while checking through their property. If you're happy you've searched them, let's just bang them up until your ready. I've got a cup of tea waiting patiently for me in the reserve room. Come and find me when you're ready to push on with this. They're booked in with the identification they had on them, so it matters not if that turns out to be false, and I take it they're each of no fixed abode. I'll leave listing their property until you've had a good look through." With that, the gaoler magically appeared from the cell passage and beckoned the three 'caballeros' to follow him to their new, less-than-plush accommodation.

Having watched them being locked in their respective cells, the officers set about re-examining what they had. Farmer quickly realised the ten pound notes which Vilabos had were also consecutively numbered; in addition to which, Bartez had ticket stub for the cross channel ferry from Calais to Dover. Paul Hazel found an identical ticket for the same ferry for the same day. The boys were satisfied they'd linked prisoners one and three together, but in order to get a conspiracy, something a little more was needed to show prisoner two was involved in the joint enterprise.

Paul, ever keen to ensure the truth didn't spoil a good story, 'for a change', removed four sequentially numbered twenty pound notes from Sanchez property, leaving the rest of the sequence in the bag. He then placed them in Vilabos' property bag, removing four from his bag and putting them back in to Sanchez' property bag. Pete Farmer and John laughed quietly at Paul's cross pollination.

"Just like that!" said Paul in his Tommy Cooper voice.

Feeling round the bottom lining of the 'Harrington' jacket belonging to Bartez, Pete could feel some small pieces of paper and what appeared in his search, to be a piece of card together with the paper. "Wait a minute I've got something here," declared Pete as he rooted around in the side pocket discovering a hole in the lining. Slowly edging the contents round to the hole in the pocket, he then removed three London Underground tickets, two tickets for the Paris Metro and a Chilean national identity card in the name of Antonio Caro.

"So Bartez, now we know who the fuck you are," Pete proudly announced to the other two, feeling uncharacteristically brave, "Here John, give me five of those sequentially numbered tenners from Vilabos' dough. I've got thirty quid in tens and four fivers. It's my pocket money for the week, they're old and all separate numbers. Right, put two of the sequential tenners in his bag, and I'll take fifty quid out. There all three are linked now." The other two smiled knowingly. Pete held on to two of the London Underground tickets and one of the Paris metro tickets, carefully placing them in a separate polythene bag, to which John donated sequentially numbered notes from the Vilabos property bag.

"Well, you never know you're luck do you? I guarantee this is just the start, so who knows who else they might be associated with when we nick 'em?" said a smirking Pete. With that, Pete took charge of all three of the prisoner property bags, pulling the numbered seals tight, but still could be reopened for the property records. He ensured they couldn't be opened again without a record of the seal being broken recorded on the custody record which went with each prisoner. He hurriedly folded the fourth bag for future use, secreting it in the inside pocket of his own bomber jacket, just as the custody sergeant reappeared.

"Right lads, where are we?" asked Sergeant Satchell, wiping the crumbs of two recently dunked Hobnobs from the front of his NATO jumper. John outlined the facts of the case. A wry smile emerged on the face of attentive Sergeant, as he listened to a familiar tale of three pickpockets, two blocking an oblivious passenger trying to board a crowded doorway of the tube train while the third moved in to 'dip' the unsuspecting victim. There were three thieves and three plain clothes officers. As was so often the case, the intended victim would either not realise they had been the subject of the thieves' quarry or they simply moved away from what appeared to be a scuffle between two groups. The Sergeant's interest was ignited though when John shared the revelation that another passenger had seen everything, including seeing the three Chileans trying to steal from a woman in much the same fashion, on the train before.

Having topped and tailed the custody records, making a careful note of each individual bank notes serial numbers, the tickets which linked the prisoners, and details of the forged passports and I/D cards, he told the gaoler to fetch them from the cells. As they stood before the desk, looking confused and sorrowful in equal measure, having confirmed they understood rudimentary English, Sergeant Satchell charged them with substantive offences of theft from the person, possession of forged identity documents, and the all embracing conspiracy to steal within the jurisdiction of the Central Criminal Court.

I waited for the boys to return to the office. Ultimately there seemed little point in me attending Bow Street nick on this occasion. They had everything well in hand — they are after all, capable chaps. The Chileans will be remaining in custody until their appearance at Bow Street Magistrates Court tomorrow, then — with objections to bail because of their ability to acquire new passports or I/D with the very real risk of them absconding — they'll stay at her majesty's pleasure until the trial date. If I've got a criticism, it's that they didn't take more time with the investigation and actually interview them with the assistance of an interpreter, if only to get an admission — or more likely a denial, but that said, because it would be a contemporaneous note interview, chances are they'd have enough thinking time to frame their answers. There's just no surprise element with that kind of interrogation, and I do like surprises! Well that's me done for the day, I'm off to something I've taken up in recent times: amateur dramatics, in the village hall near where I live. Now there's a surprise I hear you say. As if I don't have enough drama in my bloody life! The boys have invited me to a rinse at 'The Portman' a nice little drinker not far from Balcombe Street where in 1975 an IRA gang were nicked having thrown nail bombs in to restaurants in the west end. I'll leave them to it.

THE ACID TEST

"You ought to try this, Bob, you must be used to speaking in public with all those court trials you're involved in," said Polly, mother of two kids at the same primary school as Bobs' two.

"Oh. I don't know, I don't think I'd have the time what with work and running the kids to their various activities. It's kind of you to offer, but really I think my limit is bringing them to the Christmas panto," Bob replied apologetically.

Polly undeterred said, "Tell you what, the group are doing a farce in the spring, I'll give you a buzz nearer the time when they're holding auditions."

Bob smiled, realising he was beaten by Pollys' persistence, agreed to the phone call, hoping he wouldn't be in to receive it.

*

Conroy, somewhat predictably, as far Bob was concerned, had booked on at 6am to go to 'Awaits callers' at the Yard — New Scotland Yard to the uninitiated — to search for any previous history on their latest bag, the three Chileans. Then at 9am he had an appointment with the prime witness to the attempted theft, a Mr. George Dangerfield, who had enthusiastically given his business address to the boys — a rather plush set of offices just down the road from Piccadilly in Pall Mall. After his visit to 'Awaits callers' John went up to the fourth floor, and having sampled the culinary delights of the police canteen in the form of a full English, he left the Yard past the Eternal Flame commemorating fallen officers, via the exit opposite St. James' Park tube station. Having time on his hands, he elected to walk to his meeting, through St. James' Park, saying hello to the pelicans by the lake, past Horse Guards Parade, Admiralty Arch — a tribute from King Edward to his mother — and Trafalgar Square to Dangerfields' offices just off Piccadilly.

"Good morning sir," said John as he was ushered into the plush offices of Dangerfield's property development business. *Must pay well,* he thought, as he was greeted with the offer of a cup of coffee from a fit — to his mind — twenty something blonde, and a comfortable leather easy chair beckoned his arse, opposite Dangerfield. John explained the reason for coming to see him, enquiring whether he was willing to be a witness to what he had seen the three Chileans doing prior to their arrest. To John's concealed surprise, Dangerfield expressed his more than willingness to assist the police. Indeed he even went further, telling John that as a regular traveller on the Underground, he'd seen more little South American men at Victoria, and drawing on his amateur sleuth status, he suggested they meet the following day in an effort to catch them. John couldn't believe his luck. Here was a member of the public, someone keen to help the squad, pointing them out and, of course, giving a further statement. Dangerfield confined himself to his evidence to date, with the verbal promise of more to come. Conroy thought he'd died and gone to heaven, as he steered his 'model' witness through his statement, trying to curb his eager anticipation of tomorrow's operation.

*

Paul Hazel, Al Fish and Dave Champion sat deep in discussion in the café at the top of Carnaby Street, as they waited for Pete Farmer, deep in discussion about their now suspended Detective Sergeant Hunt, speculating whether he could've done what those from Complaints and Discipline investigating were now suggesting. It seemed unlikely Hunt was responsible for his partners death — but poor Basil and his family — they agreed. Then Dave reminded them of the incident when Hunt stabbed an Aid to CID in the arse because they found themselves with two lots of evidence being too similar. Apparently the Aid even agreed to being injured, but he thought he'd just be assaulted, taking one for the team; he didn't realise he'd be stabbed! Again the scenario played out like one of those bent Detective Sergeant Greg Dennison's little dramas, with a fictitious suspect committing a fictitious theft, being intercepted, then the GBH! In unison, they did wonder if Hunt was beginning to lose his 'marbles'.

*

Well, I've been caught! About time too, you might very well say, but you'd be wrong to misjudge me. You find me sat in a big circle of what I can only describe as 'apprentice luvvies' who I guess their only desire is to be noticed. This shouldn't take long. I expect it will be a large portion of 'don't call us, we'll call you', then I can go home happy that at least I turned up! Maybe a job backstage or even sweeping it. Not too much commitment to that!

Not looking good. The stage director has asked me to read again, and the female lead I've got to read opposite is a gorgeous long dark haired lady — not what I would usually go for, but hey this is only acting! Besides, I'm happy enough with my lovely lawyer who incidentally is sill trying to get me to leave the missus, and from her point of view, sees no difficulty in taking on the fruits of my loins, in other words the children. God life can get complicated, can't it? Whoever said, it's all part of life's rich tapestry?

*

Pete arrived, red faced, his high forehead a delicate shade of crimson, hence the nickname, 'Carol' after the red headed singer of T'Pau, one Carol Decker. But in Pete's case, it was a case of no hair, just a balding red head! After the usual fine of a round of teas for being late, Pete suggested working the Victoria line as there had been a couple of reports of a young blonde haired white man acting 'strange' from members of the public, to a couple of uniformed officers who had just passed through Oxford Circus station. Although it was just after Sunday lunchtime, he suggested it was better than nothing. They each agreed they didn't want it to turn into a 'dry' day for arrests. Bob Trebor had found it necessary to reinforce the rules of the game. The squad hadn't had any bodies — aka arrests — that past week, something that was quite unusual, the four in question protesting that each of them had been involved in trials and remands at court and so the opportunity to 'recruit' new defendants had been limited. But they also knew that working a Sunday at time and a half payment for overtime meant there needed to be some kind of payback. Put simply no arrests, no overtime payment, pure and simple. Bob found it worked to focus their minds on the job in hand. That said, he'd never had to implement the sanction, relying on the team to pull out the stops and get a body. Carrot and stick seemed to work, in Bob's mind.

The four musketeers walked past the entrance to Marlborough Street Magistrates' Court and the stage door to the Palladium before turning right up Argyle Street towards Oxford Circus Tube Station. The clear blue sky of the afternoon succeeded in causing Pete's forehead to turn a stronger red, as if he'd become the victim of sunburn.

"You'd better stick behind us Carol, that forehead of yours is going to act like a bright red warning light to any dips we see!" said Al to the ridiculing delight of the other two as they descended the stairs outside Top Man. "Keep moving, otherwise the drivers in Oxford Street will think they're stopping at a red light!" said Dave.

Each of the team were seasoned campaigners at culling dips. They took up their positions along the length of the southbound Victoria line platform waiting for the couple of minutes shown on the dot matrix indicator to pass before the next train arrived. The cooling breeze of ozone, electrified oxygen, preceding the arrival of the next train was a signal to the team to have their wits about them, as the carriages juddered to a halt filled the length of the platform in front of them. As the doors slid open along its length, those on the sparsely populated platform moved forward invited by the open carriages. To Champions surprise, at the double doors where he stood behind the intending passengers, was a blonde haired white man who looked a *'bit of a handful'* to Dave's mind, fitting what he thought, was the description of the suspicious character reported to the uniformed officers earlier.

Not wanting to arouse interest from the suspect, Dave peeled away, masking his movement behind the suspect and three or four other members of the travelling public. Paul, Al and Pete saw Dave pull back from the suspect at their respective positions further along the platform, and whilst they didn't have a clear view of Dave's immediate vicinity, not a problem in the great scheme of things — they could each see the blonde head in the crowd. Dave didn't move in on the suspect so the others knew there was no need to rush to his assistance, but they moved closer to cover the eventuality. Blondie, as if feigning confusion, turned and re-boarded the train. Dave followed in as if another passenger, not showing any apparent interest in his target. The other three, seeing Dave get on, knew they had to board as well. Pete and Al Fish manage to get in a the same carriage a either end with Paul in the next. The doors closed with the train sailed off in the direction of Green Park, the next station stop.

Blondie moved in close behind an old lady, struggling with her purchases proudly displaying logos of the various shops including John Lewis, Armani and Escada. *Perhaps these are the bait for Blondie to shape up behind her*, Dave thought. As they got off in unison — she searching for the exit, he being frustrated in his efforts by the on coming crowd — he turned full left, again feigning confusion, and re-boarded. Dave was already committed to getting off and so merged with the melee of passengers to the right of the door. Pete moved up to the door where blondie had entered, allowing Dave to move further down. Instead of the usual announcement warning the doors were just about to close, they did so, surprising some still wanting to board along with Dave who watched the suspect, his team and the train go sailing out of the platform, heading for Victoria. Now he had a quandary. Should he sit tight there, then change platforms — hoping the suspect, together with his team returned — or take a chance and jump on the next southbound train due in thirty seconds. He chose the latter.

Containing his competitive impatience to be involved in any arrest, his journey lasted only a couple of minutes before arriving at Victoria, although in Dave's mind it seemed to take forever. He resolved in his own mind that if he was unable to find them he'd phone into the Information Room to inform them if the team called in, then he'd return to Oxford Circus to await their return. His contingency plan was short-lived when he saw blondie, followed at a distance by his team as they crossed the circulating area at the base of the escalators, onto the northbound Victoria line. Seeing that Pete was holding back, he seized the chance to speak with him while Paul and Al were closer to Blondie. According to Pete, he'd 'shaped up' behind a lad carrying an unzipped 'Head' sports hold-all on his shoulder, but he couldn't be sure if he'd dipped him. *Typical*, thought Dave. Although he'd never made his opinion public about Pete's willingness to step up to the plate — in others words for him to take the initiative on an arrest — he'd seen on many occasions he'd hold back, preferring to play 'second fiddle' to the arresting officer. Dave wasn't really convinced that Pete had the bottle for the job.

I'd noticed it as well. It's not as if he doesn't get involved in cases — in fact, he's been witness to a couple of mine where there were loads of alligators snapping at our heels. I just wish he'd lead for others to follow. An added dimension is that he's passed his Sergeants' exam, and I think he wants to appear before his board without any public complaints outstanding, which I guess he thinks is important to him. I'm afraid it's the kind of squad activity where one is bound to get such allegations of corruption or perjury. It just goes with the turf. As I've said so many times before, it's the first line a defendant will adopt in readiness for any trial, where his brief can allege corruption by the Police, albeit untrue. Of course, the trade off is having to reveal to the court any form, or previous convictions they might have. But they need to get it in early to give it credibility even if they subsequently choose not to use it, because it means an investigating officer is appointed but no investigation takes place as it is sub-judice. It means basically the officers against whom the allegation is made, cannot be interviewed or the complaint investigated until after the trial is completed. In my experience, often the complaint runs out of steam if the defendant is potted.

The northbound platform was fairly empty as a train had just departed and the next one was hot on its heels. The team broke apart, keeping a surreptitious eye on their target. The doors opened, beckoning the intending passengers to enter. Blondie got on through a middle set of doors just as a young girl in a track suit, carrying an open raffia bag with the Ethiopian flag embroidered on it on her right shoulder, was alighting. He turned to follow in behind her, which threw the team off guard. They mirrored his move back onto the platform. Then he turned again and got back on. To a man, they were convinced he was just about to dip her, but then didn't.

The process of shaping up behind possible targets, the pulling out at the last minute went on at each stop it seemed, all the way to Kings Cross. Blondie then did the same again going back south to Oxford Circus. Paul, Dave and Pete managed to get together while Al kept his eye on the target. 'He's well at it' was the conclusion, nobody does what blondie was doing unless they're a thief, who just hasn't found the perfect victim.

Paul said, "Fuck it, let's just take him I've had enough of this," which Dave agreed with.

They looked to Pete for his confirmation, but he really wasn't sure.

"I don't know, I mean he could just be stupid. Look you two have him, I'll go witness to it."

As had been expected, Petes reluctance to take the lead on arrest came to the fore again.

The boys were beginning to get a bit pissed off with his refusal to engage. In the interconnecting passageway between the southbound Victoria line and the Bakerloo line they stopped blondie, and briefly explaining their reason, took him to an adjoining office. He walked with them like a lamb to the slaughter.

All the while Pete had been rowing out of the job until the sixty four dollar question was posed to blondie by Paul, "We saw you trying to steal from several different people, have you got form for it?"

Blondie, his head dropping with some shame, in his reply said, "Yeah, I've got three previous for dipping. I was just a bit skint that's why I was trying to nick today."

Pete, on hearing this said, "Alright lads I'll do this one if you like."

Nothing was said, but the boys gave knowing looks at each other. Suddenly Pete was rowing back in on the job again. *Typical*, they thought. Blondie had put his hands up to trying to dip, even told them which two they were, which would go down as an attempt theft from persons unknown, and Pete saved his reputation as an ace 'thief taker' on the Dip Squad.

Blondie seemed resigned to being nicked as they awaited transport to West End Central Police Station. His only preoccupation was whether he'd get bail once he'd been charged, particularly as he was going plead guilty.

Paul said, "I dunno. Depends on whether what you've told us checks out. Let's just wait and see."

Blondie appeared content with that as they cruised through the central London streets to his 'new accommodation'. The prisoner van pulled up outside the front of the nick in Savile Row, in view of being rejected from the small station yard which had a variety of CID cars belonging to various members of the Obscene Publications Squad, once headed by Detective Chief Superintendent Bill Moody who did time for corruption following his trial at the Old Bailey. The dip squad members were recognised by the custody sergeant who as a Detective Constable had worked with a couple of them before recently gaining promotion. So the friendly face accepted the circumstances of blondie's arrest and told him he'd be held in the cells while Farmer and the rest of the crew did their enquiries on him. Blondie slammed the sergeants desk with his fist in anger at being held up for so long, and demanding bail — or as a black belt in Kung fu, he'd cut up rough. He was immediately jumped on by the boys who bundled him down the passage way and into cell three, to calm down. As they returned to the charge room to an unfazed sergeant who continued with his paperwork, Farmer and Hazel discussed their surprise on how strong the prisoner had become at not getting his own way, something they'd have to watch when they got him back out for charging.

Dave and Al joined the other two in the charge room having completed previous conviction and bail suitability enquiries.

Dave said, "The pre-cons seem to stand up, but the bail enquiry suggests he's known there, but it's not a permanent one, if you get my, drift Pete. We could take a chance and bail him, but he might do a bunk. How about a bit of fun? I mean, he'll be going to Marlborough Street Magistrates

Court tomorrow morning anyway. If he fancies his chances as a tough man, let's have a competition."

The custody sergeant strolled in to the charge room, enquiring whether the boys were ready to charge their man. Dave lowered his voice to propose his game. Once blondie had been charged, he'd have to arm wrestle Dave, best of three to decide whether he got bail that night or remain in custody until the following mornings court appearance. The sergeant laughed asking if he was serious, to which Dave responded 'Absolutely'. Farmer, wasn't so confident it was a good idea but realised he was in no position to resist the 'attractive' suggestion. In the meantime, Hazel and Fish gathered some of the late turn shift who'd just finished their refreshments to come to the charge room to lay bets on the latest game of 'It's a Knockout'.

Blondie, a little more subdued to when he was first banged up stood in front of the sergeant, mystified why so many officers had appeared to have an interest in him.

"You are charged that on today's date at Oxford Circus Underground Station you attempted to steal from a female, unknown. You are not obliged to say anything in answer to the charge, but what you say may be put into writing and given in evidence. You'll be at court tomorrow, the details are on this form." Blondie remained silent as he took a copy of the charge sheet form 59. .

"Can I go now? I just want to get this over with."

Dave said, "No mate. Your address doesn't check out, are you living there or somewhere else?"

"No I am, it's just I haven't been there long. Nobody else knows me there, I've just got a room in the house. So can have bail now?"

"Tell you what, you reckon you're a tough bloke with all that Kung fu crap, I'll arm wrestle you for your bail. Best of three."

Blondie annoyed at the proposition, agreed saying, "You don't stand a chance mate. I'll take you easy."

Paul and Al pushed the charge room desk into the middle of the room, and set two chairs for the 'gladiators' to do battle. Paul appointed himself referee while Fish went round the assembled late tun shift taking their one pound bets for either protagonist, and the skipper kept a watchful eye at the station office door for the duty inspector. Within five short minutes Dave had won the bet two to one. None of the tipsters had forecast that result and consequently Al was a 'tenner' up on the deal. Blondie was not impressed claiming he wasn't ready for the final duel, but his plea was ignored by the squad who bundled him back into his cell.

The custody sergeant open the wicket gate and together with Dave, told him he'd be staying in custody overnight until his appearance the following day at the 'house of correction'.

*

I had a bit of time on my hands so I went to court with Pete to see how he would perform. What a transformation! Armed with a statement under caution from blondie, admitting his guilt on two attempt thefts from the person, not one. Pete was 'brave' enough to step up to the mark and deal with the case in the witness box. Turns out our man had four previous convictions for theft. His sister turned up at court, apologising profusely to me for her errant brothers behaviour. Even made a point of giving me her details for future reference! Well you never know, do you? Blondie got weighed off with six months' imprisonment suspended for two years, and I resolved in my own mind to unload Pete at the earliest opportunity. I've seen plenty of square pegs avoiding a round hole and then promoted to get rid, usually above their capability.

What about the drama group, I hear you ask? Damn fool of a stage director cast me as a hapless schoolteacher opposite the demure dark haired school mistress. Every cloud!

5

HOBBY-BOBBY

"Hello Bob?" The voice on his phone was familiar, as he slumped into his chair, having just performed the most important function as far as he was concerned, the feeding of the fish! It was the head of security at Pentonville Prison, Nick, who had become a good drinking buddy ever since the 'gentleman's smoking evening' aka 'stag do' about six months ago in the Prison Warders social club at the back of the prison. Nick said he had a 'guest' on his wing at the prison who was coming towards the end of his sentence, and actually allowed out on day release once a week to get him used to the outside world. He was a former heavy duty armed robber whose career reputation preceded him, this time for possession of explosives. He'd approached Nick after his day release last week to tell him of a proposed major fraud he was being invited to join. As with any information of this nature, Bob asked him what Nick thought was the motive behind him effectively 'grassing' up the co-conspirators. He couldn't throw any light on that question, something which had also troubled him. He didn't appear to have any connection to the suspects involved but he did wonder if it was somehow settling an old score from years back. It would have to be, because he was coming towards the end of a ten year stretch. They both joked how some villains hold a grudge for a long time. Bob confirmed he'd get back to Nick once he'd sorted out a bag man to come with him to the prison, and fix a date for interview. Bob replaced the receiver and quietly sat pondering the information.

Acting Detective Sergeant Brian Kent, Bob's trusted confidant on matters needing impromptu denial, or spurious explanation, knocked and entered, passing Bobs latest 'fishy' acquisitions. Sensing he was in for a bit of a story he made himself comfortable in the easy chair to the right of the guv'nor's desk.

"They look nice now guv, settled in well haven't they."

Bob acknowledged Brian's comments of piscatorial expertise, and cut immediately to the chase. He told him of his chat with the head of security at the 'Ville', and explained that a villain who was coming towards the end of his incarceration had been approached to be part of a half-million-pound fraud, and the losers would be American Express. Basically when he met with an old friend at a pub not far from where his day release work was, the proposition was put to him that a team of Scots villains had access to a top-grade printer and equipment which could reproduce forged travellers' cheques, which were so good they wouldn't be detected by banks examining them. Selling them to members of the public who wouldn't be able to resist a bargain at a fraction of the cost of the real thing, would jump at the opportunity to buy and cash them as the genuine article. What the villain was looking for was someone to buy the whole 'parcel' from the printers, and he'd then get an informants reward for propping the job up. Brian, sensing a good enquiry, offered to do the background work on the villain, and arrange a prison visit for the following week to have a 'chat' with the informant.

I think I mentioned it earlier, when I told you how my team continue to be under investigation and I have had my wings clipped, in so far that those investigating think I've been moved off my Dip Squad. However, my Commander, Eric Brown is a decent man, and on the basis that like me he thinks — in his words — it's a 'trumped up' investigation, he's given me a written direction to continue my squad work but he's now given me responsibility for a small team of officers who are usually engaged in investigating large scale frauds arising from robberies of Royal Mail in transit, which the Post Office Investigation Branch have neither the resources or capability to deal with. What some might say is above their pay grade! . Hence the information I've given to Brian for him to dig around. If I am under the spotlight, and suspect I probably am, then I can show I have diversified my interests! To add to my responsibilities further, the boss asked me to take on the role of overseeing the activities of a newly formed search team, headed by a Police Search Adviser, or POLSA for short. This was following a reassessment of Police responsibilities in the aftermath of the Brighton bombing by the Provisional IRA. It means I've now been issued with all the counter terrorism kit, including a black 'romper' suit— in other words flame proof overalls — and reinforced body armour, and of course, boots! So, no pressure!

*

As arranged, John met with Mr. Dangerfield at the sandwich bar by the bus terminus at Victoria station. As far as John was concerned, they engaged in inconsequential chit-chat over a espresso while waiting for the boys to arrive. Dangerfield's enthusiasm to give the Dip Squad assistance and direction on suspects gushed from every sentence. Ten minutes passing saw the arrival of Paul and Al Fish, who immediately ordered two more coffees for themselves albeit John and George declined the offer of replenishment. The boys were careful not to divulge too much about the manner in which they may be obliged to operate, in the company of George. It was unusual to take a potential witness, who wasn't 'of the faith' so to speak, on a covert observation — because officially it may compromise the operation; whereas in reality it might curtail the 'activities' of the professionals.

The meeting terminated with the four of them weaving their way through the buses bidding to escape on their various routes at the front of Victoria, and across to the staircase leading to the underground beneath the Victorian canopy at the front of the mainline station. The boys firstly agreed to check the Circle and District line, opting for the eastbound platform as a starter. John elected to stay with Dangerfield while Paul and Al separated as they each entered the busy post rush hour platform. George, looked every inch the man about town in his Chester Barrie suit, set off with his 'Herbie Frogg' tie, a 'James Bond' clone if ever there was one! He was desperate to give his input to the observations looked excitedly up and down the rear of the three or four deep passengers waiting for the next trains arrival. John sighed an air of resignation at Dangerfield's enthusiasm, surmising that he was a rank amateur when it came to covert ops. Unlike the deeper tube platforms there wasn't much of a rush of air preceding the train announcing its imminent arrival as it drew to a halt in front of them.

On the doors' opening, the platform of intending passengers pushed forward to get on. George tried surreptitiously indicating two short middle-aged men busily shuffling at the back of the crowd some fifteen yards away. John hit his pointing arm down, in an effort to conceal his obvious sighting of the Mediterranean-looking suspects. Al and Paul were either side of them as they moved in behind an elderly-looking city gent carrying a small rucksack in his left hand. One of the suspects, dressed in a pale blue casual jacket, barged in front of the gent while the second wearing a denim 'Levi' jacket carefully lifted the gents suit jacket flap revealing his rear pocket which quite obviously held a wallet of some description. John had to physically restrain George from making his move, opting to remain some distance the unfolding events.

The city gent, frustrated at having his boarding of the carriage blocked, pushed past he blocker and on to the train while the second 'dip' pulled back in the obvious hope his efforts at relieving the gent of his wallet went unnoticed. However, Paul and Al boarded with the two suspects and their intended victim as the doors closed, leaving John and a very excited but disappointed George on the platform.

"They were with the the other three you arrested, I recognised them straight away, especially the one in the denim jacket — he certainly looks a rough lot. Shall we catch the next train and go after them, I'd hate to think of your colleagues coming off worst with them?"

John tried to diplomatically tell him they'd be fine. They might be very good dips, skilled in their art, but violence, he said, wasn't in their library of efforts to evade capture. In fact quite the reverse, theirs was to act confused, not speak English-albeit they knew enough to get by — and probably if all else fails, they'd try bribing the police, as in their own country, to evade prosecution. So no, they weren't going to pursue them, instead John phoned in to the Information Room from the control room on Victoria Station simply to advise what had happened, and that George recognised them and would make a witness statement as to what had transpired, that way it would be recorded on the tape should a snide defence brief months later alleged they had coerced Dangerfield in his evidence. Before he could finish his briefing, was told that Paul and Al had two arrests awaiting transport at Embankment station, to go to Bow Street police station. John confirmed they'd go straight to the nick to meet up with them. To John's relief, Dangerfield told him he had to get away to his offices for a meeting, but was at pains to tell him he was quite happy to give another statement identifying the two miscreants. Conroy feigned disappointment but thanked him for his help in trapping two more, what appeared to be South American, dips and confirmed another statement would be needed which he would phone and arrange.

Bob sat back in his Captains chair, rescued from his previous office, staring at the neon tetra shoal being pursued by two very aggressive angel fish. He was in a state of shock and somewhat crestfallen. Brian Kent popped his head round the corner to tell Bob he'd organised a prison visit for the pair of them on the following Wednesday, the day after their possible informant had returned from his day release. He could see Bob's thoughts were elsewhere so he quietly closed the door leaving him in peace.

I'm gutted to tell you the truth. The 'brief' I've been seeing for the past couple of years has just given me my cards. Or at least she's given me an ultimatum, I either leave the wife or it's over. In the meantime she's told me she'd been tapped up by some chinless wonder of a barrister, who — she took great delight, in telling me it seemed — she'd slept with, and intends seeing him again. To be fair, she did tell me about him before, but I didn't take it seriously as I knew from other sources that he was a pisshead drunk and a heavy gambler on the horses. What the fuck?! So to all intents and purpose I'm in the skip at present and a 'single' man again. I just couldn't do it to the kids. When people say they stay together for the sake of the children, I get it, but can it be right that couples live in such misery. Surely it must affect the kids. Mind, I'm not at home that much so at least they don't see domestic turmoil which doesn't appear to exist to them when they're with me, which I guess is a good thing. I just wish I hadn't lost the brief, especially to a privileged turd like him.

On a lighter note the boys have just phoned to give me the good news of two more Chileans nicked. So I'm off to 'supervise' their incarceration with the little 'jamboree' bag of left over goodies from the first three charged a couple of days ago, which Farmer thought might provide some conspiratorial connection to them! Still not convinced about him.

Bob strode purposefully towards the underground for what was an uneventful journey to Covent Garden and the five minute walk to the nick. Sergeant Satchell was once again the custody officer, greeting Bob as he stepped in to the Charge Room, the two prisoners were lodged in the cells while the team were rooting through their property.

"Hey look at this ones gear. He's got five hundred quid in fifties and a couple of tenners. He's also got a cross channel ferry ticket folded inside his Chilean passport. At least it looks like him, Juan Jesus Martinez," said Al.

John and Paul looked to the guv'nor without a word, appealing to establish if he had the 'necessary' with him.

"Shall we go and have a cup tea upstairs Sarge and leave the boys to sort out what they've got?" said Bob to the skipper who was engrossed in the number of crisp fifty pound notes on his table, both prisoners seeming to have about the same quantity. He agreed with Bob as the goody bag was 'palmed' to the ever-aware Al, leaving the boys one question: whether they intended interviewing them as he knew of an interpreter, who could assist. Grateful for his assistance they continued to go through the prisoners property.

"Here, this ones got a Spanish identity card in the name of Francisco Caro. Isn't that the surname of one of those we nicked the other day? Wonder if they're related. Looks a lot like him in the photo, bit fatter in the face perhaps, I reckon they are. Paul give us a couple of those tenners from Martinez property bag," said Al, at the simultaneously relieving the same of the sequentially numbered notes from their goody bag.

John and Paul rooting through the fifty pound notes found again there were a number which were sequentially numbered, whereupon Paul did a switch between the two, exclaiming "You'll like it, not a lot!". To ensure a possible future continuity, he then took the cross channel ferry ticket from Juan Jesus's property bag and put it in the goody bag, remarking there may be more to come.

As the subdued laughter between them subsided, content in the knowledge they had linked the two prisoners together, which to their minds was only right with these professional thieves, they had now connected them to the first three. Bob re-entered enquiring whether the detectives had established connections, to be told that there was evidence to connect each of them to each other and they were in the process of getting an interpreter to attend the nick to assist with interviews.

"I doubt they'll say much — probably feign confusion, deny the offence, and apologise for any inconvenience caused. Anything more than that I'd be surprised. Still, at least it will show to the court we tried." said Bob. With that he congratulated them on their latest arrests, and said that they had a good victim statement from the city gent which would nicely link with Dangerfield's second missive.

Right I'm off homeward bound, to attend the first rehearsal of this blasted amateur drama I've been selected for! I'll leave them to sort out the contemporaneous note interviews of the two, using the services of a dear old man who I'd known from previous investigations. He not only spoke Spanish but he also knew South American Spanish as he had lived in Santiago, Chile for about twenty years earlier in his life, when he was teaching.

6

REVELATIONS

'*She used to look good to me but now I find her simply irresistible*.' boomed a smooth singer by the name of Robert Palmer Bob through his Walkman headphones, as he found himself reflecting on last nights escapades at the drama group, resigned as he was, at wading through and signing off countless crime reports.

Today's the day that Brian Kent and I will be going to that creamy white painted prison known as Pentonville, originally designed by Joshua Jebb, of the Royal engineers, in 1842, for the detention of prisoners prior to transportation, or Australia as we now call it. Now I get how Brixton prison's address is in Jebb Avenue, guess he did that one as well. Pity we can't still do that, some might say! Transportation I mean.

That stunning dark haired woman I'm playing opposite was there last night, but she didn't stay long, a bloke who I thought was her husband turned up and she left in tears with him. It was only at the end of the evening when I was having a drink with a few of the cast, I found out it was her brother! Apparently — now bear in mind I've only just met these luvvies — one of their number told me she believed her husband was having an affair with another woman in the group. The way he was talking, left me with the impression, they're all at it! Must be all that attention seeking. Anyway I got as far as finding out her name is Sharon.

"Right, what have we got then Brian?" as Bob's bagman knocked and entered the office not waiting for an invite, as he was still engrossed in the next song of being *addicted to Love*. Removing the headphones, he listened to Brian's briefing. The man they were about to see, was indeed a man with a lot of form for serious offences, he was on what was colloquially known as the 'main index' at New Scotland Yard. He had changed his name by deed poll, probably to avoid discovery when he was finally released, and was now known as Dave Driscoll. Bob suggested they just go and hear what Driscoll has got to say; not quiz him too much, but create the impression of wanting to believe everything he said as 'gospel', then come away to do more digging. He sure as hell wasn't going to register him as an informant at this stage. This, they both knew involved generating a lot of paperwork, which may never lead to anything.

Brian led the way to the new Peugeot 205GTi in the back yard, gaining approving comments from Bob as they got in for the short journey to the 'Ville'. Brian had been tasked with assessment of this quick car as a vehicle suitable for surveillance.

Their passport into the prison was via the official visitors entrance near the large wooden doors where they were met by the guv'nor's pal, Nick. He'd set it up so they could have a cosy chat with Driscoll in one the rooms where they wouldn't be observed by the other lags in the establishment. The familiar clang of gates being unlocked and locked again led them to a plain pale green door and Bobs' conclusion that it was a job he could never do. *It's almost as if you're doing time as well,* thought Bob. Nick opened it to reveal Driscoll sat one side of the table. On seeing the three he leapt to his feet, greeting them with, a morning sir! *Snivelling shit,* thought Bob. At this point Nick left them to it. Brian sat to the right, opening his portfolio notepad, while Bob sat opposite Driscoll. He came prepared with twenty Benson and Hedges strategically placed on the table for Driscoll to use as required.

Driscoll needed no encouragement to light up a free fag, or to ingratiate himself with his two 'guests', as if he was greeting two long lost pals. As with all villains, he enquired from Bob if he might know Bobs own governor from a while back. Cute to this kind of over-familiarity, he gave him Maurice Branch's name, simply because he'd headed up a large cheque fraud in the past. Driscoll immediately said he knew Bobs boss and asked to be remembered to him. Bob, familiar with this tactic from the likes of his 'kidney', took the lead playing along with the charade of best friends, simply to glean the information, while Brian sat jotting salient points from what Driscoll was saying. The story was that he met an old friend a couple of weeks ago in 'The Old Bill' pub in Greenford, seemingly named after an old steam train, and nothing to do with the officers' vocation! The second time he met him he was in the company of a couple of Scots who, had access to a very sophisticated printing set up which could produce excellent forged travellers cheques to be sold to punters at less than half the market price. The Glaswegians gave him two samples to see if he knew of anyone who could take on the parcel for which they wanted a return of thirty grand cash. With that Driscoll fished around his trouser pocket, and placed the four forgeries on the table in front of Bob, inviting closer examination.

Bob immediately saw they were of excellent quality, but not knowing if they were good enough to be passed, say, in a bank, or bureaux-de-change — but he registered no question of authenticity with Driscoll, preferring to comment on their excellent print work. Driscoll sat back in self satisfaction drawing on another cigarette, content that Bob was taking the bait.

"I want to hang on to these, Dave, if I can. As I understand it you're after the ten per cent informants fee, is that right? It's going to take me a week or so to gear up, and then have a meet with your man, okay?" said Bob.

Driscoll was content with Bobs strategy, of wanting a meet with his mate to then set up negotiations with the Glaswegians. Bobs idea was to put in a covert officer, who'd masquerade as a villain to purchase the whole package, without outlining too much to Driscoll. He responded he'd be in touch with his mate by telephone from the prison, but he knew he was a regular at the pub in the early evenings, so it wouldn't be difficult to hook up with him.

Bob made a point of overwhelming gratitude for Driscoll's help, saying he'd be in touch with Nick during the week, to facilitate the informants phone call to his mate. Brian did a bit of background chat and made notes on Driscoll's history and when he expected to be released, important to ensure Driscoll would play no active part on the deal, reasoning as Bob did, this wouldn't then compromise the arrest and subsequent trial of the villains. Driscoll was ahead of the conversation understanding the limit of his involvement or otherwise. A knock on the door, summoned Nick who told Driscoll to stay put while he escorted Bob and Brian from the prison.

They bade Nick a farewell as they drove away, agreeing that a 'lager frenzy' in the prison officer's club at the back was long overdue. Bob recounted the tale of a 'gentleman's smoking evening' at the club when one of the comedians was a bloke in a wheelchair called Tony Gerrard, who initially declared he wasn't so much meals on wheels, more muck in trucks! The evening became all the more memorable when it was discovered two News of the World reporters had managed to get two tickets to the 'concert'. In itself not too much of a problem, except the following Sunday it had made the front page, and a double page spread about this 'cultural event'. The organisers of the evening were two of Bob's officers, one of whom phoned him in a blind panic when he saw that local newsagents were selling out fast! Reassured that he he should leave falling on his sword until he'd had a chance to speak with the guv'nor, the officer rang off. Bob then made the call to his immediate boss, an old pal who had served with him when they were both junior officers. Agreeing there wasn't too much of a problem in a private function organised at a private location, the pair of them hatched a wind up. Bob rang the junior detective back, directing him to ring the guv'nor in the next few minutes.

"Hello guv, it's me, I don know if you've had a chance to see the Sunday press have you? It appears we feature in the 'news of the screws', I'm really sorry guv."

The boss then went into about five minutes interrogation on how the event came about, organisers, purpose of the event and so on, finishing with how disappointed he was with the officer.

Sensing he was in trouble, he asked what he should do.

"The next fucking 'do' you have like this, make sure I get a ticket!"

The officer struck by the demand simply confirmed there was no discipline issue to worry about, heaved a sigh of relief, and apologised profusely.

The guv'nor reiterated with Bob the conversation he'd had with the young detective, told him to piss off and be more careful in future. Drama over.

*

Brian said, "What do you reckon guv'nor, sounds tempting doesn't it? I know what you're thinking — why him, why now?"

Bob agreed, affirming he didn't trust Driscoll, especially with the kind of form he had. What he was fiercely conscious of, was putting in a police buyer into something that might be a trap. He'd give it some thought.

The rest of the journey back to the nick was quiet, as George Michael serenaded them on the radio with *Careless whispers*. Bob, assuming the position back at his desk, requesting Brian to leave his notes with him to ponder. And so the phone announced its need for attention.

*

"Hello guv, it's Paul here, I'm down at Notting Hill nick with Tony White, yeah, Angie and me. You know the new Doris we've got on attachment? We've just nicked him for attempt theft on a bird on the Central line at Notting Hill. He wants to talk to you about our business, reckons he's got information that might be of interest to us, but he won't tell me, he'll only speak to you. Okay see you in an hour, we'll go and have some grub first."

Bob smiled to himself. Perhaps this was the breakthrough he needed in the dodgy investigation he and his officers were currently subjected to. Those lowlife —to his mind — officers, Secrett, Branch, and Spooner, while Kid Creole singing about a stool pigeon, was blasting from the radio precariously balanced on the hood of his aquarium.

"Ha, cha cha cha," as he sang along while feeding the fish.

He took the five minute walk to the tube station, checking in the reflection of the shop windows that he was still that Sharp dressed man that ZZ Top sang of. *If only I had the one with the blonde hair in the video on my arm*, he mused. Twenty minutes later, he couldn't help thinking how the area had begun to transform from 'bandit country' with salubrious attractions as the 'Mangrove' club, to a more 'gentrified' suburb of west London, where Range Rovers — colloquially referred to as 'Chelsea tractors'— were in evidence on every street corner. He pulled open the large brass-handled door and wandered in to the front office of the nick. The sight of his 'black rover', aka brief or warrant card, at the front desk, granted him access to the bowels of the police station. His detective ability led him straight to the canteen where he linked up with Paul and Angie Scott, buying a round of teas for them.

"Right, what have we got? By the way, good arrest, you know Paul that I know Tony from a couple of earlier skirmishes. He usually accepts his fate on the basis that we don't catch him every time he's thieving. Usually plays ball. What's this about today?" said Bob as Angie listened intently as to how they had spotted White on the westbound Central line platform 'shaping up'— going through the preparatory stages of a dipping or theft from the person — from a couple of young female tourists. Paul, being the seasoned officer, described how White had struggled when they arrested him, but desisted when he saw he was outnumbered, and Paul identified him by using his name. It meant in Whites mind, even if he escaped arrest, the Dip Squad would be after him, with every likelihood they'd pick a time and place inconvenient to him. Hence, he went like the proverbial lamb to the slaughter. The tourists gave their details to Angie which she had recorded in her pocket book, although they had informed her they'd probably be leaving from the London Brothers hotel on Euston Road, the following day.

So Tony White wants to speak to me alone. My guess he's going to try and trade the arrest today with some gems of information on our current 'little local difficulty'. Basically he tells me something which I don't know but have suspected in return for no further action on his problem with Paul and Angie. Better be good for me to go out on a limb like that, although I am content he's an honourable thief. Can't be too many of those to the pound, can there? But care is still required.

If he's willing to grass someone else up, then he'd find it just as easy to grass me up.

Bob told the pair of them to hang on in the canteen sort out their notes of evidence, particularly mindful of the fact a 'new recruit' was being tested as to her viability of working on the squad, while he went to speak with Tony. Descending to the charge room he saw the custody sergeant, and after a brief chat with him assuring him what was about to take place wasn't a formal interview, he secured the release of White to a juvenile detention room behind the sergeants desk. This meant that nothing needed to be additionally recorded on his custody sheet because effectively he was still in the 'peter', or cell.

"Right, Tony, nice suit by the way — Armani I guess — business is good for you. What do you want to speak to me about?" said a casually enquiring Bob as if he wasn't overtly interested.

"Mr. Trebor, we've known each other for some time now haven't we. You've always been straight with me when you've nicked me, and you know I've always pleaded guilty although… well you know." Tony was waffling and Bob told him so, he assumed he hadn't called to speak to him just to tell him he appreciated the way he'd been allegedly fitted up in the past.

"What do you think will happen today?" White tentatively asked.

"I don't know Tony, but with your form I would think you've got to be going to Crown to be weighed off. I'm being straight with you."

"Yeah, I know guv, not like someone in the past.", retorted White.

"What do you mean Tony?"

"You know, Dennison," he said.

"Hasn't he been straight with you in the past then?"

"Are you kidding," as White burst out laughing.

"Guv, I don't know if you can help me but I'm on a bender (suspended sentence) at the moment. If I go down for this one, and you know I don't want to plead not guilty — but if I go down for this, I've got eighteen months to do, and I'd rather not if you get me. So I'm wondering if we can come to some arrangement?"

Bob said nothing, waiting for him to reveal before he could consider any kind of deal.

"Sir, I've known 'Mackey' —that is Andrew McMurray — since we were at school together, so a long time. You and your squad have got aggro from him when that Sergeant Dennison nicked him at Russell Square. I saw Andrew a couple of weeks later and he told what really went on."

Now Bob was interested.

"I'm not a grass, but even at the time I didn't think it was right. Andrew had been nicked by your guys, don't know who —it don't really matter — but he didn't like it. I ain't going to say it but he reckons he was fitted up by them. I don't know, but do know he had the serious arse as a result of it. He couldn't figure out, with all the money on him why he couldn't be taxed and given a life. I told him you guys don't work like that, they cant be bought."

"You're damn right, that sort thing sickens me Tony."

So he got hold of an old boyfriend of his — you know he's queer don't you? — so he spoke to Dennison. I've never like him, he took over a grand off me one time, for nothing, it's what he does. He just stopped me and shook me down, I didn't do nothing but he told me I was lucky, some fucking luck. He don't do your kind of work now does he."

"No. As I said, that sort of thing sickens me Tony."

"I can tell that guv, I wouldn't even insult you by offering it. But Dennison's different. I could tell you lots about him guv but I don't want to get involved. I know you lot are sweet, I know that."

"Would you put it down on paper then Tony?"

"No guv, I don't want to get involved. But I tell you Dennison's bad, what he did to you and your boys was way out of order."

"How does he know Mackey?"

Tony said, " He's known him ages, I think he nicked him for 'sus' (suspected person) good while back. I told him to leave it, but he wasn't having it, so that Greg Dennison met up with him and told him he could get him off the charge your boys had him on. Next thing I knew was the shit at Russell Square happened. He told me he met up with Dennison, he'd shook him down a few days before. He didn't know what was going to happen but Dennison told him to trust him. They were just by the lifts when Dennison got on his radio calling for urgent help, he shook Andrew about and the pulled his jacket off his shoulders to make it look like they'd had a 'tear up' (fight). Only about a minute went by when two old bill turned up and jumped all over him telling he was nicked. Next thing he knew was Dennison fell to the floor as if he was knocked out. An ambulance took him away and Andrew was taken to some offices — not a nick but it was that place where he had to say the Dip Squad was bent, which is what he did. He didn't know the two bods who spoke to him, but they told him what he said, was music to their ears. That's exactly what they said. He just thought he was making the usual allegation of bent coppers, but they told him they would fix the charge he was on, he had nothing to bother about."

Tony went on to flesh out the bones of what he said, at Bobs request. Then came 'killer' question as far as Tony was concerned, he needed to make a statement about what he'd said?

"I can't guv'nor, you know that. I ain't no grass, it just ain't right, that's why I've told you. What is Dennison now a Detective Inspector?

"No still, still a sergeant ."

"He's doing well though isn't he? He's working around Victoria and Waterloo isn't he guv?"

Bob said, "Is Dennison still seeing Mackey?"

"Of course, he is, why do you think he's earning so well? Dennison's given him licence to. You know he tried to get hold of me not so long ago. He actually came round my house looking for me. Told my mum some old bollocks about me being wanted for a traffic offence, told her he wanted me to go down the station. I knew it was rubbish so I didn't go."

"When was this?" asked Bob.

"Some time earlier this year, my mum can tell you."

Bob said, "Now Tony, let's get this straight, really you've only told me what I already knew. This is about you walking out of your current problem, namely the bender hanging over you. But I'm a reasonable man, so tell me what else is there you need to tell me? Why did Dennison set this up for Andrew? What was behind it?"

"I don't know guv, all I know is Andrew told me it was a way of getting the Dip Squad investigated. Dennison told him not to worry, it wasn't about him, they had other information about your squad. Not you, the word is you're straight —no it was the others. They were after getting the others, some other investigation, he just said he'd get a result if he went along with it. I'm not the only one who knows it. Some of the others know it as well."

"Who are we talking about Tony?"

"I don't really want to say. Alright, I don't like him any way, Monk, Gerry Monk."

Bob's wry smile meant the name was very familiar to him but he didn't comment any further. Again he invited Tony to commit it to paper in the form of a statement under caution, but his response was as before in that it was more than his life's worth. Bob briskly told him to get to his feet, as he was going back in the cell, without any promises to the future.

Once back in the 'peter', Bob met up with Paul and Angie once more in the canteen. The two of them were keen to find out what 'gems' of information White had imparted to the guv'nor. Conscious that Paul might be one of his squad in the sight hairs of the investigating officers, and Angie having joined after the raid in no way implicated from what Tony had said, Bob was deliberately vague about the meeting. His explanation was that White, like so many dips before, was just looking for an angle to avoid being 'potted' for his latest arrest. This seemed to gel with pair of them.

I bloody knew it! I said at the time of the raid on our offices, there was something smelly about the allegation. Apart from my idiot Detective Sergeant Hunt, I cant see how anyone else has done anything like those investigating were suggesting. I think I'm fireproof, as are the team, I just guess it'll take time to shake out. Until the investigation runs its course we'll just keep quiet. What's happening with White I hear you ask?. As they haven't got the female victims statement, I legitimately got him out on bail for further enquiries, achieves two things, first he's still on a string which I can tug anytime and second, although he wouldn't make a statement under caution, I did make a usual witness statement, which I wrote in my name about what he'd said to me. That way, if he needs to he can claim he personally didn't grass anyone. But just for the moment I'm going to keep it safe as insurance. I'll let you know when I drop the bomb.

Bob left Paul and Angie to tie up the loose ends and paperwork for the bail back with the custody Sergeant before releasing Tony White on an unsuspecting world, while he made his way back to the tube station for the return to his office. His arrival back at the office was disrupted by his phone demanding a reply.

"Oh. Hi Maria, blimey this is a blast from the past! How are you?

Just to put you in the picture, I haven't heard from her since I was a Detective Sergeant running a vice team operating around the King's Cross area of London. Must be at least a year and a half or two ago. Putting it bluntly she's a 'tom' — or a more familiar label, a prostitute — who back then I cultivated as my informant. At that time, she was strung out on crack cocaine, or was chasing the dragon, doing heroin big time —

anything up to ten or twelve wraps at twenty-five quid a pop, a day. The 'Cross' was the only place you could buy crack on the street. Italian pushers were bringing it in to the country through Ramsgate. They figured it was a safe route for them from the continent. They'd usually base themselves at the seaside then come up to town with the gear. Maria was in a mess when I first nicked her for being on the game as it's called. She had to earn at least two hundred and fifty pounds a day just to feed her habit — charging twenty five pounds a 'trick' or a 'short time' in other words sex or a blow job(oral sex) with a condom of course — before she could then live and pay for her food. You'd be forgiven for thinking she'd perhaps been abused or from a broken home. No, her family were actually quite well to do, living in the posher part of Tottenham. She was attractive at one time, enjoyed the attention of men, but a short trip from alcohol to drugs saw her now injecting the 'fix' in her feet as the veins in her arms and hands were shot to pieces. Back then I actually managed to get her on a drug dependency reduction course. She did really well, getting the habit down to two wraps a day. But then she couldn't make that final fifty percent cut to one wrap. In no time at all she was sadly back up to double figures. When she phoned I was surprised to hear her gruff voice. I thought she'd probably be dead by now! Anyway, knowing what I'm doing now, she reckons she has some information for me. I'll meet her in the Burger King later.

7
MEETINGS — BLOODY MEETINGS

The day started with the guv'nor of the nick, McVicar, barging into Bobs office and remonstrating that his squad had emptied the fire extinguishers in a pissed-up battle with one another in the middle of the night, yet again. Bob side stepped his obvious irritation first by saying he'd sort out the culprits, and then by sharing the fact that he'd met with a prostitute yesterday evening down at Kings Cross. The guv'nor's attention was immediately tuned into this nugget of information as Bob knew he'd served in that area as a uniform Inspector. He then waxed lyrical about his time there, and how he'd enjoyed — if that be the word— working the streets and nicking the 'toms' aka prostitutes. The offer of him coming as a 'guest' to the Friday afternoon 'debrief' when copious bottles of Lambrusco red would be consumed, seemed to dampen his annoyance at the squad indiscretion with the fire extinguishers, yet again!

*

Late afternoon saw Tommy Francis and 'darling' Clementine meet up in the Nags Head, inspiration for the *'Only Fools and Horses'* boozer, just north of Camberwell Green. The day had come when Eddie Moody was to be challenged about his 'unfortunate' oversight in not repaying his debt. In the company of Tommy was another trusted pal, whose only job was to drive them to near Ladbrokes in Walworth Road, drop them off while they had their meet with Moody, then pick them up just in Carter Street, near Manze's pie and mash shop.

"Alright, Roger, this is our wheels for the job," as he introduced him as his regular driver otherwise known as 'Ferdie'.

"Quick rinse at the Nags Head before we go. Eddie is where I thought he'd be, cleaning up on a couple of bets. I don't know where he gets his tips from but it must be good," as Tommy outlined the plot. He reckoned they had about thirty minutes before Eddie would be leaving Ladbrokes. They will wait at the bus shelter opposite, and as he goes past them on the blind side they drop in behind him, about ten yards back as he goes up Carter Street. It's not until they reach the garages by the flats they will challenge him with the shooter Tommy has with him, and relieve him of the expected ten grand he'd have on him before issuing an ultimatum of fourteen days to find the rest. He'd just show him he's 'tooled up' in case he thinks well-reasoned argument might save him from losing his profit for the day.

A quick drink later and a cruise up Walworth Road saw the car being parked up just along from the front door to Carter Street nick. Tommy and Roger wandered off down to the end of the street, turning left to where the bus shelter would give them cover while Ferdie drove back down Carter Street parking further along Walworth Road in case of any difficulties. Just then, a crack of thunder announced rainfall. Tommy looked across the road to see Ladbrokes' door open and a very happy Moody step out, shoving a large wad of notes into his left over coat pocket before pulling up his collar shielding the back of his neck as he darted in between the passing traffic, making his way in to the street ten yards from the interceptors. Tommy and Roger fell in unnoticed behind him as he strode purposefully towards the police station to his left. Tommy reminded Roger that from the money relieved from Eddie they'd get a 'bag of sand'— a grand, or one thousand pounds in layman's terms — between them, bringing a smile of approval from Roger.

Moody made his way into the cul-de-sac of garages where he fumbled for his keys for his Rover P6 —same as the police motors — parked across two garage doors at the far end. Unaware of company he casually walked towards it when he heard a voice he recognised behind him.

"Eddie, hows it going, I thought it was you walking up here. Funnily enough I was looking to have a word with you." Seeing he was in company with Clementine, he tried casually asking what's up.

Tommy, outlined 'the case against him' as they gathered together. He looked first of all for an explanation, before assuring Eddie how this was now going to be resolved, as the heavens opened up again with a large crack of thunder.

"Come in here out of the rain Ed." as Tommy pushed the up-and-over door to the garage next where the Rover was parked. His sinister tone indicated to Eddie this was turning nasty. He saw a single chair positioned in the middle of an otherwise empty garage save the puddles of water increasingly gathering size from the constant drip-dripping from the tired corrugated asbestos roof. Eddie, not wanting to confront Tommy's frame as he stood in the way of his escape, complied with Tommy steering him to the chair, and firmly planting him on to the seat, guided by Roger, who stood like an expectant barber at the rear of the chair.

"Alright Tom, no need to act hasty. I'm sat here all ears. What's this all about? I ain't trodden on your toes have I? I mean, I'm sure we can work this out."

Tom leant forward, filling Eddies face so the only thing he could see was Tommy's bloodshot eyes staring into his. His attention was distracted by Roger deftly taping both his wrists to the chair arms, securing his position as that of the condemned man in the electric chair. Happy that he now had Eddie's undivided attention, he produced a gun from the rear waistband of his trousers, and poked it under Eddie's nostrils to emphasise that this wasn't just a minor problem.

"How much have you won today? Five, ten, a score? Now listen Eddie, it's official, you are a piss taker. You know you owe my people, and they're getting fucking impatient waiting for you to weigh in. You get me? So what I'm goin' to do is relieve you of your winnings and then I'm goin' to help you recognise that as a result of you getting the rest of what you owe, you won't need to fill out the menu card at hospital or worse still, have a label tied to your big toe showing your membership of the fucking mortuary. Are you understanding me?" said Tommy as he waived the pistol under Eddies nose.

Eddie nodded silently, in an air of resignation for his predicament, he realised his new found wealth was about to be removed from his possession. He appealed to Tom to remove the gun from under his nose, at the same as his inside pockets were being fleeced. Tommy's chubby fingers started counting the twenty pound notes as he juggled holding the pistol in his other hand. Roger watched dutifully from behind the chair, not realising what was about to happen. The cheap insulating tape used to restrict Eddie's escape was beginning to lose its bite, as the previously tightly bound wrists found they had more movement than was bargained for. Tommy declared he was satisfied with the haul as a sizeable down payment, but to ensure he kept Eddie's attention and his continued commitment to repaying the rest of the debt, he jammed five hundred pounds back into Eddie's inside pocket.

"Right there's a monkey to keep you going," said Tommy as he stood over Moody, still brandishing the revolver. He bluntly told Eddie he was being given a chance to redeem himself with another two weeks grace to find the remaining money owed, in Tommy's mind there was no point in harming Eddie's health any further, as it would defeat the point of the debt collection.

Eddie nodded acknowledgement of the five hundred pound donation, sensing his chance perhaps to escape, or to take his money back, barged forward from the chair freeing the tapes that held him. Roger fell forward trying to pull Eddie back in the chair, as Tommy fell backwards as the gun still cocked fell from his hand. All three watched as the gun floated seemingly in slow motion in a rainbow arc, unable to resist the force of gravity any longer, striking the ground just to the right of Tommy's foot. The previously cocked gun fired without a finger on the trigger, prompting an immediate yell of excruciating pain from Eddie as he looked down at his left foot. The randomly fired bullet had succeeded in penetrating his Chelsea boot, and had exited through his instep leaving him rolling around in pain on the floor of the garage.

Roger kicked Eddie in the head as if taking a free kick at Fulham, preventing the injured Moody making a grab for the gun. Tommy stamped on his hand, increasing his pain and enforcing the message he wasn't going to win this particular skirmish. The scramble came to an end as Tommy picked up the gun and jammed it back in his pocket, careful to ensure no further accidents.

"That's your fucking fault Eddie. I warned you, now sort yourself out. It ain't that bad. More blood than serious, get on with it. What I'll tell you is if you want some more I can let rip again if you want." He fired a second shot at his right foot, which missed as it bounced off the concrete floor, finding a way through the asbestos roof to be lost outside. Eddie continued to scream. The blood formed a puddle around his foot as he lay on the floor trying to deal with the pain.

"Just so you know things ain't no different just cos you've got a scratch. Two weeks, or more of the same, and you better not say a fucking word about this or I'm coming after you pronto, you're a dead man limping."

Tommy and Roger laughed as their sense of humour grew more faint as they walk briskly back down Carter Street towards Walworth Road. The sound of the gunfire didn't seem to register with anyone close by, not even at the nick no more than fifty yards away, the cloudburst of thunder and lightning seemingly masking thoughts of anything more serious. Happy they'd made good their escape from the scene the pair nonchalantly wandered into the evening population of Manze's pie and mash shop. Roger sat at a long bench at the back of the shop, his hands sensing the cold marble table as he waited for Tommy to arrive with his two pie mash and liquor.

"That fucker better not bubble us." as Roger expressed concern about Tommy's gunslinging techniques, first querying the need for the he gun, and secondly his ignorance that the bloody thing was loaded. He assumed it was just to be a bit of flash, a scare tactic.

"You reckon he's not going to say anything Tom?"

"Not if he values his fucking life he won't. His problem is he thinks he's more clever than he really is. Well, now he's got a limp to remind him to weigh in when he owes. Fuck him."

As they started their pie and mash, Trevor sauntered in, having been told earlier in the day by Tommy to meet up with them. After usual exchange of insults by way of mutual banter, Trevor sat down, waiting to hear why Tommy had asked for the meet. But nothing was going to happen until Tommy and Roger had their fill, followed by a portion of jellied eels.

*

"Hello Greg, nice to see you. So what you doing here?" said Detective Inspector Walker, as he leant back in his chair, surveying those under his command in the general CID office at Waterloo nick.

Truth be told, it wasn't the best of accommodation in that it was stuck in the middle of a busy and vibrant main line station in much need of rescue and refurbishment, neither of which were imminent. And so the police were stuck with a low grade establishment which the wealthy landowner railway companies would rather lease to commercial interests giving them a greater return on the space. The flip side was that it was handy to have law enforcement to call on, consequently a necessary evil in a way.

"Hi guv, no problem, I was just passing through, I've been at Southwark Crown Court this morning, and I just needed to use the phone — got a couple of follow-ups from my case," said Dennison.

Walker deep in thought, said, "Here Greg, you used to do dips didn't you. When you've got a moment after your enquiries, look in, I want to pick your brains."

"Ok guv, funnily enough I bumped into, you know their boss —D/I Trebor — the current head of the Dip Squad down at court today. I'll look in after."

As Dennison reappeared at the governors door Walker said, " Greg, it's probably nothing, but do you know the crew of the current Dip Squad?" Dennison confirmed he knew Trebor as they'd worked together before, but the rest of them were mysteries to him. His question as to why the interest met with a smoke screen of casual indifference from Walker. He figured there was more that Walker wasn't telling him but he knew not to ask further as it would be met with a wall of silence, and he wasn't really interested in mixing a potion for Trebor, as he knew it would come back to 'bite him on the arse'. He tried again to no avail, and so Dennison left Walker, still ruminating on his enquiry.

As the day had finished, as far as Walker was concerned, he locked his drawers, checking twice to ensure the contents — a number of empty wallets and some embarrassing papers — wouldn't be discovered in his absence. He heaved on his beige raincoat, the kind that seemed to be the issue of the American secret service, and set forth for The Wellington pub across the road from Waterloo station for a drink with his 'informant', Trevor Jones aka Sutton.

*

Maria was struggling to stay awake as she looked out from the Burger King window at the familiar vista of her 'beat' on the busy Euston Road. A continual procession of traffic paraded in each direction past the front of Kings Cross railway station. The pedestrian forecourt was busy with tired passengers seeking fresh air having disgorged from their newly arrived trains. Needless to say they were going to be disappointed with the polluted exhaust filled air at the front of the station. Dozens of people continued in their determined march back and forth to their places of employment while amongst the melee a few 'ladies of the night' plied their trade as a couple of drug pushers continued their deals, selling crack cocaine on the street. Maria knew the various players involved in both occupations, although the rest of the general public were completely oblivious to their activities, preoccupied with getting from A to B with the minimum of fuss, not wanting to hang around the dusty and dirty strip any longer than they needed to. She hoped it wouldn't be too long before Bob appeared. She was coming down off her fix, her body telling her she needed another 'hit', fiercely aware that she also needed to earn in her nominated occupation to pay for it.

Five minutes elapsed as Maria's need for 'speed' increased when to her relief Bob pulled back the tired buckled aluminium door and sauntered in. He nodded to her, enquiring if she needed anything while he ordered two menus, of cheese burgers, fries and coffee. As he returned to her shop window location, she eagerly seized the food and drink as if she hadn't eaten for days. It was no surprise to Bob as probably that was the case.

"You're a boss now" she said in the familiar gravelly voice acquired from years of booze and drugs.

Bob confirmed her enquiry as he likewise ate his food, and enquiring why she needed to see him now after all this time. *There must be an angle* he thought to himself. His suspicions were rewarded with more information about the raid on his squad.

"Bob I'll always remember how you helped me when you were working round here and you got me on that drug rehab. I know it didn't work out, I really tried honest, but I just couldn't do without that hit. It's what gives me the buzz, you know?"

Bob stayed silent just listening to her thinking, *sooner or later she's going to get to the point. I bet she's got two or three court appearances coming up at Clerkenwell Court, and she wants my help to avoid going inside. Here we go, I thought so!*

"You know the old lady on the flower stall outside St Pancras Station, well she's a mate of mine. Honestly, I've known her for years. I don't think I'm giving anything up when I tell you she's helped when I've been working, letting me know when the Old Bill have been about. You're nodding your head, Bob, I know you know that and I guess you know she's got a boy who ain't, well, the most honest. He's a bit of a grifter (*aka con man*) but he does some dipping as well."

Bob told her to get to the point, confirming he knew exactly who she was talking about, and that he wasn't stupid. *It's why I'm a detective, for God's sake!*

"Her boy was there at the stall helping his mum out when I saw the pair of them. Must have been a couple of weeks ago I can't really be sure. I can tell by you nodding now you know him. Well his mum told me that a mate of his told him about some squad getting nicked. He said it was some sort of Crime Squad or Dip squad or something I don't think he was any more exact than that. But he said it was a set up by some dodgy detective who knew the guy who had been chawed (*arrested for theft from the person*). Everyone knows it was fixed so he could make corruption complaint against the squad, so they could be fitted up. I don't know why it had to be done but even the boys didn't think it was right 'cos the detective who did the nicking is well bent. He's been on the take for years. Now, can you help me with my little problem?"

Well there we are then. I guessed she wanted a 'lift' on her Clerkenwell Court appearances, so I'll have to do some homework on that. She's been straight enough to tell me what I already suspected so if I can ease her problem then I will. You've probably guessed it, I know the dip she's talking about, he's a gobshite but I reckon what he's saying is right. He's big pals with another white dip I've had dealings with, that obnoxious fucker who goes by the name of Gerry Monk. The pair of them are like peas in a pod, they've both got about the same amount of 'form', but Gerry is about ten years older. I think I can assume that unless he's nicked by us he's not going to voluntarily chat to me, so I'll just store it in the old memory bank and wait my time. At least it confirms everything I thought about the fit up on us. Stinks doesn't it!

Bob told Maria he was leaving her, so she had the chance to make her exit without being seen with him. He offered another meal, which she declined, so with that he dropped a twenty-pound note on the table for her, with the assurance he'd try and do what he could on the court appearance. He thought, *at least she could buy another wrap of crack cocaine if needs be, before she'd go working the streets again.*

8

MEXICAN STAND OFF

"Alan, come in sit down. Turn down Bob telling me he doesn't like Mondays on that radio will you. You're at Clerkenwell with Harrison this morning aren't you?" Bob enquired.

Fish leant across the top of the aquarium switching off the Roberts radio. Silence fell on Bob's office.

"Yes guv should be for a Section one paper committal. Why is there a problem? There's only two statements to commit him to Southwark Crown on. I'm serving Dave Champions statement additional, nearer the trial. Don't want to give defence too much of a clue on the full story."

"I need you to do me a favour." said Bob.

He first made the point of Fish undertaking to not reveal what he was about to ask him to do. Al believing his loyalty to D.I. Trebor and the team was beyond question, and so he was happy give that assurance. Bob then told him the background to Maria, how in the past she'd been an informant of his when he was working vice around Kings Cross and how he'd met up with her the day before.

"What I need you to do after you've done your committal is to nip into the gaolers office, and have a root through the remands list find out when Maria's next up, and who the officer is dealing with her. I want to speak with him about offering no evidence if its an option, in return for what she's just told me." Bob then went through how she'd told him their little local difficulty, shall we say, had been a fit up from start to finish. Dennison's assault and arrest of McMurray had just been a vehicle to start a criminal investigation into the alleged corrupt practices of the Dip Squad. He then went on to tell him how the white dip whose mum runs the flower stall at St Pancras station, told her he knew it was a stunt, and in fact, most of the usual dips in London also knew.

*

Al emerged from the Circle line at King's Cross onto the familiar concourse at the front of the station. As he strolled in the direction of Gray's Inn Road, it occurred to him that all life was revealed here, if only the public could see it. Crack cocaine wraps passed across to their purchasers once the purveyor had been to a local drop, sometimes in the base of a lamppost, or a hide in one of the many and various bits of street furniture. His mind was playing Eric Clapton's song *Cocaine*, as he resolved not to bother with as far as he was concerned, the little shits, knowing they'd reliably be there the next time he passed by. A couple of 'battle-weary' prostitutes leant against railings on the corner of York Way, obviously negotiating with their pimp on how much of last nights takings they could keep, their habits demanding the lion-share of any income. Al continued his route across

Pentonville Road past what used to be the Lighthouse Insurance Company building, then La Scala cinema club before turning up Kings Cross Road towards Clerkenwell Magistrates Court next door to — as was so often the case — a police station, that being Kings Cross.

*

"I assume you're not in charge of the Pickpocket Squad any more and that you're just here to collect those files and paperwork we've now decided isn't central to our investigation, so that those cases can be progressed at court?"

The question was being levelled to D/I Trebor by Acting Detective Chief Inspector Secrett, who was self-assuredly leaning back in his office chair at headquarters. Bob had gone there to retrieve some of the case files which were seized on the day of the raid. Since that time, although the squad had been told to continue with their work, the seizure of various court files made it almost impossible to progress various cases. The devil in Bobs mind thought, *Maybe I should just let the various trials get thrown out at court. Then he could blame the consequent internal enquiry on those arseholes who, with absolutely no evidence, had raided his squad!* But his own conscience couldn't let the villains get away with not facing trial simply through their police investigators incompetence.

So he found himself trying to make peace with a shit of a governor suffering small-man syndrome whom he little time for, simply to get some of the files and paperwork back, to progress through the wheels of justice. Secrett tried making it as difficult as possible for Bob by quizzing him on each batch of paperwork. Bob had the upper hand as Secrett didn't really know what he was looking at. Bob wondered why the Sun page 3 calendar had been seized from the squad office, but resisted questioning Secrett as to what evidential value there might be in it. So it was restored to him together with the more urgent files that needed addressing for forthcoming court appearances, assorted correspondence and some photographs of various squad members at a get-together. One of their number thought it might be fun to get a Christmas card printed to send to the many and various lawyers they'd done past battles with using one of the group photos. Bob had actually blocked the novel idea, as he felt they could fall into the wrong hands, such as the very villains they were seeking to catch. So the idea was shelved, the pictures being displayed on the notice board just under 'Linda Lusardi' advancing her 'fine form'.

"Are you in a position to tell me what's happening with me and my team? It's been some time and we haven't heard anything," asked Bob who was doing his best to strike an air of casual indifference as if it didn't matter, but trying to trade on his earlier working relationship with Secrett. Bob knew from experience that once Secrett had the bit between his teeth, it was very difficult to open his eyes to the reality of the situation. The door to the office shared with Acting Superintendent Spooner flew open banging Bobs heel as Spooner swanned in.

No apology, barely an acknowledgement as Spooner said, " Need to speak to you Mr. Secrett when you've got a moment. I'll be in the bosses office."

The intervention prompted Secrett to take his eye off the ball, and promptly brought his investigation of Bobs motives to an abrupt halt. He simply demanded signatures in the property book for the paperwork Bob was taking away. Spooner avoided eye contact with Bob, who returned the compliment by ignoring his presence. He was mindful of a friendly officer letting him know what Spooner thought of him. At the time of the McMurray allegations at Headquarters, Spooner's — along with Branch's — reaction was to say, 'This is pennies from heaven, McMurray's has made my day!'

I told you I didn't like him. Spooner is a dodgy bastard and he's using me and my squad as a punchbag to avoid discovery of his own conduct. He's a big pal of that bent D/S Brian Western, mentioned in the 'The Fit Up' who I believe was busy tipping off the dips when we were out working, the result being no thefts or suspicious persons operating when we were out in the field. This whole business of Branch, Spooner, Secrett, and Dennison and the need for such an extreme investigation, when really the only matter which might require further investigation is that against Detective Sergeant Hunt and his alleged assault on Basil Chakrabati has a very smelly aroma to me. I've dropped off my statement about the meeting Tony White where he alleges that we've been fitted up, with the staff officer to the deputy head of Complaints and Discipline. That'll put the cat amongst the pigeons! The staff officer, asked me if I knew what I was doing, My answer to him was simple; 'Yes', I said, 'I'm telling the truth!' Enter one whistleblower! Not easy doing it on your own, but fuck them, they asked for it.

Bob dropped the box of files and correspondence in the boot of the car in the yard at headquarters. Paul Hazel sat listening to the radio blasting out, *'It's final countdown''* unaware of the significance of the meeting the governor had just had with Secrett and Spooner.

As Bob sank into the passenger seat, and said, "That's about fucking right Paul" pointing to the radio and Europe's analysis, "Secrett hasn't got a clue, he didn't really know what he was looking at in the files. He wouldn't give me any idea when we might hear what was going on. I don't reckon they've got anything on us you know, and I think that's why they're scrambling. That nonce Dennison is behind this I'm certain. Let's do some more digging on McMurray, 'cos apparently they've given him some kind immunity from prosecution in return for a statement alleging we're all on the take. Right, back to the nick, Paul. I'm interviewing Frankie Dobson with his brief about his attempt at bribery of John Conroy. Let me guess what his response will be." They both chuckled in unison at Bob's sarcasm.

As Bob held the front door of the nick open while Paul struggled through with the recently retrieved box of case files and so on. Just inside on he bench seat he recognised Dobson sat with his brief, a regular combatant of the squad by the name of Charlie Dickson, although his card used his formal title of Charles Oscar Dickson LLB, known colloquially as the Cod, or 'cash on delivery' which is probably nearer the mark! Bob acknowledged their presence while informing them to wait five minutes while set up the interview room. To his annoyance, someone had already booked the room so Bob had no option but to use his own office. John Conroy, realising this, had set up the office with the requisite number of chairs for the interview. He led Dobson and the Cod to Bob's office, where on entry the Cod seemed more interested in the aquarium and its residents rather than the matter at hand. *Kindred spirits, perhaps,* thought Bob.

Dobson was a white man in his late fifties, thick set, who gave his employment as a retired fish porter, his story being he ceased trading when Billingsgate shut down. The reality was that sitting before Bob was a career criminal with many convictions for theft-pickpocketing, on London's Underground, the London buses, and at various horse-racing courses — in essence, anywhere that he and his cohorts could prey on unsuspecting members of the public. Bob mused, *How does this lawyer sleep at night? He knows his client is a shit of a thief, we both know he's dishonest, and yet here is a lawyer will argue his innocence with all the vigour he can.*

It was late afternoon when the contemporaneous note interview commenced, with D/I Trebor using John Conroy to record the written questions and answers. Bob started with the caution, "You're not obliged to say anything unless you wish to do so, but what you say will be taken down in writing and given in evidence. Do you understand?"

Dobson looked at the Cod for some guidance to which he nodded, then said, "Yeah."

"A week ago today, at about 6pm, you were arrested at Regents Park Underground Station together with one other man for attempted theft. I'm not concerned with events leading up to the arrest or the arrest itself but merely with the events subsequent to the arrest. Firstly, do you agree you were arrested on that date and time?"

Dobson quickly agreed, "Yes."

"Do you remember being taken to an office at Regent's Park station and later searched?"

Dobson sighed and said, "Vaguely."

"Do you agree you were searched prior to your arrival at the police station?"

Dobson looked to Cod who surreptitiously shook his head, and said, "No comment."

"You were arrested with another younger man, were you the spokesman for him as well?"

Dobson responded, "No comment."

"Do you remember this officer, Detective Constable Conroy, being present when you were arrested?"

Dobson said, "No comment," to the nodding approval of his solicitor.

"Did you have much money on you at the time of your arrest?"

Dobson sensing the questions might get more direct, made no reply.

"Would you dispute that you had somewhere in the region of £170 on your person?"

Dobson said, "Sounds about right," feeling comfortable knowing this what was recorded on his charge sheet at Marylebone Lane Police Station.

"When this officer, searched you prior to going to the police station, you said 'It's yours if you want it, you know, a favour for a favour'?"

Dickson shuffled forward on his chair, and coughing, prompting Dobson.

Dobson made no reply, believing it to be his best course.

"When the officer said to you that what you were saying sounded like an attempt at bribery you said, 'take it, but call it what you want', do you admit that?"

Dobson made no reply, preferring not to commit himself.

"You then went on to say, 'it's all yours if you want it, if you'll let us walk', do you remember that?"

Dobson said, "No comment."

"Am I right in thinking that you do not intend to reply to any questions put to you?"

Dobson confirmed saying, "That's correct."

"After you had attempted to offer this officer money, he quite rightly repeated it to his colleague, and you said, 'I can't believe you won't trade, I'm one of you lot, I can do lots of favours.' do you remember saying that?"

Dobson, despite Dickson's disapproving cough said, "Yes the last part."

"Which part do you remember?"

Dobson clammed up again.

"In fact when you were told you'd be reported for attempting to bribe the officers you said, 'I can't believe it, you lot are so stupid,' do you remember saying that?"

Sensing he had a problem Dobson remained silent.

"Do you dispute what I say?"

No comment from Dobson.

"Can you think of any reason why these officers should deliberately lie, because I cannot?"

Again no comment.

"Is there anything you want to bring to my attention that I've not asked you about?"

Dobson shuffled uneasily on his seat.

"Do you appreciate the implications of this and the seriousness of these allegations?"

Dobson said, "No comment."

"These matters will be reported, is there anything more you wish to add to this, this is perhaps your last opportunity?"

Dobson said, "No I don't think so."

Bob wrapped up the interview by inviting Dobson to sign the notes as being a true record as to what had been said, but Dobson sensing any kind of conformity might be misconstrued, he refused. Undaunted, Bob invited the Cod to sign, and stupidly he did.

Why was it stupid I hear you ask. Because that arse of a brief Dickson by signing, could no longer represent Dobson because he now becomes a witness for the prosecution. Fuck him! Now what you've just read is the kind of offers made on a fairly regular basis by the older generation of dips who figure that paying the arresting officers was a way out of prosecution. It was something which was commonplace it seems back in the late sixties and seventies. My team just get the buzz from nicking them and putting them away, a regime which they couldn't comprehend and were unable to breach.

9

OLD HABITS

Bob returned to the nick at Baker Street, cursing the benefits of his new fitness regime. He'd recently realised that continual drinking was beginning to take its toll, so his resolution was to use the shower and changing room facilities in the basement following a gentle jog round the outer circle of Regents Park. Feeling better in himself for having exercised, but knackered, he flopped back in his chair, waiting for Brian Kent to arrive back from Brighton. He had signed off some crime reports, which had been determined unable to investigate any further, and two cups of coffee, when a knock on the door announced the presence of Brian.

"Hi guv. Got an update on the forged traveller's cheques."

"Come in Brian, what's the score then?"

"I went down there early this morning for a meet with the expert. She looked at our two samples and she reckons they are top-notch. They'll fool anyone in a shop, either home or abroad, and probably most banks who in all likelihood wouldn't have the time to scrutinise them too closely. I told her as much as I could about our informant and reassured her nothing further would happen until we'd set up the job to purchase them. Obviously they were concerned about a load of forgeries being 'put down' without their knowledge but I said as we were going to be the buyers so to speak, of the package, then we'd have control over them," said Brian.

Bob was pleased with Brian's opening enquiries at American Express, and told him to set up another meet with Driscoll to set up the first introduction of the 'police buyer' to negotiate with the villains. With that Brian went back to the general office, and Bob finished off his paperwork before feeding the fish and taking a reflective five minutes watching on the feed, and mulling over in his mind who he'd utilise as his 'buyer' of the travellers cheques.

*

Three of the squad decided late afternoon was going to be the best time to strike, and so Dave Champion, John Conroy and Al Fish loaded up with their wallets, pocket books and handcuffs in readiness for the eagerly anticipated arrests for dipping. Agreed they'd go down to Oxford Circus and trawl the central line back and forth through the West End passenger traffic. As they left they bumped into Brian Kent, who would've loved to have gone out with them hunting, but today he was working for the guv'nor on something they'd soon know about. With that the three 'musketeers' made their way to the bowels of the Bakerloo line, heading two stops south.

The three of them separated as if not knowing each other as the southbound train entered the platform recently upgraded with Sherlock Holmes silhouette tiles adorning the walls. Conroy and Champion boarded in the centre of the train taking up positions either side of the double doors. Al Fish boarded via the end single door of the same carriage. Most of the seats in the carriage were occupied with just a few people standing holding on to the rails above. It swept out of Baker Street into the darkness of the tube, south towards central London and the next station, Regents Park, about a minute or so away.

The train ground to a halt with apparently no passengers wanting to alight. As the doors opened, Champion watched a woman approach the open doors from the left side. She was *very smartly dressed,* Dave thought, carrying an open shoulder bag over her left shoulder. Her effort to get on was interrupted by a young man who pushed in front of her, from her right. He then stopped with one foot on the carriage and feigned confusion as if lost. John Conroy stood immediately in front of the pair of them watching what was happening. Dave saw a second older man who he thought he knew from intelligence reports as Frankie Dobson, move in behind the woman struggling to get on. He had a 'Burberry' style coat which was open and at first glance looked as if his hands were in his pockets. He watched as Dobson's right hand emerged from beneath the coat and plunged into the woman's open bag, clearly rooting around. The woman was completely unaware of his activity, more perplexed as to why the younger man was still blocking her ingress.

Dobson said, "No Terry, leave it."

He pulled away and the first man stood back, which enabled the woman to board. John and Dave stepped off to follow the pair who by now had gone to the single door at the opposite end to where Fish had been. The pair broke away and ran along the platform to the next carriage, prompting reaction from the three detectives, who blended with the boarding passengers as they followed their prey. At the first doorway was an elderly Indian looking man in a suit being blocked again in the same way, by 'Terry'. Dobson was seen to move his hand underneath the rear flaps of the man's jacket, going for his rear pocket.

John Conroy grabbed Dobson round the neck and in pulling him away said, "You're arrested for attempt theft, Frankie."

The Indian man frustrated at his path being blocked barged past 'Terry' and onto the train, as Champion seized Dobson's partner in crime. Al Fish in the meantime re-boarded the carriage scouring its occupants for the first intended victim.

Conroy said, "Leave it out, calm down."

Dobson annoyed said, "You leave it out, I'm one of yours, I'm one of yours guv."

Fish triumphantly holding a business card with the woman's details, joined the two officers as they made their way to an office near to the entrance to the station to await transport to the local nick. Out of the view of the passing public, John told Dobson to turn his pockets out, in readiness for a cursory search for weapons as Dave did like wise with Terry.

John checked Dobson's back pocket and felt a large amount of paper money. "What's this, how much is there?" asked John, believing it to be the proceeds from a theft, reasoning that any lawful owner would be in a position to know roughly how much they had, coupled together with the fact that he didn't put it on the table with the rest of his possessions.

Dobson said, "I don't know, but it's yours if you want it, you know a favour for a favour."

John said, "Explain?"

"You know, it's yours." Dobson winked and smiled.

Conroy was mindful yet again of corruption there had been in earlier years, counted it and said, "Is it all yours?"

Dobson thinking he was negotiating his freedom said, "No it's yours if you want it, you know for letting me walk."

Conroy said, "You've backed the wrong horse mate, this isn't the good old days, you're nicked and you've attempted to bribe me in the presence of my colleagues, so you're nicked for that as well," and cautioned him.

Dobson said, "I can't believe you won't trade. I'm one of your lot, I can do you lots of favours. I shouldn't be here, if you sheet me I'll be in trouble. I'll give you someone to contact."

John said, "Talk to the duty officer at the nick, you'll be reported for attempted bribery," cautioned him again.

Dobson said, "I can't believe it you lot are so stupid. It's a fair cop guv."

And that's how I came to be involved in the case. The duty officer contacted me and agreed it should be me who should conduct the interview of Dobson prior to submitting a report to the Director of Public Prosecutions. It's an offence that requires that level of approval prior to prosecution. After my interview the two thieves appeared at Marlborough Street Magistrates Court and pleaded guilty. They both had plenty of form, or previous convictions as we call it, and were sentenced to nine months imprisonment each. I submitted my file with a strong recommendation that given Dobson's propensity for corruption witnessed by at least two officers, it was an appropriate case to go forward for prosecution; if only to send a clear message to others that the days of bent coppers taking bungs was over. Now have a guess what the response was. How about this; in view of the fact it was an isolated incident arising out of Dobson being prosecuted for a substantive offence, and the likelihood of no greater penalty of imprisonment should he be convicted, reasoning any sentence would be concurrent, it is not in the public interest to prosecute him. I know, what's the fucking point? So much for the legacy of successive Home Secretary's cracking down on criminals and corruption! You really couldn't make it up.

*

"Take a look at this," said Spooner as the kettle boiled on the ad hoc tea club set up on the draw pack next to the window, now misted, announcing its readiness for tea bags. He gave a copy of Detective Inspector Trebor's statement detailing the meeting he had with Tony White, to Secrett to read.

Spooner fumed, "That fucker Trebor, he's trying to mix us a potion, it's his bloke Hunt who murdered Chakrabati, we fucking didn't."

Secrett was absorbed at the content of the statement, as he read it through three or four times looking for errors, but none were readily identifiable.

Secrett chose his words carefully, not trusting, in his view, the firebrand Spooner said, "So basically he's saying the arrest and assault on Dennison was all contrived between him and McMurray. I suppose the first thing to check is whether Greg knows anything about this, and secondly how tight are the two statements taken from Sutton. We need to keep those completely quiet don't we, if we're going to rely on McMurrays allegations of fit-up. Does Mr. Branch know of this hornets' nest? He's going go fucking mad when he finds out. I think the business surrounding Hunt could be dealt with in isolation, couldn't it?"

Spooner agreeing with the overall proposition expressed by Secrett might work, but for it to succeed, the best thing would be for Director of Public Prosecutions to come back with a quick decision to prosecute Hunt. He reasoned that this would then give credence to the suggestion there being no smoke without fire, therefore the whole squad is crooked in some shape or form.

"I'll have to register officially, the receipt of Trebor's statement, but Branch isn't in until tomorrow. I'll speak to him then."

*

Fish wandered through the double swing doors into the vestibule of Clerkenwell Magistrates' Court. They closed behind him, cutting off the early sunlight seeking to make its presence felt across the terrazzo floor leading to the two courts at the far end. The area was buzzing with defendants, sat on benches around the walls looking like expectant fathers waiting to be called into the delivery room to be told the joyous news of another hungry mouth to feed. Others more experienced with appearance at court, mooched around *like wandering Jews,* Al thought, waiting to be spoken to by the officer in their case or some legal hack grafting on legal aid. He moved through the sea of faces, spotting the reason for his attendance, one Delroy Harrison, leaning against the oak panelled wall within the glazed portal leading to court one. As the court hadn't yet started Al was able to open the swing door to where Harrison stood alone, sucking through his teeth on the arrival of the 'tec' who had *fitted him up, bent bastard,* he thought.

"Alright Delroy?" said Al not expecting a positive response from the prospective defendant.

Harrison repeated his disdain through his teeth saying, "What's happening, I'm busy innit."

Fish explained to him that this would be a simple straightforward committal for trial. The statements just need to be served on his defence solicitor, and everyone could then go home.

Harrison told him he hadn't got one so now what?

Al went into court with Harrison having been called by the court officer. Al went to the witness box while Harrison wandered casually into the wrought iron clad dock, his disdain of the judicial system immediately apparent to the magistrate, Mr. Burke.

"Your worship, this is the second remand in this case, and the court was assured the defendant would be represented today for a paper committal for trial at Crown Court. The defendant I believe is asking for the committal to proceed with the witnesses being called. However I'm given to understand court time would not be able to accommodate this today. In view of this, I would ask for another remand for three weeks, a date suitable with the court list, so that the defendant is represented. There is no objection his bail continuing in his own recognisance and not to go within fifty yards of any Underground station in central London, as before sir."

Burke looked over his half rimmed glasses, and enquired, "You've heard what the officer has said, is that correct?"

Harrison told to stand by the court officer, said, "Yeah, whatever."

Mr. Burke, realising the belligerent attitude of the defendant was not going to resolve matters on this hearing, granted the remand, pointing out Harrison's obligation to obtain legal representation for his next appearance, but sensing his words might be falling on stoney ground.

Fish closed the file of papers resting on the witness box, nodded to the female clerk whom he remembered from last Christmas's court drinks when she and he had a wine fuelled dalliance in the clerks office at the front of the building. He made his way to the back of the court holding the door open for Harrison to exit before turning to offer a bow towards the magistrate.

Harrison stopped just outside in the glazed booth, and turning to the officer said, "You fitted me up, you bastard. You know I didn't do nothing when you stopped me. You told me you just wanted a word, so we went into that room then you told me I was nicked. What for? Nothing. Then when I was in my cell at the nick, the door opened and a fucking great pink rabbit came into my cell and battered me and whacked me head, made me mouth bleed. Now you want to go for trial on this bollocks, I ain't done nothing you cunt. You and those fuckers Champion and Farmer."

Al thought back to the evening at the Police Station. While he was sat doing the paperwork for Harrison in the Divisional Surgeons room, one of his pals from another crime squad heard he was in there so decided to pay him a visit. It's true to say he was dressed in a bright pink furry suit complete with 'Bugs Bunny' head which he'd hired to attend a fancy dress party with a cartoon theme. When he'd learnt it was Harrison who was subject of Als attendance at the nick, he'd told him of an incident a couple of months before where he'd assaulted 'Bugs Bunny' and escaped arrest. Checking it was ok to have a 'chat' with the prisoner, he went to his cell and administered a 'positive' payback. He complained to the magistrate and he ignored him telling him he was mistaken or hallucinating!

It's true, I remember Fish telling me about the alleged incident! Couldn't possibly have happened could it? A six foot pink bunny bangs a prisoner? Surely not! Mind you Harrison's a shit, so a deserving case of robust retribution. Gives them something else to make a complaint about — but of course it lessens their credibility too.

Fish stared at him, unmoved by his outburst then said, "Listen very carefully I shall say this only once. You were nicked fair and square. You were trying to dip that lady with the raffia shoulder bag with the smiley face on the side of it. So just suck it up and take your medicine. You've got loads of form. So just shut the fuck up about what's what.

You were at it, we know you were at it, you've got no other reason for being on the Underground. This ain't like the old days; you can't buy yourself a life. We don't trade."

Harrison exclaimed, "What fucking woman, I bet you don't know her, cos she don't exist. It's a fit up and you know it!"

Fish tiring of Harrison's attitude leant forward to stare him in the face said, "Listen you twat, I've got a crystal ball, and I've looked into it. And it tells me that if I see you anywhere on the Underground you're going to get nicked. If you think this case is bad, just wait until the next time. It will be your worst fucking nightmare."

Harrison stepped back, holding on to the exit door, and with his right hand reached in to the inside pocket of his bomber jacket. With a triumphant cheer, he produced a mini cassette recorder, of the type used for dictation. "You're fucked now, copper, got you recorded," and waved it in front of Fish.

He made a grab for it, but Harrison was too nimble, jamming it in his pocket, and running across the vestibule and out the front of the court building. Fish, not wanting to cause a scene, simply walked out of the building in a confident manner as if nothing had happened between him and the defendant. He then turned back on himself to do the enquiry about Maria for Bob Trebor.

He quickly confirmed she was only on remand for the one offence of 'tomming', the colloquialism for prostitution, and saw the the officer in the case was a Crime Squad Constable operating in plain clothes who he knew. Noting the details he resolved to get back to the nick as soon as possible, not only to give the guv'nor the details, but because he was worried about the stunt Harrison had just pulled.

*

I'm waiting on Fish getting back to me, but in the meantime I've had a call from my 'co-star' at the local amateur dramatic group. Just to fill you in; we had to give our contact details to the nominated production director so we could be contacted in case of changes to rehearsals or script and that sort of thing. You'll remember I was told her old man is seeing to some other woman in the group, leaving this dark haired beauty feeling somewhat abandoned. At the rehearsal last week she asked if I fancied a drink. I told her we'd be going for one after the rehearsal, but she said just us two. Ding dong! So on the pretext of wanting to discuss the script with me, she says she's on her way up to London to see me and will be with me later on this afternoon. I've told her to meet me at the front of Charing Cross station, by the Eleanor Cross at the front, and suggested perhaps a drink or two. She jumped at the idea straight off, telling me she didn't need to be home until late as her husband was working away for the week! There's no urgency in us meeting to discuss the play so she must have another reason and so are you thinking what I'm thinking?

The knock on the door announced the presence of Al Fish with two mugs of tea.

"Hello guv, I checked out your tom. She's on only one appearance at the house of correction. I know the bloke who is the officer in the case, he's on the local crime squad so I don't think there'll be too much of a problem dealing sensibly with the job. Here's his details." With that Al gave the guv'nor a piece of note paper with all the details neatly recorded.

"Thanks, Al I might ask you to have a word with him in the first place. I'll give it some thought. How did the committal go. Straight forward?"

"Um not exactly guv."

Fish went on to explain how the defendant Harrison hadn't got his arse into gear to be represented so a section 1 committal, ie. a paper process where prosecution statements are served on defence lawyers and the originals lodged with the court, couldn't go ahead. The next kind of committal, a section 2 usually requires witnesses to attend to give 'live' evidence and can be cross examined by defence lawyers or the defendant, before the court decides if there is sufficient evidence to commit the defendant for trial at Crown Court. It's invariably a lengthy process taking up a substantial amount of court time, so consequently that couldn't go ahead that morning either.

The story of how Fish assured the defendant would have a very difficult future, was met with Harrison waiving a micro cassette recorder under the officers nose claiming he'd recorded all the conversation and he threats. Bob listened to Al's confession and plea for inspiration on the confrontation outside court.

He looked to the ceiling then across at his fish, before giving guidance. "Right, first of all you're an idiot for getting caught out like you have. You reckon nobody else either heard or saw what was going on, so there's just you two. Now this is the bit you need to pay attention to; I am assuming from what you've told me, you were aware that he had the recorder with him because you'd seen it when he was holding it prior to going in for the remand. Most importantly he kept switching it on and off and cursing the fact that he would accidentally either rewind or fast forward it, something which you witnessed before and after when he ran out of the court building. Is that right? The importance of what I've just said, is that any recording produced at any court hearing could not be described as a clear uninterrupted version of events, and could not have any probative value for Harrison. Got it?" said Bob delivering Fish a 'Get out of jail free' card.

Fish heaved a sigh of relief as he listened to his guv'nor's analysis of what he assumed was his death knell in the job. "Thanks guv. Is there anything I should do at the moment?"

Bob said, "Yeah, you record the whole incident of the remand, including the 'bland' verbals I'm sure you'll recall that you made in your pocket book, chopping up your actual words so they become innocuous. You'll make a similar entry in your diary, not necessarily with the verbals, that would look too contrived. But will record the fact that you tried to find the Court Inspector to no avail the tried to phone me here to immediately report what had transpired but there was no reply, and the reserve officer on the switchboard couldn't find me either. Now sod off and do it now, so that any unannounced visit won't cause us a problem. Then bring both to me so I can countersign them, recording my knowledge together with my verbal instruction on the committal strategy, which needless to say will look nothing like what we have just discussed. Got it?"

Fish feeling a great weight had been lifted from his shoulders, knowing Bob was putting himself on offer, thanked him, promising a fresh cup of tea in his 'Jaguar' mug, the last going cold in the heat of conversation.

10

THE NAKED TRUTH

Boles barged into Branch's office, and seeing he was obviously stressed Branch replaced the phone.

"Yes sir, what can I do for you?"

"Have you fucking seen this statement that was dropped off yesterday to us from Trebor? Read it!" said Boles, almost spitting out his words to Branch. "And when you have, you tell me how you hope to deal with it because it looks as if that smart-arse is trying to up the stakes. I want to know what we have, to rubbish this, because otherwise we've got Trebor as our first fucking whistleblower, I want him thoroughly gone over." Having thrown the copy across Branch's desk, he turned, storming out of the room slamming the door behind him.

The Detective Chief Superintendent carefully read through the statement, taking in the impact of its content. He summoned a coffee on his intercom, then re-read it and resolved in his mind the enquiry into the Pickpocket Squad needed to dealt with quickly. Spooner and Secrett were summoned to his office like two naughty schoolboys and waited for inspiration.

"Right what I want know is, what dirt has Trebor got on White. Is there anything there in that relationship that we can pressurise White with? Because you two are going to see White to test the strength of what he's said in this pile of shit. Trebor is not going to become a whistleblower otherwise we'll have the press all over this, so he's got to be neutralised, you got me? Second, how are we doing with any evidence of corruption against any of the squad members? We need to divide and rule on this when it comes to interviews. I know we've got Hunt pretty much out on his own with the suspicion of manslaughter on Chakrabati, but can we link any of the others with him? But what is important is that they don't get wind of the existence of Sutton. Now fuck off and get something put together, use Dennison as well if you need to, but we keep this tight. Right?"

Secrett stayed quiet while Spooner gave Branch the reassurance he was seeking. However, Secrett remembered an incident back when he was doing observations on Royal Mail thefts. He and another had nicked two black villains from south London. They had them in custody, and Secrett was about to interview his prisoner, when Dennison suddenly and surprisingly appeared in the custody suite. His appearance prompted an immediate violent response from Secrett's prisoner, who leapt to his feet to assault Dennison, causing him to make a very quick exit from the room. In an effort to try and calm the situation he asked what had caused such a response from his prisoner. The prisoner gave an account of when he was about fourteen years old, Dennison had fitted him up on a 'sus' charge, in other words being a suspected person loitering with intent to commit theft from the person. In short, dipping, for which he was given Borstal serving nine months before he was released.

Until the statement from Trebor had arrived at their door, he hadn't given the earlier incident much thought, believing it was just a case of sour grapes. But now he began to have misgivings about Dennison's credibility and trustworthiness, something which he didn't think was wise to mention to Spooner, or indeed, anyone else at this stage. His preference is to wait and see.

I'm just on my way to meet my theatre group acquaintance who was most insistent in meeting up with me! I don't know what she wants, but I wouldn't mind betting reprisal or revenge is on her mind for her husbands current dalliance with someone in the group. Or maybe it's just a shoulder. I really don't know her at all well, I mean, my only acquaintance was when we read for our parts in the farce, and me seeing her run out in floods of tears with a man I at first thought to be her husband but I now know to be her brother! Just walking past the tell tale aroma of Burger King on the corner. There she is. Bloody hell she looks fit, long dark hair, black mackintosh, and the first thing I noticed about her, long legs!

Sharon was tired from her West End shopping expedition, as she wandered down from Covent Garden towards the Strand. She had found out her husband was having an affair with an older woman in the amateur dramatic group of which they were all members. Her emotions were torn between devastation at the discovery and a resolve to gain revenge for his infidelity. As she wandered past the shop fronts offering perfumes, makeup, handbags and the latest fashions, she chanced upon an Ann Summers shop offering something a little more exotic. *Why not?* she thought, having never entered such an establishment in her twenty six years.

She emerged into the late afternoon sun, sporting her new purchase in the tell tale pink carrier bag.

Bob wandered up to her, unseen in the crowds making their way towards Trafalgar Square. She turned to see him as he spoke her name. Her instant smile showed she was pleased to see him. She flung her arms round him, kissing him on the cheek.

"Hi Bob, how lovely to see you, let's go for a drink shall we and have a chat. I've got plenty of time. Do you know anywhere around here?." she said, clearly in the 'driving seat' of this meeting.

Bob said, "Yeah sure, there's a nice little wine bar I know, just five minutes away."

Sharon warmed immediately to the idea, thrusting her arm under his as he directed their stroll down Villiers Street towards Embankment tube station at the far end. She said very little, except to say she'd been for a job interview with the employment agency she'd signed on with, hence her reason for being in central London, but making it clear she enjoyed her regular trips to the capital. Bobs knowing smile signalled to her that he was pleased to meet up with her.

"Here we are." The darkened doorway of Gordon's Wine bar revealed their descent into the cellars of the establishment, Bob lead her by the hand down the stairs to the candle lit recesses looking more like catacombs.

A bottle of Malbec and two glasses saw them seated at the rear of the bar, as he explained the place had no electric lighting other than behind the bar. Sharon liked the old-world charm of the place, seemingly left still in the last century, when they were the 'go to' importers of booze into the capital when the Thames used to rise to point in the gardens just to its left. A second bottle saw her enquiring if Bob knew of anywhere they could go to be private.

This is new. Usually the man does the chasing but she seems very keen to cement relations! I know just the place.

The pair of them stumbled back up into the street, turning left and a walk through Embankment station booking hall, and more steps they found themselves on Hungerford Bridge. As they wandered south towards Waterloo, Bob regaled Sharon with the night he was called to the pedestrian bridge to a man who had been found dead about halfway across, having been stabbed several times, without any obvious reason why. Her senses veered between shock and fascination that Bob had effectively 'seen the world' a life well lived for someone so young. The thought attracted her more to him. Her conscience didn't feel compelled to ask further. As they took in the view of the Thames, a light breeze refreshed them, as they walked towards the Royal Festival Hall. This concrete edifice had been built in celebration of the post war era and the festival of Britain. Bob intrigued her with a story of his youth when as a Sea Scout he slept on Captain Scott's ship *Discovery* when it was moored adjacent to Cleopatras Needle. On one occasion he fell from a pontoon next to the ship into the river. Several gulps of water and he was rescued. More recent times had seen the river much cleaner, but the riptide was still a danger, as many attempt suicides had learnt, to their tragic cost.

They continued in light laughter and conversation towards Waterloo, on the promise of Bob showing her the sights. Turning left into the smoke filled 'Whole in the Wall' pub, their resolution undaunted, saw two more rounds of drinks. By this time Sharon was feeling the effects of the wine, and enquired if they were going any more private, her passion raised combined with the fleeting thought of her feckless husband, and revenge fast becoming the order of the day.

I don't need telling twice! I'm taking her round to the Union Jack club, a tower block hostel available for a variety of military personal, just round the corner from The Wellington pub, and for coppers on showing their 'brief' (warrant card) can also gain entry to the bar, and for a small back hander fee can rent one their bedrooms, for more private social intercourse! And so we fell out of the nicotine drenched pub, and into the salubrious establishment, and knowing the guy on reception I'm now the proud owner of a key to paradise I hope! One more red wine then up stairs to 'Bedfordshire'!

As Sharon sat in eager anticipation, nursing her wine, she adopted a casual air as she enquired what the evening held. Bob declared it was about time for a bit of a rest in the room he'd booked which drew a knowing smile from her. They went out to the lifts still guarding the rest of their red wine. Up six floors, the lift doors slid open beckoning them to the room opposite, and with a turn of the key they were in.

"I need to use the loo, I won't be a minute," as she closed the door still clutching her recent purchase from Ann.

Bob sat at the end of bed, like a naughty schoolboy waiting outside the headmaster's office, wondering what punishment awaits, glancing out of the window at the passing trains below. Feeling the effects of the wine, he leant back, laying flat out with his feet touching the floor at the end. The bathroom door opened to reveal Sharon in a black and red basque and black stockings, suspenders, and the heels she'd been wearing earlier. The fine wisps of hair defining her fanny made clear her intentions for Bob. He thought all his birthdays had come at once as she slowly and seductively walked towards him, a wry smile and enquiring whether he approved. Pointless question he thought but worthy of considerable praise as she fell to her knees between his, slowly undoing his trousers as he quietly called for his god. Her mind was on revenge for her husbands infidelity. It was her first experience of anything like this, as was the oral pleasure she was about to give, although resolving not to go the whole way when the moment came.

Their lovemaking continued for some time, Bob stripping off, hoping she'd still find him attractive, while she was on a mission for him to come inside her. She leant over on the bed still standing, as Bob stood behind as he reconnected with her as he gently caressed her pert arse. His mind was racing that this might be the one and only time he might experience this, and so was keen to put in a good performance. As they continued, he looked across towards the door into the room and saw a full length mirror, attached to it showing every move they made. She let out a whimper signalling for Bob to do the same, as he thought to himself the last time the mirror was called upon was probably a squaddie in full uniform adjusting himself for parade! They fell to the bed, embracing each other post intercourse, laying there for an hour to recover.

Goodness that was good, she's got not only a stunning body, but is great company too. Lucky boy. Better still she's wanting to do it again. In those circumstances I don't feel used and abused, well not really!

What's happened to the wife? She's finally had enough of me, so she says, and run off with a long distance lorry driver from Norwich. She's taken the children with her as well. Now I've started divorce proceedings but of course that will take some time. The children are of an age that they seem okay about the situation and are at a time in their schooling where it won't be too difficult to change schools. Meantime, there's no restriction on me seeing them according to her. We'll see.

*

'I make this statement of my own free will. I have been told that I need not say anything unless I wish to do so, and that whatever I say may be given in evidence. *E. Phyle. R. Trebor.*

'I have been pickpocketing for a number of years, about seventeen years. I have been arrested for this type of offence on many occasions in the past. Today I was arrested at Holborn station. When I got to the room with the officers, I asked about the suspended officer and the others what were being investigated as I knew you was all from the same place. The reason I asked was because I had met one officer previously and said that he had been suspended. I was shocked because he had been suspended because tried to figure out why this happened to him, as all of this time I have been nicked by him he has never accepted anything from me. I have always known him to be honest. So when heard about this I just could not believe it. Through the years I have known a hell of a lot of pickpockets and we talk, and we have always said those transport guys are cunts, because they don't take, and it makes hard for people like me to earn a few bob. I say it, knowing it to be true and I am willing to swear by it. The reason I am making this statement now is because I have always been sweet with the squad as I have been around for a long time, and I could not believe that someone like Dennison could be involved in stitching up another copper when he has always been so bent, I mean dishonest, and queer in the past. I mean I had dealings with Dennison before, a few years ago. I met him through Alan Bell who is a dip I work with or used to work with. He got arrested by Dennison and he bunged him, and he was the one who told me that he was alright, and I could give him a drink, so as not to be arrested. I have met Dennison because Alan showed him to me when we was out dipping. I first met him when I was out dipping with Alan and we was jumping in and out of the trains looking for somebody to dip. When we got to Hyde Park we was stopped by Dennison and another copper and he said we was going to be done for sus. We tried to make out we was doing fuck all but he said we would be done. Alan said listen don't do us, as we could have a drink for you and you have done me before. You owe me one, so he said listen man, we have a hundred for you if we can stay cool. We was sitting on a bench at the time, so we took out the money and gave it to him. He said afterwards he can't protect us from other coppers, but if he sees us it would be alright. So we took the train and went. Dennison took the money from us and put it in his pocket. We was well pleased to do a trade with him, as we knew from other dippers he was cool. I did not see him again for a long time, I'm not sure how long, and I didn't care cos I knew we could always trade again. Some time later I met him, I'm not sure how long, down at Bond Street and he was with somebody, I did not know him. He stopped me on the the platform and asked me how I was doing. I said not good at all and that I had not done much but he said what have you got on you and I said seventy quid. He said, not much at all is it and I said listen man leave me with something in case, so he took fifty out of the money I gave him. The other copper was there but took no notice of him, then I took off. That was the second time Dennison took money off me. All this happened before you took over guv. I know of bent coppers at West End Central on other dip squads like Dc Cork and Morris. I think they're out of the job now. Just to say the reason I'm making this statement is because the officers of your squad don't deserve this shit, you've always been fair with me. As there are coppers and coppers, some I like and some I don't give a shit for, but you lot didn't deserve what's happened. Just there is criminals and criminals, and that bent bastard Dennison is a criminal."

I have made and read the above statement and have been told that I can correct, alter or add anything I wish. This statement is true. I have made it of my own free will. *E. Phyle. R. Trebor.*

What you have just read, is yet another pickpocket after Tony White to tell me the ruse used by Dennison to have us raided by Branch and those other two shits, Spooner and Secrett, was a fit-up job. My conclusion is as it has been all along: Dennison is bent and doesn't want to be discovered. The others simply want scalps! Now this particular dip I'm with wasn't arrested for an offence, it was just a couple of the lads and I saw him on the platform at Holborn tube station. So essentially there's no mileage in it other than voicing his annoyance at Dennison's antics. I'm quite sure he's 'at it' as the expression goes —probably his targets would be the foreign tourists and punters going to the British Museum. So I guess I've saved them from the plundering of Mr. Ernie Phyle, a middle aged West Indian man with loads of form for dipping, but a pussy cat, and not violent at all. His comments when we stopped him were very interesting. He had nothing to gain from us, but readily agreed to come with us to the local nick to make a statement under caution about what he knew, unlike Tony White who wouldn't commit to paper himself. Now just to give you an insight, usually there is a caution at the start of the statement and a declaration of its truth at the end which would ordinarily be written by me or whoever the officer is taking the statement. However in this case Ernie was quite content to write the whole damn thing from start to finish. In fact my only involvement was to dictate the first and last bits and to counter sign Ernie's signatures. So there you have it. Now my quandary is how to ensure it gets to the right people whilst maintaining its integrity.

11
LOYALTIES

"Here you are Trev. Now's your chance to do me a favour after all I've done for you," said Tommy as they sat across the marble table in the pie and mash shop in Walworth Road.

Clementine sat in silence as he watched Tommy pass across a plastic Tesco bag wrapped around something bulky within. Sutton, realising he was under obligation to the pair of them, surreptitiously slid the bag towards himself then cradling on his lap under the table top. He realised by the weight and it's shape, it had to be a gun of some description. He enquired what he was to do with it. He'd fenced many things for Tom before but this was a first. He could feel the outline of what felt like bullets, and there were only four of them. His concern was immediately raised that maybe there were still two in the chambers, but was reassured by Roger that it was in fact empty.

"Get rid of it will you Trev, babysit it somewhere safe."

Sutton, not wanting to resist this instruction, confirmed his willingness and obligation to help. He didn't know what it had been used for, but he was no idiot and assumed it had been used as the 'muscle' Tommy and Roger had just been engaged in. About ten minutes past as Roger 'polished off' the last of the pie on his plate, they each rose and left the pie and mash shop. Trevor went south towards Camberwell Green while the other two jumped in Ferdie's car, driving off north towards the Elephant and Castle.

*

Bob leant back in his chair, looking across at two tiger barbs ganging up on a guppy swimming past minding its own business as Donna Summer seductively sang *The Deep's* theme tune. His daydreaming about Sharon, was interrupted by that little shit Secrett appearing without knocking in his office.

"What's this, another fucking raid? Oh no you haven't got a gang with you this time have you. Just you and me. You'll never take me alive copper," said Bob in a sarcastic tone.

Secrett resisted the urge to pull rank on Bob, as he needed something which had been restored to him in error the last time they locked horns. He reasoned that he needed the group photograph of the squad taken at a social event be as it would greatly assist in eliminating most of the squad, including Bob, from any further suspicion. It was more to do with the identification relative to the unfortunate death of the squad member Basil Chackrabati. Bob toyed with the idea of saying it had been destroyed but he weighed up what might be good for the team, so opened his desk top drawer, selecting the picture from underneath other paper work. Secrett leant forward in the hope he might see the contents of Bob's drawer without success, so expressed his gratitude as he carefully placed the photo in his portfolio case. With that, he left as quickly as he'd arrived, leaving Bob wondering if he'd been duped.

Bob wandered into the squad office, and beckoned Kent to join him with the paperwork he had on the American Express enquiry. He'd had the opportunity to select a covert officer who was 'level 2' and would be perfect as the buyer of the package of forged travellers cheques. It was Shaun Bennet, known to both the officers, who was on his way over to the nick when he got delayed in the City of London.

What is a 'level 2' officer? I hear you ask. It's basically an officer who has undergone some form of interview and psychometric testing. This would occur following their application for a particular post such as operating as a covert officer, infiltrating criminal enterprises possibly gaining the trust and familiarity of known criminals or suspects engaged in crime. They'd have to undergo assessment through psychometric testing including verbal, logical, diagrammatic reasoning, and spatial reasoning. Now all that sounds like some kind of gobbledygook, but it basically means you've picked the right person for the job, who understands the parameters in which they're expected to operate. Sounds complicated but it's not really, just means they know how to operate — within the law, of course!

"Hello guv, sorry I'm late I got a bit held up in the city," in answer the Bobs greeting and introduction to Brian Kent.

As it turned out the two of them knew each other from a joint enquiry they'd been involved in, in the past.

"You won't believe what happened, it's a bit of a laugh really. I'd just come out of a little greasy spoon, and was walking up that little shopping arcade opposite Liverpool

Street Station, you know, it's called Broad Street Arcade. I don't know if you know, but at the top end is a jewellers — think it's a Ratners or something — on the left. I was only about five yards from its front door when a bloke dressed in black with a robbers mask bolted from the shop. I jumped on him and whacked him a few times with my stick until he said he'd give up. With that I turned him over and cuffed him, told him he was nicked, I thought for blagging the jewellery shop. Three or four blokes came running towards me, and I thought *That's good, usually members of the public run in the other direction!* So I pulled him to his feet, helped by one of the blokes who started making a fuss of the bloke I'd whacked who by this time had claret pouring down his face from injuries he'd sustained, I don't know how, if you get my drift. Then they told me I was nicked!

I thought it was a bit rich, given what I'd seen and what I'd stopped, only to be told that the 'victim' of my interception was actually a City of London police officer re-enacting a robbery five days earlier for the benefit of Police 5 who were filming just out of sight at the top of the arcade! I had to go with them back to Bishopsgate nick to see their guv'nor who was actually as good as gold. Told me I was being recommended for a Commissioners commendation for bravery and my prompt action!"

Bob and Brian by this time had collapsed into fits of laughter, speculating that Shaun was going to be commended for GBH on a police officer. Now that must really be a first!

Having called for celebratory cups of tea all round, Bob calmly outlined what they had so far. It was his intention to get Shaun introduced to the villains through his Pentonville snout, who would make his excuse and leave the negotiations to buy the package at this point and play no further part. Driscoll's legend or story would be that he was so close the end of his sentence, he dare not risk involvement, but in the interests of success he introduced his old mate who had 'fenced' for him many times in the past, and had always come up with the right amount of cash without quarrel. The meeting finished with Bob saying they'd have another meet with Driscoll at the prison who would meet with Shaun at some place convenient so they could get to know each other before the meet at the 'Old Bill' pub with the villains.

*

Secrett and Spooner were deep in discussion about what they believed was Trebors latest stunt. The Phyle statement under caution had arrived on the desk of Maurice Branch, which was all the more alarming, full of allegations about Dennison and scattered insinuations about what had occurred when McMurray was arrested at Russell Square. No sooner were they aware of its existence and content they were summoned to a conference with Branch. Their offer to see Phyle fell on stony ground.

"I'm not happy about Trebor's latest trick. He's got to be taught a lesson not to take us on. If I had my way you'd be going to see both White and Phyle to kick their allegations into the long grass, but I've had a meeting with Mr. Boles this morning. He has a different view I'm afraid. He is recommending this whole affair be pushed over to another force to investigate.

His initial enquiries with CIB2 at the 'Yard' has met with a positive response and so by tomorrow they will assume responsibility for the whole investigation. Thanks to Commander Eric Brown's insistence, the investigation is likely to include an unannounced visit on another office."

Spooner and Secrett leant forward in their chairs, doing their best to appear unfazed, enquired what had prompted the course of action when they were firmly convinced they'd said nothing to anyone about the existence of Sutton and his earlier allegations. It was dawning on them they'd have to watch their backs as it seemed the senior officers were in danger of feeding these two together with Dennison to the wolves if they were not too careful. Apparently, Boles inadvertently let slip to Eric Brown about the unknown Sutton as far as Brown was aware, bleating to another officer about the Dip Squads activities. It prompted a firm response that there was undoubtedly a need for any allegations to be treated with the same vigorous enthusiasm as that meted out to his own officers, stressing that actually nothing irregular so far had been established against any of his officers, save the almost routine of allegations which any number of pickpockets make against their arresting officers usually at the time of their arrest. Boles, sensing that the manner in which the enquiry was being conducted, and to date nothing of substance had been uncovered to warrant criminal or discipline proceedings, feared it might impact on his chances of selection for a Chiefs job somewhere else in the country, if it were to grow arms and legs and walk towards him instead of away. Essentially he'd lost his 'bottle' although of course he'd never admit that, opting to lay responsibility for any shit storm to be dumped on more junior officers.

Secrett, in an effort to establish the extent of what Branch was telling them, made the point that he and Spooner had been back to see Sutton in Pentonville with the photograph of the Dip Squad members to identify who he says were involved in corruptly taking money. It seems it was a waste of time, although Trebor and his merry men didn't know that. Sutton thought he recognised Trebor but couldn't be certain and one other who actually had a beard at the time, and all the others were mysteries.

Branch couldn't contain his anger saying, "Who the flying fuck told you to go and see that fucker in Pentonville? And you've told him what? That he's not going to be prosecuted for the Conroy job. You don't have the authority to do that you fucking idiot, who said you could speak with the Director of Public Prosecutions, that's my fucking job. You mister are taking the piss. Spooner leave us for a moment I need to speak with Secrett alone."

Spooner counted his blessings he hadn't gone with Secrett to the prison that day, but couldn't say that Secrett was lying about that little tête-à-tête. He said nothing but slunk out of Branch's office, carefully closing the door behind him, like a concerned parent not wishing to wake their infant child. He'd thought it a bit risky when he found out about it, but said nothing to anyone in case of repercussions. His only thought was that Secrett was going out 'on a limb' by interviewing Sutton alone, but figured he was looking for a bit of glory by showing his initiative. *Wanker* he thought.

And of course he was right!

Branch listened to Secretts repeated pleas that he was just trying to look at the bigger picture and tie up loose ends so the enquiry could proceed without any confusion on the McMurray allegation. He reinforced his trust in Dennison, claiming he'd always found him to be honest and trustworthy.

Branch cynically said, "If that's the case, how have we got two dips so far both saying he's taxed them, taken money off them in the past. They've both, separately, been given a 'life' — in other words, they have been let off — in return for the money they had on them. Now I don't know what you call that , I but I call it perverting the course of justice and theft, and fuck knows what else. Now don't interrupt, you've fucked up big time, and I've got to do something about that without it showing out. You see that cheese plant over there in the corner? Now every so often it gets 'too big for its boots' and unmanageable so I have to cut it back so it doesn't get to big for the flower pot, just like you have. Imagine you're that cheese plant, what's the moral to this story?

Secrett was confused at the analogy, so he said, "Don't get a cheese plant sir?"

As he finished the sentence Branch hurled a series of expletives at him, followed by a very stern, "Get out of my fucking office." Licking his wounds, he returned to the office with Spooner, trying not to show he'd been roundly bollocked, and try to calm Spooner who had every reason to feel he'd been verballed by Secrett.

*

"Hello guv," said Sutton, nursing the last of his pint as he saw Detective Inspector Walker enter the pub and walk towards him. The juke box blasted out another Police record demanding not to stand so close. He sat at a high table carefully holding a rolled up bag under the counter top concealed from the general public gaze. Walker greeted him with the offer of another pint, removing his trench coat as he did. As always, as seemed to be the case, Sutton wasn't in the habit of turning down free drinks, so he'd confirmed another would do very nicely. Trevor was building himself up mentally to ask a big favour of Walker, far more than the usual plea of restoring a number of purses and wallets to victims of dippings on the Underground, which his 'mates' had relieved them of. Walker returned with the beers, seeing that Sutton was still caressing the rolled carrier bag under the table, but intuitively knowing, given the past, what the request would be, so he sat patiently for him to go through the usual story.

"Ah thanks guv. Thanks. I um, have a bit of an extra problem in the bag under the table. There's six purses and wallets there like before, but I've got something else, and I'm shit-scared of doing the wrong thing with it. I just thought you might be able to dispose of it for me through your official channels if you get me. It's not a problem, it hasn't been used if you get my meaning. It's just the old boy had it at his home, and I told him I didn't think he should have it after all these years. I mean, the Second World War has been over for a long time ain't it? He just had it as a souvenir from those times. He was in the army, see, so he figured he could just hang on to it."

Walker grew impatient to see what it was Sutton was blithering about, thinking maybe it's rusty old bayonet or something similar. To avoid attracting attention Trevor passed the rolled carrier bag across to Walker seated next to him, who surreptitiously took hold of the bag and contents. To his concealed surprise he felt the soft outline of what were obviously purses or wallets, and from past experience knew what to do with them, but the obvious weight of the gun fell to the bottom of the package, revealing that he was not, as he assumed. dealing with a knife or bayonet of some description.

In a low voice he said, "What the fuck have I got here Trevor? It feels like a fucking pistol, and my guess is, the little metal bits are some ammunition for it. Who's is it?"

Sutton repeated the story of how he thought he was doing the 'old boy' a favour by handing it in to the Old Bill. He figured Walker would know how to dispose of it, as it hadn't been used for a long time, it just needed getting rid of. His continued pleas of help eventually convinced Walker to take it into protective custody, on one condition — that he would subsequently sign a property disclaimer and disposal form, so that there would be no problems with its destruction. Trevor readily agreed to this, just relieved that he'd actually got shot of Tommy's problem without revealing to his tame detective the truth of its origin. Walker instructed Sutton to get the beers in, while he tightly wrapped the bag concealing it under his rain coat, looking around to see if anyone was looking what nefarious activity had just transpired. Instead of leaving the Wellington to go home, he realised he'd have to return to the office to secrete the bag and contents, locking them in his office desk, until he could deal the contents the next day.

*

Late afternoon saw Bob slavishly going through a backlog of crime reports each requiring his reading and then signed off as no further police action. The numbers being disposed of occasionally sent him on a bit of a guilt trip, together with his annoyance his team were unable to take the enquiries any further, and no arrests would ensue. His frustration he and his team were somehow letting the public down, but then realisation would take over and galvanise his resolve to catch more thieves, to keep sending that message out that his boys were on their case. Just then the door knocked and slowly opened to reveal the 'brief' standing there. She entered, pausing only to admire the aquarium Bob had told her of.

"Hello, Detective Inspector Trebor. I was at Seymour Place juvenile court, and as I hadn't heard from you for a while I wanted to see you."

Bobs offer of coffee was politely declined. "What's wrong? Why have I got a strange feeling about you being here today. Do I detect from your straight face I'm about get bad news?"

"Bob you know I had been seeing that barrister, I'm just so confused over you. I've always wanted to be with you but I can't go on like this, living a life of sometimes seeing you, sometimes not. I don't want to hide any more, so really the ball is in your court."

"Do you love him, the learned barrister? No don't answer that. It's strange isn't it, I love being with you all the time and at the moment I can't, you're seeing him which I can't stand the thought of it but cannot object, I don't have the right. You're like sand slipping through my fingers and I seem to be unable to stop it. I'm trying to do a good job here, and balancing the kids well-being at home, but really wanting to be with you full time to make you proud, but I don't seem to make it mean enough. Please will you still see me?"

"Bob I'm confused, I can't give you that commitment. I'm sorry. I must go."

With that she turned, leaving him leaning back in his chair, the wind taken out of his sails. He sat dumbstruck, with thoughts of resentment and regret welling up inside him. *How pertinent* he thought, as Joy Division came on the radio lamenting love would tear them apart again.

12

THE PLOT THICKENS

Daybreak.

I'm back in the office, writing off more of what I'd call no hope crimes. It's usually where the victim of the theft isn't really sure where they'd lost their property between points A and B, but by virtue of the fact they travelled on the Underground, that's where it must have happened. They have nothing constructive to add, which might help with suspects for their loss, , simply what I've just related to you. Now, a half reasonable copper might do some investigation of the crime the moment its reported to them. But no, invariably it was the first uniformed officer they saw, and so reported the crime. Sadly, in so many cases the officer does nothing to investigate, just accepts the allegation at face value. 'What good is that?', I hear you ask? Absolutely none, the victim might just as well have just reported it to their insurance company, and just cut out the middle man. But they know they're going to need a crime reference number hence our involvement, otherwise they don't get paid out by the insurance company, and I wouldn't might betting, in that case, they wouldn't even bother telling us. It's a travesty, because all it does is increase our crime numbers without any hope of us catching anyone, and it puts up all our premiums, yours and mine, and it's too damn late. Sometimes though, a conscientious officer will dig a bit deeper and we might get some descriptions. At least that's a start, and with our analysis of locations, times of day, and modus operandi, and so on, we might actually be able to build up a strategy to capture the thieves. And that, my friend, is why the make up of the squad is so crucial to its success, and why jealous people with the wrong motives want to be a part of it, and it's why there is no less than the most scrupulous officers working for me. Putting it simply, there are no bent bastards on the take on the team, which of course is the reason we're being investigated to such an extent by those I suggest who have something to hide from their own skullduggery, which they're are desperate to conceal.

Right I'm off to the car pool to pick up the London cab we have. Excellent bit of kit for getting close up to target criminals without them 'sussing' what's going on. Sharon from the drama group has just called me, wanting to meet later. I'm taking the cab home with me tonight, the garage man has asked me to put a few miles on the clock, as it's not been used for a while. Two birds, one stone! Deep joy!

Bob waited on the rank waiting for Sharon aka 'the naughty school mistress' to arrive off a train from London. She'd been to the capital for yet another interview, and keen to reunite so to speak. It was Hazel who gave her the nickname, and this instance seemed be entirely appropriate thought Bob. A sound of the horn and a wave in her direction saw her recognise Bob although the mode of transport was a new one on her.

"Where would you like me to take you madam," he asked knowingly.

Somewhere quiet where they could have a quick drink and chat, a country pub somewhere, ensuring they wouldn't be discovered. She got in the passenger part of the cab. Bob checked the mirror and could see she was seated, leaning back on the seat, treating him to a view of what she had in mind. All modesty abandoned, she declared she was without knickers but was wearing stockings, the white flesh revealed the route to pleasure. Doing his best to focus on his driving in the late evening sun, their conversation fell silent as he wormed his way through a series of single track country lanes, while Sharon pretending to squirm, writhed on the rear seat faking an orgasm for Bobs pleasure. He turned into the car park at the rear of 'The Old Mill' pub, happy that they were sufficiently off the beaten track from discovery and yet so close to home for the pair of them.

As darkness fell, Bob realised he was not in for a drinking session, particularly as he had the 'job' taxi; after all, what would it look like if he was to get stopped and bagged by local plod, or just as bad, be involved in a collision with a fine upstanding member of the public? However, his moral high ground didn't extend to the naughty school mistress who in his mind was '*up for it*' and who he was resolved to loosening her inhibitions even further, albeit she appeared to need little encouragement. Within the hour they were back in the cab, she having told him she'd secured a modelling job with a fashion house called Cojana in Marlborough Street, so good news, she'd be in London regularly!

They adjourned to the back seat, the car park being almost empty. Sharon checked Bob was 'feeling' ready as her hand deftly opened his flies, and she rubbed him into life.

Bob suggested they move to some railway arches nearby where they'd remain undiscovered. She agreed, sensing her juices were flowing. Five minutes later saw them once more on the back seat. The school mistress dropped to her knees, pulling his trousers lower to suck on his now swollen manhood. She groaned in unison with Bob as he watched her mini skirt ride up to reveal her suspenders straining to hold on to her stockings as she pulled back his foreskin hard to lick and suck his swollen helmet. She rose to sit astride him to carefully guide his cock into her tight fanny, and then ride him, selfishly gaining ultimate pleasure, while Bobs focus was on her pert nipples having released her lace bra. As the windows of the cab began to mist up his mind was filled with Tina Turner singing about steamy windows. Her confidence had grown since their last coupling. She pulled clear, leaving Bob wondering what was next on the agenda. She dropped to her knees again, and pulling back his foreskin, she gorged on his cock, sucking it so hard he was unable to prevent the inevitable in her mouth. Sharon withdrew to reveal a thin trace of Bobs 'pleasure' dribbling from her mouth as she swallowed.

"That's the first time I've ever done that. Am I a naughty girl? she smiled up at Bob looking for a reaction.

Bobs only response was to say how fantastic it was as he laid back trying to recover, vowing to do it again, but she told him she'd have to make tracks for home.

*

Daybreak again saw Bob waiting in the rank outside Kings Cross railway station for Brian Kent to arrive. Fifteen minutes passed as Bob turned down several fares waiting for Brian to arrive.

"Sorry I'm late guv the tubes are up the spout this morning," as Brian jumped into the back not knowing what a scene of unbridled passion it had been just twelve hours earlier. Bob resisted the temptation to bollock him, choosing to set off for the pub in Greenford which would be the location for the 'exchange' on the forged American Express travellers cheques. He explained the strategy of how Shaun Bennet would be conveyed by Brian in the cab to the pub and be dropped off outside together with Driscoll who'd do the introductions to the villains before leaving again in the taxi. He'd then be dropped off at Greenford station to make his own way back to Pentonville prison. He'd then wait for however long it took for Shaun to gain the confidence of the 'targets' and set up the deal to purchase the parcel, emphasising his preference to do it in west London, somewhere near Baker Street. This would then enable Bob to get sufficient resources, or manpower in 'old money' together, to do an ambush in one of the little mews just off the main road. They pulled up outside ' The Old Bill' and plotted up on the building, access points, roads, pathways and anything else which might present a challenge to a successful operation. As the time got to eleven Brian left the cab to have a quick look inside just as opening time unlocked the doors to the establishment.

"Looks alright, boss. Mainly bench seats and a few tables and chairs. No security cameras, which is a bit of a surprise as its in the middle of this shitty council estate. My guess, most of the punters are going to know one another but if

Shaun is going in with a 'face' it should be alright," as Brian continued with his briefing to the guv'nor.

*

A degree of panic had set in with Secrett. His own sense of self-preservation started to kick as he detected in his mind, Spooner was attempting to divorce himself from the day to day investigation of the Dip Squad. His mind drifted back to a time when he was in charge of Trebor. But now that young detective sergeant he used laud it over had morphed into a fire spitting dragon, who far from simply defending himself from an allegation of corruption, now seemed hell-bent on fighting fire with fire. The two statements of pickpockets White and Phyle had thrown a low ball into his strategy. Having known Trebor when Bob worked for him for about three years, both qualifying as surveillance instructors from the same Regional Crime Squad course, he'd become fiercely aware of his capabilities. Even from the time learning of Sutton's original allegation of corruption, supplemented by Dennison's attempted arrest of McMurray, his gut feeling that whatever the truth of the matter, he honestly couldn't believe that Trebor was involved.

Moreover, his mind went back to a time when he and Trebor were engaged in investigating registered mail bag robberies, which were occurring while the bags were in transit on the rail network. The bags usually contained high-value mail or correspondence, often jewellery, or cash or blank travellers cheques, the paying public, or large companies believing their 'registered' mail would be safely couriered by the Post Office. The Serious Crime Squad, of which the two were senior members, knew differently, to such an extent they thought it perhaps safer to use the conventional mail conduits of first-and second-class post! On this occasion following some diligent investigative work by Bob, he'd establish a pattern of thefts occurring on a late-night train from Victoria. It seemed each time they were violated and established packages missing, the means of opening was either a sharp knife or a lighter to melt the seals.

*

Secrett dressed smartly in a two piece suit as if he'd been out for the evening, boarded the 11.30pm train from Victoria going to the south coast, while other members of the team were due to ride the later train looking for targets. He sat in a compartment of the first-class carriage, which connected with the mail van, the compartment just behind his. Bob, dressed casually, and not in company of Secrett boarded and sat in a second-class compartment, of the same carriage, the front section being separated by a swing door in the thin corridor, with a sign on the window indicating that 'poor' people could stray no further towards where Secrett had positioned himself. Prior to boarding Bob watched members of the Post office load about three dozen registered mailbags in the cage just behind where Secrett was seated. He indicated they'd been loaded and the cage containing them, he believed, had been locked. They both knew and were able to identify the high-security bags, by the colour, the distinct label attached to the top, and the tell tale use of either plastic or nylon ties ensuring the various contents remained secure.

The journey proceeded uneventfully, Secrett recalled in his mind, with only a stop at Redhill and Gatwick on the trains route south. As it slowed to a stop at Redhill, Bob looked out along the platform and saw the only passenger to board was a man who looked about forty years, dressed in black and wearing a vicar's collar. He headed straight for the carriage where the mail cage was, observed by Bob, who rapidly came to the conclusion this was no vicar, the tell-tale broken nose, weather-beaten face and his continual furtive looking about himself. He briefed Secrett as he went past, continuing to follow the 'vicar'. Bobs view of the 'vicar' saw him lean against the cage door, succeeding in slipping the latch and looking up and down the length of the corridor before moving inside. He left him to get on with what believed to be thefts from the bags, and retreated to tell Secrett what had just transpired. They returned to the cage to find the suspect sat on three or four of the bags. Realising he was being arrested, the vicar accepted his fate without question as he was handcuffed to prevent escape.

Secrett said, "Right, what bags have you opened?"

The vicar protested his innocence, saying he'd only gone in to sit down, believing there were no seats available further along the train and so sitting on the bags seemed a good option. In the meantime, Bob checked to see if any seals had been broken, but it seemed they hadn't. Maybe they'd intercepted too early, not giving their suspect a chance to perform. Having got this far, Secrett was determined not to let the arrest falter, for the sake of concrete evidence of a theft as the train pulled in to Gatwick airport, where postal staff waited to unload the registered mailbags destined for more exotic locations overseas once re-sorted. Bob felt obliged to go along with Secrett's plan, not least because he was junior in rank. A search with the supposed innocent man in an unoccupied office on the platform revealed he was neither in possession of a knife or lighter, or indeed anything which may place him in the category of going equipped to steal. In fact his only 'offence', if Bob could call it that, was of impersonating a man of the cloth. His details, which couldn't be verified by anything on him, revealed he had no form aka previous convictions. This still didn't satisfy Secrett, as he now had the bit between his teeth and wasn't about to let go. He was a determined officer, who, having sold on an idea was very difficult to shake off.

Away from the suspect he said, "You have this one, Bob. We can help him reconcile himself with truth. He's got to be at it, we just jumped in too early."

And I thought, hello, what's this stunt he's pulling. I expect he's right, the bloke was well at it. Nobody gets dressed up as a vicar if they're not one, unless of course it's one of those kind of parties! No he's definitely a 'wrong-un' but we've got nothing on him. His identity checks out, but he's got no form, and nothing with him, knife or lighter to assist in the commission. So why nick him? I'm not into tucking someone up just to save my embarrassment. It's just not right apart from perverting justice. So I told him I wasn't interested, but if he wanted to do the script I might be able to follow his lead. Guess what? Secrett bottled it and backed off, and so we let him go, leaving him in no doubt he was very fortunate to be walking. I could see the situation where if I'd nicked him, I'd be the one with the complaint for wrongful arrest and a 'shit-storm' of an investigation, and I wonder if he'd stick by me, or duck out with some statement that doesn't even come up to proof. No, he showed his lack of metal when I reverse the situation. Glad I did, dodgy bastard. He never mentioned it again, but I knew, and he knew that I knew!

A shiver went down the spine of Secrett as he thought of another occasion when Bob saw what kind of senior officer he was. At the time, Trebor was a Detective Sergeant engaged investigating Royal Mail robberies and thefts. Secrett had just joined the squad as the Detective Inspector in charge of Bob's team. Keen to impress on the junior officers that he was a shrewd senior detective, he'd learnt from one of the intelligence reports passed by the the Post Office Investigation Branch, they were concerned about a particular postal worker who appeared to have a lifestyle way above what his pay grade would seem to support. He guarded the information jealously, making the necessary enquires about the suspect, without the knowledge of any of his team members. He went with Bob and a couple of other detectives armed with a warrant to search the suspect's address, a second floor flat on the Guinness Trust estate on Stamford Hill. Secrett had been tipped off, the post office worker was on his way home after his shift. He didn't have enough time to obtain an actual search warrant from a local magistrate, thereby causing delay in the search, so cutting corners, as he had before, he used a copy of his own gas bill for his home, which he would flash quickly to the suspect, claiming it to be a genuine warrant to search. The suspect opened the front door to learn that Secrett, together with his team, were going to search his home. Believing the gas bill ruse, they entered and commenced the search. Secrett delegated the various rooms for the officers to search while he told Bob to take the suspect into the bedroom to commence his search in there.

In the confusion entering the property, Secrett had managed to slip into the bedroom and carefully place a key, easily identifiable as belonging to the Post Office, in the bedside drawer. The key was of a specific size and shape, and was used to secure the cage doors in the brake van on the train where the high value mail would be loaded. He left the room, allowing Bob to commence his search. It was quite apparent the suspect had been living way beyond his means. The wardrobes were full of Armani, Versace and Gucci clothing and shoes, with no visible means of support other that his postal loader's job, it was obvious to Bob they'd got the right man. He then went to the bedside cabinet where he discovered the key. It's difficult to determine who was more surprised, as Bob declared to Secrett what he'd found.

Sensing he was about to lose everything he owned, plus his liberty, the postal worker protested, "Hang on, that's not my key." He led them to the lounge, where on the coffee table he pull a plant up by the stem. "That's my key there." Bob, looking into the base of the pot found an identical key to the one Secrett had planted. The suspect was grandly told he was being arrested for various thefts from the Royal Mail, while Secrett retrieved his key from Bob, who thought it a completely unnecessary stunt and told him so. So fed up with the trick Secrett had played he told him he wanted nothing further to do with the job. It wasn't how he worked, to his mind, it wasn't *noble cause policing.*

The postal loader put his hands up, even made a statement under caution admitting what he done, in return for some of his clothes being returned to him. At Crown Court he pleaded guilty and got two years. This was just another incident demonstrating I should never trust anything Secrett says or does.

Secrett quietly reflected on what evidence there was on any of the Dip Squad and it seemed there was none, other than a couple CID diaries which recorded each officer's duties on a daily basis, were found to be a couple of days out of date, and a couple of bits of procedural crap which didn't really amount to anything. It meant he was going to have to get together with the others to manufacture enough for an internal discipline hearing to save their blushes! Just then, Dennison knocked and entered together with Spooner. They sat thinking how to progress the investigation, each putting in their suggestions but not really coming up with anything concrete. Their problem, they agreed, was that the raid on the squad was carried out before they had even obtained a witness statement from McMurray, and they'd already been told by Branch to leave Sutton's two statements out, which again had been obtained after the raid, not to be mentioned. Leaving DS Hunt to one side, and Spooner told them Branch had instructed him to interview Penny from the list office at Knightsbridge Crown Court, the supposed witness to Basil's fall down the escalators, they needed to create a valid reason behind what seemed an extreme course. Apart from a few administrative questions they really had nothing. To compound the situation, McMurray had been told, he'd no longer be prosecuted for the Dip Squad arrest, or indeed, the attempt theft and assault on Dennison.

*

"There he is, Al. There's Harrison at it, further down there can you see him?" said Dave Champion.

The pair were at Temple tube station, on their way back to the nick from a case conference at Queen Elizabeth building, in Middle Temple, famed for its Middle Temple Hall, in that Shakespeare first performed *'Twelfth Night'* there. It's hallowed turf for many a barrister, punching above their weight! Fish saw Harrison dashing in and out of the intending passengers, eager to gain one of the last remaining seats on the westbound Circle line train. The lunchtime delays to the trains had created dense overcrowding on the platform, enabling the officers to get close to the subject of their attention without being seen by him.

"He's got to go Al. He's taking the piss, I'm sure he's got bail conditions not to be on the Underground. What do you reckon?"

" Yeah, he got them when I committed for trial from Clerkenwell the other week. He reckons he taped me at court admitting I'd fitted him up. As if! I don't know if he did or not."

"C'mon Al, can't let him front you out like that. Tell you what, I'll lead the charge, you just come in as witness. I'll do the business. Besides it'll come up at Crown, after the other job any way, won't it.?"

Fish agreed with Champions assessment of the situation. They slipped in behind Harrison to watch more closely his 'shaping up' behind a victim. They felt the breeze of the next train coming into the platform as Harrison pulled his blouson jacket down over his right shoulder, concealing his lower forearm and hand. As the train ground to a halt, using the jacket to mask his movements, he shuffled in behind an Asian looking woman, holding a toddler's hand in her right hand, trying to steady the child's entry on to the train, as she corrected her shoulder bag on her left shoulder, clearly focusing on boarding the crowded carriage. Oblivious to Harrison's close proximity to her, she was unaware of his hand fishing around the top of her bag.

He turned, having failed to secure any of its contents, coming face to face with Dave Champion who said, "Have a guess. Yep you're right. You're fucking nicked."

Fish barged in to prevent his attempted escape. He called to the mother and child, who had not realised the reason for the scuffle behind them. Al used all his persuasive tendencies for her to alight, which she duly complied with. After a brief chat during which she continued to extend her grateful thanks to these two 'heroes', she was once more on her journey home, with her bemused child. It was difficult to know who was the most surprised by this appeal — Fish, Harrison or Champion who had by now secured custody of the prisoner with a very quick click-click of handcuffs. Harrison simply remained quietly docile as he could see on this occasion, a protest of his innocence would be to no avail. A short assent up the stairs found them in the booking hall, where Al summoned a uniform van transport to take their 'prize' to the local nick. They toyed with the idea of going to the nearest police station, but opted for their favourite haunt at Bow Street.

"Told you I had a crystal ball didn't I? So that's two different trials your up for now, you fucking loser," said Al to a rather fed-up Harrison.

There was no response, needless to say, as he thought how he would spring the tape trap at his trial.

*

Boles sat back in his office as a rare treat of early morning sunshine made its presence felt, creating shapes across the grey carpet in front of his desk. He could barely conceal his anger as he learnt of the resultant raid on Detective Inspector Walkers office, where a perfectly serviceable revolver — together with four live bullets — were found, courtesy of the search by CIB2 officers. Boles quickly realised, what had started of as a raid on the Dip Squad, perceived as a thorn in his side, together with allegations of corruption from two professional pickpockets about officers he'd appointed to do his dirty work, the plot had certainly thickened!

13

HOMEWORK, HOMEWORK

Sir Timothy Humphries, a newly recognised member of the aristocracy of this green and pleasant land, wondered to himself how it was that his clerk of chambers had dumped a seven-handed conspiracy to steal within the jurisdiction of the Central Criminal Court, together within various substantive offences and forged passport counts. To cap it all he mused, *they're all bloody foreigners, from the sunny uplands of Santiago in Chile. Doubtless the whole blasted trial will be through an interpreter! What a slow and ponderous procedure* he thought. His usual fayre was to his mind, that of a good GBH, robbery or sexual assaults. His chambers thought it would be a bit of light relief for him as he sat in his room, impressively bedecked with all the judicial references one could imagine, awaiting the arrival of the officer in the case, one Detective Inspector Trebor together with his side kick DC Paul Hazel. This was to be what is known in the trade as a 'con'. No not a confidence trick, although some may disagree; this was to be a case conference with the sole intention of ironing out some the wrinkles in the case.

A knock announced their attendance as they were ushered in by the clerk who extended the usual pleasantries of afternoon tea for the officers, which they gratefully accepted. Bob immediately apologised for their lateness to the elderly gent in his late fifties, occupying what seemed an oversized office overlooking the cobbled square, as Head of Chambers at 4 Kings Bench Walk. He waived the platitudes away as of no consequence, having been back for about ten minutes from the Central Criminal Court from another victory. The con was something invariably held back in chambers, usually after four o'clock, after the day's skirmishing and posturing for the benefit of a jury.

"Right, gentlemen, I've had a look through the papers and I've drawn up the the indictment for the seven defendants on the premise that each of them is known to at least one or two others in the group. As I understand it, three were arrested, then two, then the last two who were actually arrested after the first five had been committed, but it appears they've now been joined to the first five, and so we have seven appearing on the same indictment. To save time, there is the overall conspiracy to steal within the jurisdiction of the Central Criminal Court, which lumps them all together in one large wheel with several spokes to it. Then we have a number of smaller conspiracies to steal in each of the groups, and also substantive theft or attempt theft offences the Crown will say, plus finally various passport offences, theft of identity documents and so on. Does that sum it up Detective Inspector? Here, this is a copy of the indictment containing all the counts. As you can see it runs to over fifteen. But of course when we come to the day of the trial we may be able to slim down some of it having dealt with the various defence representatives, and of course we might get a steer from the judge. What say you officer?"

Bobs mind was elsewhere although he was doing his best to appear as if he was listening to the 'invaluable' assessment by the learned gentleman sitting the other side of the rich mahogany desk with most of its luxuriant deep green hide inlay covered in books, papers and other unrelated files. In an attempt to prove he was on top the case he said, "Yes sir, that's about right, I think all the angles are covered. I guess the next thing to wait for is probably communication from those representing them, what their various positions are, and hopefully, some sort of fixed date from the Bailey."

Humphries said he knew a couple of the barristers who'd been pencilled in to conduct defence for them. Seemingly they were alleging some kind of 'fit-up' , in as much as they were claiming that none of them knew anyone else in the conspiracy and were at a loss how the Police could be so corrupt as to round them all up into one big enterprise. As far as they were concerned they were simply confused tourists from the same part of the world who the authorities were taking advantage of.

The very idea, officers of mine indulging in the dark art of corruption ? You'll notice there's not one allegation they've had anything including their large amounts of cash, stolen from them. These sods are the best in the world at thieving, they just don't like it up 'em, Captain Mainwaring! I've sent of for their previous convictions from around the world, which isn't an easy job in itself to do. Any enquiry of this nature has to go through Interpol at the Yard, who then get in touch with their respective counterparts in the countries we're making the request. As it stands I've asked for anything in Chile, obviously, but then I've included Columbia, and Europe in particular as they seem to work our part of the world in the summer months. Interpol reckon it might take a few months as some the countries, Chile in particular, aren't keen on dropping their own in the proverbial unless they absolutely have to. I've already been to the Chilean embassy in London, trying to circumnavigate the request, but I should've known — he was a very nice man, but he just went all political on me, and advised me to use the the usual channels. When I enquired what they might be, he didn't have clue! Bet he knows his way to the Ambassador's pile of Ferrero Rocher!! So it leaves me just a couple of things to do, not least the interpreter for the trial, I think the lovely Fiona will be ideal. She's well 'pro police', and I wasn't able to use her for any of the interviews when this bunch of lost soles were nicked. It can't be the same interpreter you see. Mind you, if there's any loss in translation, I have every confidence whatever she relays in court will be to our benefit. Otherwise she won't get an invite to the next squad soirée! I'll deal with the run-through of the evidence and the cross-pollination of various exhibits nearer the time. Now I'm off to meet the naughty schoolmistress, I'll tell Paul to tidy up anything else with Humphries clerk.

*

"I don't like this Greg, I've gone through all the stuff we seized on the raid of the Dip Squad, and really apart from a few internal discipline matters which really aren't sackable, we're a bit stumped. Is there any chance your man McMurray might have forgotten something, like perhaps that a couple of them were on a regular pay-off from him? Or he'd been given a life, something like that?"

Dennison listened intently to Secrett, who to his mind was beginning to lose his nerve. *It wasn't really his bag, this kind of stunt,* he reflected. "I can speak with him guv, it might be that in the heat of the moment he forgot what I told him. Might it not look a bit rehearsed though?"

"Greg, let me tell you in confidence where we are. McMurray has made his allegation, and as a result he's been given immunity from prosecution on the Dip Squad job. So essentially there's nothing outstanding against him. Here's the problem: we've now got two different dips come forward to say that you're bent, on the take, and that the whole incident at Russell Square was a set-up just so he could make his allegation. To complicate things further, D.I. John Walker, who I know you know well has also been raided, because that fucking idiot of a deputy chief, Boles, let it slip to the Commander Ed Brown that a white Dip by the name of Sutton, had also made allegations of theft by one of the Dip Squad."

Dennison looked quizzically at Secrett, as if to say, *another good allegation, what's wrong?* He was about to learn. Secrett chose his words carefully as he told Dennison that Sutton's two statements, one of which he knew the content of, from his visit to Pentonville prison with Branch, whinged about his arrest by the Dip Squad who he maintained were corrupt, taking money, or 'taxing'. What followed, was now the problem. D.I. Walker had called into headquarters to see someone in the Intelligence section when he bumped into Branch and that was how the subsequent interviews in prison took place. The raid on Walkers office by officers of CIB2 found a couple of real problems for him. He had a number of purses and wallets in his drawer, which apparently he would deposit at the Lost Property office at Waterloo. Sutton told him that cohorts of his had nicked them and he was just being a 'Good Samaritan' in returning them, minus any cash of course. Worse still, they found a revolver and bullets for it in his top drawer. And so far no explanation. This was why something a bit stronger from McMurray might do the trick. Dennison got up assuring Secrett he'd see what he could do.

*

Paul Hazel sat in the toilets, behind a locked door, vowing in his mind never to get so pissed again, or shag the lovely Valerie Pike, his squeeze from the Stock Exchange, he'd met with Trebor when they interviewed her following a 'tail off' robbery. He tried to focus on his current predicament, but his mind kept drifting back to the day he met her in the George public house near London Bridge. Her assurance she was wearing no knickers, was confirmed by Paul on each and every occasion he met up with her. And wet…boy was she wet! As he sat in trap one he knew his seated occupation would be for some time, not because nature was continually calling, but for a somewhat urgent reason. He'd been caught — in every sense of the word — with his trousers down! A dip by the name of Parnell Perkins who he'd nicked the week before at Edgware Road tube, on the District and Circle line, had arrived at Marylebone Magistrates court in the morning and although not represented, had declared that he had the temerity to plead not guilty to the charge of attempt theft from a woman unknown. *Fucking outrageous* thought Paul, as the clerk of the court, believing he was making good use of court time saw that an avenue of opportunity had arisen in the court list for the afternoon, declaring that Court 2, normally reserved for traffic offences had suddenly become clear, which presented Paul with a big problem. Instead of Paul seeking a quick remand to get the evidence together for either a trial or committal to Crown Court, he found himself with a 'not guilty' fight that afternoon. The defendant playing the system and wanted a summary trial which would be held at Marylebone. The option was to go 'up the road' for a jury trial, probably months later.

Left with no alternative but to fill the 611 otherwise known as the Case History folder with something other than a few blank sheets of paper to make it look to the casual observer, as if this was a serious villain, he sat pondering the 'script' for Perkins. Also, as was often the case, the booby trap of a porno picture of some fallen Madonna ripped from the latest edition of *Mayfair*, had been carefully slotted among the pages of the prosecution file. Conscious he still had another arrest to record in his official pocket book which of course he would swear been made at the time of the arrest, he realised that it would be out of sync with the dates. He'd acquired a couple of Incident Report Books or IRBs from Paddington Green nick which had been issued on the day of Perkins arrest. The IRB was a very handy thing to use in as much as it was used throughout London to record incidents of varying kinds or arrests. This meant they were in the right time frame for him to write his 'original notes' in one of them and then claim they had been made at the nick shortly after the time of arrest! He cursed the helpful clerk of the court and Perkins as he commenced writing the evidence leading to the arrest and subsequent charging of the thief. But within about fifteen minutes he cobbled together a scenario for the attempt theft, and how it was that he was unable to get the female victim's details. Curiously, he'd found, that last point was often the case, even with 'straight up and down' jobs; on many occasions there was either difficulty gaining the victim's attention as they boarded the Tube, or they were reluctant to get involved as they hadn't realised they had been targeted. But Perkins needed to take a fall. He was a violent shit with a load of form running into a couple of pages, which meant he had something like fifteen previous convictions for dipping, attempt thefts and lone robberies.

*

Dave answered the office 'Trimphone' to John Conroy who was in the list office at Southwark Crown Court trying to sort out a couple of trial dates, when he saw the name Harrison on the card and the word 'fixed' underneath it. Normally this wouldn't be too much of a problem, other than sorting out witnesses, police officers dates to avoid due to holidays or leave. What would have been considerate would be to speak with the officer in the case who would have insight. Sadly some *ignorant shit* John thought, had just gone ahead and fixed the trial date. To try and break a fixed date usually meant going in front of a judge, and that's where it would all get complicated, the judge crusading on not wanting to waste money from the public purse. Nonsense, of course, because like buses, there was always another trial right behind that could be slotted in.

Dave said, "Here Al I've got John on the blower here. He's says the Harrison trial has been fixed."

It did not register with Fish at first, as his undivided attention was drawn to the 'Dear Deirdre' page in the Sun, and the confession of some bloke called Bucky who was into dressing in women's clothing, particularly Laura Ashley numbers, and smoking a pipe while watching the tv. *What the fuck is all that about* he thought to himself, then registering the urgency of Dave wanting to speak to him.

"What you on about Dave, who's on the other end?"

Dave clued Fish in on the conversation he was having with John Conroy at Southwark Court list office. A problem now presented itself. The second arrest of Harrison which had since been committed as had the first, but to Inner London Crown Court had for some reason jumped the queue in order of appearance at court and was now at Southwark. In the ordinary course of events this wouldn't really cause much of a problem to Al's mind, but his mind raced as to why the second one was fixed. Was it a test, was he being investigated for the taped recorded threats he'd made at Clerkenwell magistrates court, and the powers that be just wanted to get the second one out of the way because there was a victim and another officer, anticipating a plea of guilty? *Fuck it* he thought. *I can't start enquiring reasons behind the two trials now at the same court, or that the second fixed trial will obviously now come up before the first. Just have to go with it and wait for the 'alligators' to come snapping!* He told Dave to tell John, there was no problem, he didn't want the profile being raised in the List Office.

*

Spooner slowly wound his spoon round the top of his cappuccino as he sat at the corner coffee bar in Harrods' food hall. He mused at the wet fish display on the far side, wondering what giant specimen was being gently caressed within the display's water spray. Today was the day when he'd visit Penny in the List Office at Knightsbridge Court Court, just round the corner in Hans Crescent, He needed to pin her down on detail surrounding Basil Chakrabati's ultimate demise, having fallen from the top to the bottom of the escalators, at the Underground station. The question was, did he jump or was he pushed? If it was the latter, was it the dip Heath in his bid for freedom, or more likely — as he suspected — Detective Sergeant Hunt was to blame? Now that Basil was dead, he tossed around in his head as to whether it was murder or manslaughter. *Twenty more minutes to kill,* he thought to himself as he ordered another extortionately expensive coffee. At least he got a dinky little biscuit to go with it. He read through the photocopy of the statement Hunt had taken, making some notes down the margin of the salient pints he felt needed clarifying with Penny as she appeared to be the only independent witness to Basil's fall. He hadn't spoken to her for about a week but as at her request he delayed seeing he until after ten thirty once all the courts had 'kicked off'.

"What do you mean she's left?", Spooner trying to contain his frustration at having his meeting with Penny thwarted.

It transpired that she had put her notice in some four weeks ago, and had fulfilled her lifelong ambition to move to Australia! The List office supervisor had no idea where she had gone or indeed any forwarding address details, and — worse still from Spooners point of view — couldn't comprehend why it was so important she tell him she was leaving. *Fucking civvies* he thought to himself. *They just don't get it, not like the old days when you'd have a couple of old officers coming toward the end of their service, who were conscientious enough to recognise the potential of such behaviour. The jobs well and truly fucked* he thought to himself.

As Spooner dragged back up the Piccadilly line to headquarters, he knew the case against Hunt relied on Detective Sergeant Hunt's dubious account as well as the late Basil's statement, together with a defence allegation from Heath. He knew it meant the chances of potting Hunt were becoming severely weakened. The message wasn't well received by Maurice Branch, the boss, already pissed off with Secretts unilateral 'no further action' deal with Sutton and also Boles' apparent attempt to separate himself from any involvement in what was now looking like a dogs dinner of a raid on the Dip Squad. He was now dealing with two Dips who were less than complimentary about his Detective Sergeant Dennison, and claims that the attempt theft and assault at Russell Square was a fit-up, with the sole purpose of discrediting the squad by way of a corruption investigation.

*

Bob was running late after his 'con' in Kings Bench Walk, for his secret assignation in the form of the naughty school mistress as he walked up to the front of the Theatre Royal, Drury Lane. There she was, fresh from a catwalk modelling job in Marlborough Street. He was conscious of the time, knowing she only had a small window of opportunity until she'd have to make her way home, not out of any sense of guilt, just wanting to catch her husband out. He nearly didn't recognise her in the blonde wig and heavy make up — the demands of the fashion house. But there was no mistaking those long legs, American tan stockings and high heels. Again he thought to himself, *I must have died and gone to heaven,* as he greeted her and she immersed her tongue in his mouth.

They walked round to 'Rumours' opposite 'Brahms and Liszt' bar restaurant overlooking Covent Garden, as Bob impressed her with his knowledge of the area.

"You know that theatre is the oldest one in London. If fact it's rumoured there's a secret passage underneath it with access from the royal box. It's believed Charles the second used to use it when he got bored with the play. The other end comes up in what is now the Nell Gwynn pub, in Bull Inn Court where he would meet up with his lover for a different kind of entertainment. She used to call him Charles the third as she already had two other lovers with the same name."

She laughed at the thought that what they were hopefully going to do was no different centuries later. *The whole world is at it* she thought to herself, as they stepped out into the early evening air, and walked towards the 'Coal Hole' pub on the Strand. She remarked on the unusual name as Bob again gave her benefit of his knowledge.

"It's on the site of what used to be a giant coal hole, taking deliveries from merchants, of coal to heat the many rooms of the Savoy hotel. When he pub was built they just kept the name." Another 'pit stop' saw them fall out of there and making their way to the Embankment to the Tattershall Castle paddle steamer, the former Humber ferry now permanently moored between Embankment and Westminster.

I'm not expanding on what happened next, all I'll say is that we went the Union Jack club again. By this time she'd decided her 'old man' wasn't worth chasing, but happily mine was! Within a short period of time she was eating me again, but with an extra twist. She insisted on all avenues being explored. God knows what books she'd been reading, but fuck it, a deals a deal and so I duly obliged, even though it is still a criminal offence for a bloke to do it to a woman, unlike the buggers charter of 1967 which allowed males to do whatever to each other. Her insistence of blowing me afterwards did surprise me however! Two hours later we parted and made our separate ways homeward.

14

LIES AND DAMN LIES

"I swear by almighty God to tell the truth, the whole truth, and nothing but the truth. Paul Hazel, Detective Constable, Central London Pickpocket Squad, your worship." Parnell Perkins sat in the dock, listening attentively to every word uttered by Paul as the late afternoon searched through the high windows to shed some light on the imminent proceedings. Over the lunch break Perkins had the opportunity to speak to a lawyer, otherwise known as a 'hack' in the trade, who was able to take instructions and advise her, now client, to plead not guilty, with the benefit of the legal aid system.

'Legal Aid' is a vehicle by which any person in the street can get free legal advice and often representation at court if required. All the client needs to do is sign a couple of forms, usually completed by the lawyer, confirming their declaration of no means or little income was true. Hey presto, he or she is represented courtesy of the British taxpayer! There's no such thing as a free lunch; sooner or later someone has to pick up the tab, just as long as it's not the one who really should be paying. A duty solicitor at a mornings court attendance can in a very short time become very well paid for very little effort. All they

have to do is look at the court list for that day and then trawl round the various defendants encouraging them to sign the legal aid application forms. It's a win win for both parties — the defendant who will always see the opportunity to either delay or defeat the system as much as he or she can, and the lawyer, who, whilst adopting the high moral ground of justice for all, also sees an almost unquestionable business opportunity. In many cases it doesn't really matter if they don't use their 'services' after the first appearance; the lawyer still gets paid by the Legal Aid Board. It leaks money like a sieve. I know of at least two briefs who have boasted they now have no mortgage on their houses, and drive around in the latest Porsche! One of them, believing they were giving me a treat, took me for a ride all round London in their new BMW. To look the part they put on a stylish flat cap and wore the old string back gloves, surely a hangover from grander old days when the man about town drove a Jaguar or Bentley!

Hazel wasn't represented by a lawyer. Nothing unusual about that; officers are expected to carry out their own prosecutions at the lower courts — the magistrates' courts in other words. In the main, the only time legal representation would be given is where the case was complex or perhaps multiple defendants, or where there is a public interest which might attract media exposure of the case. Lawyers love a bit of public attention, particularly where it might lead to more and better work for them. And so the uneven wheels of justice started rolling.

Paul commenced relating the activities of Perkins at Edgware Road station which drew him to the attention of the officer. It followed similar circumstances to many other dips arrested before, particularly when operating on their

own. He was no different. In summary, he drifted in and out
of the crowds on the platform, made up quite obviously by
a large proportion of foreign tourists having left large hotels
like the Metropol on the corner of the A5 Edgware Road,
and were excited to start their exploration of the capital's
attractions. In the ordinary course of events, his actions could
be described as those of an innocent disoriented passenger. As
Gandalf said in his letter to Frodo, 'not all those who wander
are lost' as was the case with this thief, who was familiar with
his surroundings. He moved among the crowds allowing two
or three trains to pass, making no effort to board and was
unnaturally close to the backs of a number of young females
carrying shoulder bags with open tops, just begging for the
unwarranted attentions of one Parnell Perkins. Knowing the
antics of another 'black dip' who's real form was that of a
'bustler' intent on indecent assault, Paul stressed how Perkins
preparatory steps to commit his offence were markedly
different. On a couple of occasions he'd pulled at the top of
their bags in the hope of finding his quarry in the form of a
purse, without success, so there could be no mistake in Paul's
mind that he was watching a dip at work.

Finally Perkins struck; the young lady engaged in animated
conversation in a foreign language, *sounding perhaps Spanish,*
thought Paul, boarded through the double doors in the centre
of the carriage, blissfully unaware of the suspect's right hand
digging deep inside the bag. Paul could wait no longer, he
grabbed Perkins round the trunk in a bear hug, announcing
he was a police officer not only to Perkins but also to the
surrounding crowd, hoping that perhaps the young lady who
had been the subject of the thief's attention might turn round

to see what was happening. In the immediate melee which ensued, Paul managed to handcuff Perkins, much to his obvious anger — which he expressed in the form of a tirade of abuse and the somewhat predictable claim that he was the victim of racial selection by the 'pigs'. Regrettably, not only did the female not realise how Paul had come to her rescue, but also the carriage doors had slammed together shut and its passengers were now being whisked in their unfettered journey towards Baker Street, the next station.

The commotion had by now attracted the attention of a London transport employee. Once he'd satisfied himself of Paul's credentials he summoned further police assistance from the nearby platform telephone. In the meantime, between bouts of Perkins doubting Paul's parentage, he was cautioned as to why he'd been arrested. Hazel went on to detail how they were taken to Paddington Green Police Station, where Perkins was charged without interview — this to Paul's mind, was a pointless exercise. He was kept in custody until his cameo role today, and with that, Paul declared he had concluded his evidence.

"Officer, I represent Mr. Parnell at this hearing", said the familiar face stood in front him, the brief that Bob Trebor had been 'seeing to' for the past couple years.

Dirty lucky bastard thought Paul as he prepared for the onslaught. It was no surprise to him she was representing Perkins as she had been he duty solicitor on duty at court that morning.

"Officer, I see during the course of your evidence you have been referring to your pocket book. Are the very recent events not clear in your memory?"

"They are your Worship" , answering her questioning through the Stipendary magistrate who sat on his own on the bench monitoring the proceedings.

At the lower courts there are two kinds of magistrates benches. One is made up of what a known colloquially as 'lay' magistrates, invariably local members of society who have been selected, having applied to be Justices of the Peace. They are then qualified to sit, not alone — usually at least two, although more often than not in threes — with one being elected as chairman of the bench. They have all powers of a Magistrate vested in them by the Lord Chancellors office, to hear case and decide on someone's fate whether that be innocence, guilt, or if they feel they have insufficient powers to impose the appropriate sentence, they can commit them to the higher court — that is Crown Court — for sentence. To ensure accuracy when hearing a case and any decisions they make, they are assisted by a clerk of the court seated just in front of them. This person will be a legally qualified person either approved by the Law Society, or a qualified barrister of some years experience. The Stipendary magistrate is someone who, as the name suggests is a paid member of the judiciary, appointed by the Lord Chancellors office, usually of seven years experience as a barrister before taking up the post. Officers who regularly attend a particular court can often strike up quite a rapport with the resident magistrate simply through frequency of visits, with many being able to read their mindset without actually saying a word. So it was with the elderly gent sat on the bench, dressed immaculately in the traditional pin-striped suit and sporting the bud of a red rose in his lapel, something of a signature adornment. It seemed Paul had appeared before him on countless occasions, and always found him fair-minded, attentive of the evidence, and sometimes a merry quip from him which invariably lifted the heavy air of proceedings.

"With the courts approval, can you pass it across to me?" He looked to the magistrate for a nod of approval, which he gave, and passed it across, but with a stare of 'don't go on a fishing expedition'.

The court usher wandered across to the 'oak-effect' witness box, and without the court being aware, winked at the officer, intimating 'here we go again mate' before taking the Incident Report Book. Paul didn't know him, but seemed to have the demeanour of a retired police officer who he assumed *needed to top up his meagre Police pension,* to give him a reasonable standard of living. She took it from the usher with a gracious air of '*thank you my man*'. Paul knew, as did the magistrate that some time would pass before she'd launch her tirade of questions, following her pseudo examination of its contents. Paul's only concern was that the biro ink globules interspersed among the 'original notes' had dried sufficiently to avoid any suspicion.

'Thank you officer," passing it back to a waiting Paul. "Now Officer, you are an experienced officer of some year's standing, and my understanding unless I'm mistaken, is that you have been a member of what some would call the infamous Central London Pickpocket Squad for some time. You are no stranger to the rudiments of how a pickpocket goes about his nefarious activity. Fair?"

Paul confirmed what she had said, wondering where the line of questioning might take them. "My instructions are that you know my client. That is why you've concocted this 'fairy tale' account of how he's had the misfortune to incur your wrath. You saw him, knew him, knew that he had previously been convicted of similar offences of dishonesty, and this was a text book example straight out of the Dip Squad manual of guidance. However, he's turned his life around, and on the day you arrested him was on his way to a job interview,"

The magistrate confirmed now the 'cat was out of the bag' that Perkins previous convictions were available for the court, as defence went on the attack to allege a fit-up by the prosecution. Paul denied such a monstrous suggestion, feigning as best he could his indignation that such a suggestion could be made. The brief's challenges came thick and fast, taking issue with each of Paul's replies, ultimately with him admitting that he did know Perkins but he was not arrested simply because it was 'his time'.

"And you you have known my client for some time, spoken with him before, what was your impression of him when arrested?"

"I'm sorry your worship, *pause for effect*, I don't do impressions.", said Paul, deliberately misunderstanding her point but reducing the court room to fits of barely concealed giggles. She sat down deflated, the magistrate looked across and with a knowing smile, knowing the only opinion any police officer could give, is whether or not someone is drunk. He released him from the witness box. This was followed by the brief rising to her feet again driven by the magistrate glaring at her as if to say, *well what happens next then?* Paul found his way to the rear of the court, musing at *'the briefs beautiful* arse' and again thinking what a lucky bastard the guv'nor was.

"Sir, my client will not be giving evidence in this case", she declared, confirming to the magistrate that probably she had very little to go on other than alleged corruption by the officer, which in her mind, being a 'season ticket holder', so to speak, in matters of this kind, he'd rebuffed her challenges.

It did mean however, that Perkins previous convictions, many of which were now in the mix, were related to the court. To no surprise to anyone in the court he declared the case proved. A review of his previous indicated this man is a habitual thief and robber deserving of a harsher sentence than six months, the maximum he was able to impose under current legislation of the time.

"You'll be committed in custody to Crown Court for sentence. Can the probation services arrange pre-sentence reports please?" said the Magistrate, directing his request to the man seated adjacent to Paul, who nodded in anticipation of such a request.

Perkins shouted, "This is a-fit up, just like all the others. He knows me, he told me it was my lucky day, no more lifes for me. You want to look at them judge they're all bent on that squad."

The brief went to the dock to try to calm things with her client but he persisted in remonstrating his innocence as two burly dock officers having heard enough of his *'crap'* led him away to the cells.

Paul in the meantime approached her and not wishing to miss a chance said, "Coffee". She expressed a sardonic smile and declined.

Outside in the near empty vestibule of the court, a large black woman leapt to her feet, marching purposefully in Hazels direction. *She looks like the old girl out of the Tom and Jerry cartoons* he thought as she voiced her opinion of him.

"You's a liar, you's a liar. My boy is no teef" , she said barely a couple of feet from his face, her garlic breath driving him back. "I'm his mother, him a good boy, not a teef. You's a liar, you fit him up, init."

Paul grasping he was now confronted by the mother of the errant Perkins, said, "Look at his form lady, are all these people liars as well?", as he shook the form 609 Previous Convictions sheets under her nose. Leaning forward out of earshot, of a couple of casual onlookers he said, "Now fuck off and find someone who cares what your saying. He's a looser, a robber and a thief, and not a very good one, and the sooner you realise it the better the world will be. Now fuck right off."

*

The time marched on, with autumn threatening it was going to give way to winter chills over the next few weeks as the clocks went back ensuring in those serotonin levels of summer sun would be severely curtailed. Boles sat at desk pondering why this job as deputy chief had got so political. His father who had likewise been a senior officer in another force told him *'son take the exams, sergeants and inspectors, after that it's all political, but the further up the tree you go, the more you get paid, and the less you have to do for it!'*. It didn't feel like it at the present time. It struck him he had amateurs working for him, and they weren't junior officers either. *Must have been promoted to get rid of them, and way beyond their capabilities.* The only one he had any time for was Maurice Branch. He seemed a seasoned CID guv'nor who could do the job, and not somebody he would want to cross. Boles knew his own capabilities all too well. He shone on writing or telling others how to do the job, but never, ever getting his own hands dirty, which was why he sat in silence wondering how to deal with the running sore he was presiding over.

Ten minutes and a phone call prompted Boles to first summon the attendance of Branch over his office intercom, content that he had resolved how he was going to absolve himself from any responsibility for the Dip Squad enquiry and screw everyone else, apart from Branch of course!

"Afternoon Maurice, come in, sit down. Coffee?"

It wasn't unusual for Branch to be summoned by Boles to have a 'chat' about various aspects of policing or, as he was head of the department, the strategy for dealing with a particular problem. But his radar was immediately on the alert as Boles was not given to offering coffee as a precursor.

"Maurice, *(immediate suspicion at the familiarity)* thanks for coming round to see me so quickly. The reason I wanted to speak to you is over this fucking Dip Squad question.".
He sounded like a Goebbels dealing with an eradication, or irritant to a final solution.

"I haven't spoken to Spooner or Secrett personally — *(that's a lie,* he thought*)* — but you know, I've heard through the jungle drums we've got nothing if not very little evidence — of wrong doing against any of the squad other than Detective Sergeant Hunt, and even that is looking weak now that our young lady from the list office at Knightsbridge Crown has done a bunk to the other side of the world. There's not a chance such expenditure on a trip to find her would be sanctioned even if we had found her location. Add to that we we have Detective Inspector Walker engaged in some kind of 'good Samaritan' enterprise of accepting property from a known thief who was on bail, believing he's doing the losers a favour by lodging it in the Lost Property office. Worse still, he's in possession of a Section One firearm, together with ammunition, found in his top drawer, without any explanation, other than it seems the thief — or Dip call him what you will — says he took it from an old boy who had it as a souvenir after the fucking war! These finds as you know, are courtesy of CIB2 at the yard. To compound matters, apparently forensics have found the gun has been used in a couple of armed robberies in south London! So now we have two parallel enquiries conducted by two separate professional standards offices. We add two known pickpockets, who it would appear volunteer knowledge that not only was the Russell Square arrest by Dennison a contrived incident, a means to 'fit-up' the squad, but also that the officer himself has been engaged in corrupt activity in the past, as well as taking money from the thieves, a point it seems which is well known. And last of all I have a belligerent team of officers, lead by that young upstart Trebor, who are not only bucking the system with their 'no comment' interviews, but their sense of injustice is so great they have engaged a firm of West End lawyers to sue the force for unlawful arrest, false imprisonment, and malicious investigation, and that's just for starters I suspect. Now, somehow I've got to progress this's to a satisfactory conclusion, with the least amount of damage to your department, the force, and beyond."

Branch, slowly drinking his coffee, sat quietly pondering Boles 'dilemma', which was quite apparent, he obviously wanted to dump in his lap. Maurice glanced across at Boles seated behind his big self important desk, thinking what he'd said to a junior officer before, *'No matter how high up the slippery pole you climb, there's always a wanker boss!'*

Boles frustrated at Branch's silence at the complexity of the challenge said, "Right, here's what I'm going to do; Clearly I can't ask either investigative team to take over the whole enquiry as it might be construed as a cover up, particularly by the lawyers representing the Dip Squad. So I'm going to ask the Inspectorate at the Home Office, to appoint an outside force to come in and investigate the whole shooting match. Therefore the responsibility is taken away from all concerned. The only immediate difficulty I can see is their questioning of you as to your decision to pursue the course you did, coupled together with alleged dishonesty of officers under your command. Obviously I was only able to react to what was presented to me. What do you think Maurice?"

Are you having a fucking laugh?, thought Branch as he polished off the remainder of his coffee. *I'm being hung out to dry by this clown, I'm not having it,* he thought.

"I think that's probably the best course for you sir. I'm sure when it comes it, I shall have a plausible and accurate account of events, as you will.", which Boles found unnerving to hear, but was in no position to take issue with at this time, but it sounded as if his head of CID wasn't going to support his boss in any ensuing shit storm. In conclusion Boles emphasised how important what they had discussed should go no further, the other officers, Spooner, Secrett, Dennison and Walker not told of his decision at this time, to avoid any scuppering of evidence; in other words things magically disappearing before investigators have a chance to seize them. And with that Branch assured Boles of his confidentiality and left the office.

*

Paul's arrival at the office prompted the usual ritual of abuse saved for those who hadn't been in the office all day, doubting Hazel had been working but out on a 'jolly'. He ran through how he thought he'd only be at Marylebone mags for a quick remand which turned into a monster of a not guilty fight with the guv'nor's 'trout' representing the dip.

John Conroy, in a broad Irish lilt, said, "You've interrupted my story on the home front. You know I've got that dopey wolf of a German shepherd, he's fucking useless as a guard dog. Once it gets to about seven in the evenings he figures he's done enough guarding for the day and so he goes upstairs and falls asleep on the landing. Lazy arse! If anyone knocks at the door though, he springs into action barking and rushes to get down the stairs. Only problem is, because he's half asleep he falls from the top of the stairs to the bottom and arrives in a heap whimpering. Useless fucker. I had to take him to the vets the other day, he wouldn't stop whinging, he was off his food and didn't want to do anything. Then when we got back he disappeared behind the shed at the bottom the garden, and all I could hear was him whining. After about ten minutes it stopped and he came back wagging his tail and full of beans. When I looked behind the shed I saw he'd had a crap. Sitting on the top of the turd was one of the kids dinky toys! Idiot must have been in agony. And I got a vets bill for fuck all".

Paul, Dave and Pete fell about laughing, just as Brian Kent came back in the office.

"Right who had this last," holding a VHS tape in his hand. It was common knowledge among the squad that one of the Divisional CID officers had seized a load of porno tapes from a pervert they'd nicked for 'flashing' aka indecent exposure. The officer in the case made it know to the boys on the squad, if they carefully removed the loose seal on the top of the property bag when they were next in the property store, then they could have a look at the material on the tape overnight only, purely for educational purposes of course!

Brian had acquired it from the store and thinking it might spice up the love life for his missus he had an overnight 'rental'. Imagine his surprise!

"I was just settling down with a bottle of wine, hoola hoops, peanuts, and a frisky wife when after about five minutes of nature study it turned into an episode of fucking 'Pot black'. They weren't the balls the missus was expecting! Who did it?"

Conroy wasn't about to put his hands up, although he knew he'd been the last. The others just laughed at the thought of 'Sargy' suffering erectile disfunction as a result of the missus going off the boil.

The guv'nor entered the office a declared it was beer o'clock round at the Allsop Arms, and it was a duty commitment as he had some important information to impart.

15

MORALE BOOST

Hi there. You find us quaffing copious glasses of the amber nectar in the form of Budweiser on draught. I've just briefed them that our Commander Ed Brown is paying us a visit at ten tomorrow morning, after all that they've been through — their operational successes and, of course, the shit-storm of a raid, our unlawful arrests and false imprisonment. He is simply visiting one of his nicks for which he is altogether responsible for, and hoping to give them some visible support that they've not been forgotten. I've dared any of them to be later than nine in the morning so they can tidy up anything which might compromise our otherwise impeccable reputation! It's a good move on his part, despite the groans when I first told them, it'll give them a boost and it reaffirms my opinion of him that he is a decent guv'nor. I'll let you in on a secret —no, not that, little shit — I've still been having my 'fireside' chats with the Commander. He's been giving me inside track information on what those corrupt bastards at headquarters have been up to. You see, Boles has to attend regular monthly meetings with representatives of the Police committee. These are the people who have ultimate accountability to the government of the day for the effective running of the Force, it's the same with all forces throughout the country. My boss Ed Brown shows me copies of the minutes of their meetings, which give a flavour of what they're thinking. As a commander he gets a copy of them. It appears they're are very concerned at the slowness of the investigation and the lack of anything really concrete against the squad. Better still, they've given Boles an ultimatum that he he either sorts it double quick or his job is in jeopardy! I do hope that hurt, the incompetent twat! I couldn't conceal a wry smile when I read it, but I didn't want the boss thinking I would go off the deep end with the knowledge of such gems. Just nice to know.

*

Bob was in the office 'early doors' after a surprise phone call from the brief just before he headed to the pub last night. It seems she's not given him up completely, because after the drink he met up with her and they adjourned for a lovely Italian meal at the Spaghetti House in Goodge Street, before a late night chat back at her place, where she divulged that things weren't going well with the barrister 'beau' who apparently had some curious peccadilloes, including dressing in her underwear, a rather small penis which he couldn't get up because of his booze intake! It meant that she and Bob spent the night together in a more conventional performance before his dawn commute from Waterloo to the nick as she was appearing just down the road, at Horseferry Road court that morning. He skipped up the stairs to the third floor, where his first call of duty was to the fish, rising to the surface for their breakfast, as the radio blasted out UB40 claiming the red, red wine had gone to their head.

Bob looked into the squad office, heartened on seeing that the 'troops' had all made it in early to have a tidy up.

"Here guv, did you here about Farmer last night? I must tell you before he comes back from the bogs," said an excited Fish, hardly containing himself.

"You know 'Jackie-broken-nose' often sorts out a lot our statements for court?"

Bob irritatingly confirmed the fact, particularly as it was he who had set up the deal with the guv'nor McVicar in the first place.

Just to clue you in; she's a 'P A' to McVicar the boss of the nick, but he's said we can use her if we get overwhelmed with typing which needs doing urgently. She's a woman in her early fifties who still has a stunning figure, but sadly her facial features didn't match the rest of her form when viewed from behind. It looked as if she'd been hit firmly in the face with a shovel! None of us are portraits, but someone said she abuses the privilege!

Fish went on, "Just after you left, she rocked up in the Allsop, she'd been working late catching up on our backlog of statements, bless her. Anyway, she had to speak to Farmer about a couple of files he'd put into her that didn't make a lot of sense to her mind. Anyway, suddenly after a couple of drinks the pair them went missing. We didn't notice it at first but eventually we all left to go back to the nick and kip on the fifth floor in the canteen."

*

The squad carried on drinking towards closing time, their behaviour coming more and more boisterous. Angie

Scott the new attachment to the team, fell into deep conversation with Fish as he stepped behind the bar to sell drinks to the remainder of the pubs customers, relieving the landlady — who had retired upstairs to watch a late night film leaving Al to lock up at final bell — of her duties. She was curious about the guv'nor's domestic situation, which grated with Al as he thought he might stand a chance with a nice bit of posh. Angie clearly came from a privileged background prior to joining the 'job', obviously public school-educated, making him curious as to why she'd joined the force. Her pragmatic explanation was to be a police officer for no more than five years, while she continued to study for a law degree. Then, armed with her LLb she'd move on to do her 'bar' exams to ultimately become a barrister. He did his best to create the impression he and the guv'nor were good friends, telling her about his nice house in the countryside, having a bit of land, fruit trees and bushes and so on. He boasted that among them he had four blackcurrant bushes. She told him her daddy had blackcurrant bushes as well. The difference was, he had acres of them — he supplied Ribena! With that Al knew he was beaten. She knocked back the last of her gin and tonic, declaring she was on her way home. Deflated, Fish told her he'd enjoyed their chat and hoped she'd have a good time with the squad.

The team staggered back to the nick, resolving they were each too late to get home and so would rely on the easy chairs in the canteen on the top floor. As they wandered across the station yard they were obliged to pass in between the uniform Police Carrier, a long wheelbase 'transit' and the observation van, an old smaller van with no windows on the sides, used for covert operations.

"Hang on a minute, look the 'obs' van is rocking, must be someone inside. Who is it?, said Dave Champion.

They resolved to check to make sure it wasn't being nicked from the yard. They gathered round the rear doors, and on a quiet count of three they flung them open.

"What the fuck," said Paul as they each were, unusually, lost for words.

"Hello boys," said a drunken Pete Farmer with a silly grin on his face as he laid back on the long bench seat while an equally drunk Jackie broken nose was kneeling in front of him with his member of the force in her mouth. She waived to the audience, carrying on in her quest to finish Pete off.

*

You must think us awful people, but hey it takes two to tango, you know. Stop the victim-hood, it doesn't cut any ice. If you insist, then I'm a victim too. I remember a night at a 'job' disco when I have to confess I got a little bit squiffy, and one of my detectives gave me a blow job! I know, it sounds bizarre but I'll tell you what happened. We had a temp typist come and work for us, and she seemed to warm to my appearance at her office door when she was audio typing, in fact she'd come to my office too, touting for work from me. I took her for a drink on a couple of occasions and she divulged how she really wasn't getting on with her boyfriend at the time. All unsolicited I do assure you. Anyway, come the night of the disco I went outside and found a set of stairs to sit and recover in the cold night air. She followed me out, I guess, not wanting to lose sight of her target. Within moments I came round to see she was kneeling between my legs, giving my old chap a morale boosting talking to! I didn't like to interrupt so I just laid back and thought of England or something. At the end, so to speak, I told her I was off home to my failing marriage. She told me she fancied a boogie and would stay for bit longer. I thought no more about until one of the lads told me they'd seen her dancing very enthusiastically with a Detective from Divisional CID, finishing their dalliance with some serious deep throat kissing. When I saw him I dropped heavy hints that he'd stolen my woman, much to the amusement of others, then the bombshell that he'd in theory given me a B J by proxy!! Well it was wasn't it?

*

"Fish, very good, but you're fined for grassing up a squad member! You know the rules. Right, John, well done, I see you've tidied up your desk from war zone to just chaos. What's the tap doing still screwed to the wall next to your desk with the Guinness label over it?"

Conroy apologised for not removing it before Ed Brown arrived — lack of a screwdriver was the reason. After the night Bob had just enjoyed, he gave up trying with the team this morning. Things will have to do as they are, with Farmer still missing from the office, presumably trying to sober up in the basement shower before making his appearance.

Ed Brown arrived at the nick, his driver going round the offices letting as many know as he could, that the boss was with McVicar taking tea. Farmer's head was no better when he came out of the basement shower as to when he went in. He didn't feel up to glad handing the boss, although he realised it was good of him to come and give them all a boost in morale. Considerable time had passed since the day of the raid, and none them were any nearer to knowing their fate, but the team were as one in their support of Bob who had been the prime mover in getting allegations of corruption going back the other way, with the hope the investigators would become the investigated.

Trebor left his 'pets' gorging themselves on their twice daily dose of Tetra min fish food as Commander Ed Brown entered his office, leaving a greatly relieved McVicar, that the squad hadn't emptied all the fire extinguishers in their latest overnighter at the nick. Bob had primed the boys to look busy when he and the boss entered, and they responded to his demand acting as if model schoolchildren, all except Farmer who was still missing post *coitus interruptus*. Ed Brown moved from desk to desk chatting with boys individually coming finally to John Conroy next to the wall.

Farmer had the 'devil' inside him. He'd managed to acquire couple of feet of hosepipe and jammed a funnel into one end. What hadn't been realised by anyone was how thin the stud wall next to Conroy was. Pete could hear the boss chatting to John in the next office along, which was the sign for him to push the other end of the hosepipe into a hole in the wall. He then commenced pouring a half empty can of Guinness down the funnel. Within seconds Conroy's tap sprung into life, emptying a dark brown liquid over his case papers transforming his desk into a sea of brown sludge. No amount of 'oh fuck' from Conroy seemed to make any difference as he reached across to stem the flow. Too late;

that part of the office stunk like a brewery. The Commander realising a stunt had been pulled turned away so he could claim he didn't see anything, walking back out of the office, giving them a 'well done officers, I see you're keeping your spirits up'. Bob, cursing to himself the situation, led the boss back to McVicars office. On his return, Farmer had appeared and was seated at his desk, seemingly unaware of what had just occurred, and in true Dip Squad tradition he denied all knowledge, albeit he found it as amusing as the rest of the office, all barring Conroy who was 'vocally negative' over the need to get about a dozen statements re-typed.

Trebor entered the squad office to a subdued squad intent on portraying a conscientious team intent on getting their paperwork completed. It didn't fool Bob.

"Right you fuckers, I just wanted to say thank you for keeping the credibility of the team at an all time high. Now Farmer you're fined two rounds this evening for the unfortunate episode of the leaky tap, Conroy has to dispel the myth in the future that he's not a piss head when he commits his 'customers' to Crown when next at court. The boss was very happy with what he saw, albeit he ignored the your efforts Farmer. He asked me to say thank you to each of you for continuing to suppress the scourge of the Undeground network. Well done. Right for the rest of the day, office work, and send Angie out for the Lambrusco and nibbles from Threshers. As soon as the boss has gone Mr. McVicar will be joining us for an office meeting."

With that Bob left the chaps to sort themselves out, while he returned his office to kill off some no-hope crime reports.

I had a quiet word with Ed Brown. He hasn't heard anything about our 'difficulties' from the big house, so I thought I'd mention we were about to sue the job, seeing as they continue to treat us like shit, seemed to like the sound of that. He was able to tell me that apparently the star witness against Hunt has disappeared from her job at Knightsbridge list office, so that strand of their enquiry isn't looking too strong. Without her, the only witness statements against Heath are that of Hunt and Basil's, which he signed before his untimely death. Therefore as it stands Heath might take a fall, pardon the pun, and Hunt, if he did it, will get the biggest 'Get out of jail free' card. We as a team have had a couple of conferences with our brief, so all being well, in a week or so the civil action should be under way. Let's hope it has the desired effect. To allege that we're corrupt is one thing, and nothing unusual in villains putting in that 'banker' if their trial needs it, but to learn that it's being levelled at us by bent officers who it seems are far more corrupt than we could ever be, is to say the least, a bit rich! We're noble, they're just fucking bent, trying to hide there own corruption by doing us. Bastards. Right I'm joining the chaps before they get too boisterous and Fish has the chance to tuck into Angie. Well someone's got to stop him!.

*

The day of Harrison's first of two trials arrived. Fish was a little wary of what might occur, given the supposed taped threats he allegedly issued. He mulled over that he'd done everything he could according to the guv'nor's game plan so now it was alligators and denial. This trial was the one he'd had with Dave Champion, so he felt less isolated in the house of correction. The curse of Southwark Crown Court, Mr.Mario Bergamot hovered outside court 6 like a preying mantis waiting for its next victim. Al wandered along the corridor outside seeing his enthusiastic combatant, together with a scowling Harrison, but concerned he'd yet to see someone on his side.

"Mr. Fish I see you come along to give your opinion on this little challenge my client has. I trust neither you or Mr. Champion haven't been put to any inconvenience have you?" , he said sarcastically.

Time for fight back, "Oh no sir, it's the merest of pleasures to be here to share with you and of course the court, the veritable cornucopia of criminality against your client. As far as opinions go, I'd just say they're like arseholes — everybody has one, just some are full of crap!"

Bergamot, enjoying the banter roared laughing at the riposte, unlike Harrison who simply sucked through his teeth making a sound like a budgerigar

*

Bob checked his watch for the third time as he waited for Detective Sergeant Kent to appear in his office, to drive him in the new Ford Sierra CID car to Euston Station, where he was to board the train to Glasgow. He was due to meet the Procurator Fiscal, in essence the same as the Director of Public Prosecutions, the following morning, before jumping on the train back down south. The purpose of the summons by the Fiscal was because the team of Scottish villains on the forged American Express job, had got nervous last minute and wanted to exchange the 'parcel' nearer to their home ground in Glasgow.

A hesitant knock on the guv'nor's door some forty-five minutes later than expected announced the arrival of Kent. "Where have you been Dave, you know I've got this train to catch?"

"Yes I'm sorry guv, bit of a problem. You remember yesterday when you said I could take the Sierra home following the 'spin' me and Billy Spencer were doing? Well we didn't finish until very late, so we set off for our homes. Billy was driving so I dropped off asleep on the way. All of a sudden the car speeded up and then went down a hill as I woke up. Bill had gone agricultural and had dozed off as well. We were now in a middle of a field next to the dual carriageway. Local plod turned up, and sorted us out. They called out a truck which pulled us back out on the road. Luckily no damage was caused, so I put the car through the car wash this morning on my way in. Hence the reason I'm late, sorry guv.", said an apologetic sergeant.

Bob feigned annoyance, but smiled to himself as he boarded the train to Glasgow having been deposited by Kent.

*

Southwark Crown Court saw the arrival a young barrister Stephen Smythe tracking down Al Fish and Dave Champion in the restaurant overlooking HMS Belfast, indulging in a more upmarket cup of coffee and to their mind more expensive but no better than the Police room ten pence cup!

He'd had the chance to chat with Harrison's representative, Mario Bergamot, who'd indicated his client would be pleading not guilty to the count on the indictment. With that he disappeared again to the list office in the hope of getting the trial on quickly, and the detectives deciding the reason was because they'd managed to secure the alleged victims details. Harrison obviously was in the mood for a not guilty fight even where the risk of his previous convictions might mean a certain period of imprisonment. What seemed more of a surprise was there appeared no mention so far of Al's supposedly covert recording of fortune telling, albeit the boys could hardly broach the subject, which might reveal Fish's concern the threats were going to be revealed to some sort of fan-fair.

Well here I am, wending my way to Glasgow on the American Express job, first class of course. I managed to blag the upgrade on the basis that I've got sensitive material I have to read and write about prior to my arrival. Bloody Billy Spencer, honestly. At least there's no damage, and local plod haven't recorded it officially, so as Shakespeare has it, all's well that ends well.

So to bring you up to date on the 'sweaty socks'(jocks)… The meet between my man posing as a 'buyer' of the parcel of forged traveller's cheques went really well at the 'Old Bill' pub after he'd been introduced by Dave Driscoll. They were very happy to deal with him, and gave him another couple of samples which they suggested he try and cash somewhere in London. He didn't, of course, but when he had the next meet to confirm the final purchase price, he told them all went well.

Then a bit of a surprise occurred. The villains told him they wanted him to go with them to Glasgow to meet the printers, but he feigned illness and didn't travel. I needed to know where they were going as this might be the trip when they brought the consignment back to London to arrange the exchange for their cash. So I put a team of surveillance officers on the train north with them. I then had all sorts of aggravation trying to convince officers of the Regional Crime Squad in Glasgow that I needed their assistance with what I assured them was a good job. It seems their only concern was who was going to pay their overtime, and how, if the ambush was to occur in London, how they'd get any kudos out of it. I had to confirm in writing by fax that my office would fund any costs and they'd get recognition following the arrests and convictions. It wasn't until they had that undertaking would they give my guys assistance to continue the surveillance. To cut a long story short, the villains went to various addresses which appeared to be various relatives, and also an industrial unit on the outskirts of the city.

Two days later, the four targets boarded a southbound train to London. My surveillance team followed them. The problem was at this stage we were no nearer to knowing if they had the parcel or part of it with them in the holdalls they were carrying. I arranged a 'pseudo' security scare, not officially declared, but it meant uniformed officers could check the passengers and contents of their bags leaving the train on its arrival at Euston. Bit risky I know but it worked. Two things; first we were able to confirm their true identities without them suspecting any police attention to their true activities and second, a search of their holdalls revealed they had returned to London with nothing more than a change of clothing and dirty washing!

The following day my man got in touch with them and arranged another meet to see how their trip to Scotland had gone. It was obvious the security scare search had rattled them as they no longer wanted to do the exchange in London but Glasgow instead! So that put pay to my ambush which was going to occur in a mews just off Baker Street.

As I said at the outset, you now see me travelling to Glasgow to link up with my RCS colleagues north of the border to sort out a game plan. More importantly, because I have what is called a participant officer in the middle of the crime, I have to go and see the Procurator Fiscal for Scotland, firstly to confirm my strategy but secondly to enable my officers to operate as police officers in Scotland, otherwise the whole operation would be deemed unlawful. Now you know I'd never do anything unlawful, particularly in bandit country!

*

"The Fiscal will see you now sir," said an officious-looking clerk as he observed Bob checking his watch again, knowing he had a couple of hours to catch his train back south.

"Good morning, Detective Inspector Trebor, take a seat. Now I've looked at the report you kindly prepared for me, which is most helpful, but I always think with these types of cases it's so much better to have that face-to-face chat with the officer in the case, which is you. It helps to ensure there are no misunderstandings as to our respective responsibilities. I've ordered coffee, I assume you like some?"

Bob sensed a friendship otherwise missing from his earlier experiences with his Scottish counterparts. To further expand on his report, he outlined how Driscoll came to speak with him, and how the subsequent police 'buyer' was embedded to execute the transaction to purchase the parcel of forged American Express traveller's cheques from the suspects who appeared to number some four, to be arrested. He then went on to explain how the original ambush was to be in West London, but following a trip by the suspects to Glasgow they inexplicably got 'cold feet' on their return and wanted any transaction to occur on what they regarded as home turf. He suggested that perhaps the reason was that the printer who was obviously based in Glasgow, wanted to be near his share out after the exchange had taken place. No honour amongst thieves, Bob dared to suggest. Whist no final date had yet been arranged, Bob wanted to have the whole case reviewed so that he had the 'green light' from the Fiscal for his officers to operate in Scotland, which would require them being sworn in at court, and for there to be no difficulty in having his man conducting the purchase.

"That all seems fine Mr. Trebor. Now just one thing, when the suspects are arrested at the point of exchange, what will happen to your purchaser — in other words, your man on the inside?", seeming to Bobs mind a little pedantic.

"Well sir, he can run faster than the rest of us, so he'll evade capture as far as the suspects are concerned."

He dropped his half glasses down his nose, stared at Bob and said, "Oh no. We're not having any of your 'Sassenach' ways up here."

Bob quickly replied, "I understand sir. How about if we arrest him as well. Then when they've all been placed in cells, we tell our man through the wicket gate that he is wanted for a murder in another part of the country, but within earshot of the others arrested. Then we simply spirit him away?"

This satisfied any misgivings the Procurator Fiscal had, and in celebration he invited Bob for a Sherry before leaving to catch his train south once more.

16

ALLIGATORS!

Harrison's day started at eleven after the judge, Recorder Vickers QC, a female judge recently elevated to exalted ranks of being in charge, had 'weighed' off a couple of bail applications and two for sentencing. From what Al saw, she seemed pretty tough on the various defence counsel, giving him hope she might be a bit pro-police when the accusations started. He'd learnt that apparently she didn't even have to do the job, coming from an extraordinarily wealthy family. It was more like a hobby for her as she was married to an Old Bailey judge, and together they were loaded. But then he'd heard the salary wasn't that good anyway; any brief, particularly defence could earn fortunes more that way. So it seemed only judges who could afford to be judges bothered with the higher accolade.

The jury were sworn in, in readiness for the 'not guilty' fight. As usual the case was opened and the first witness was the ever-grateful Indian lady, the alleged victim in the second arrest of Harrison. Her evidence went unchallenged, save Mario Bergamot confirming she knew nothing of the commotion behind her until an officer identified himself and took her details. She wasn't able to help with the identification of the person arrested — as far as she was concerned she'd not seen him do anything. Her evidence was short-lived and Madam Recorder thanked her for her willingness to attend court and give evidence, as she commented how important it was that members of the public come forward and assist the Police in the investigation of crime. Al, as the officer in the case, wondered if the learned judge had been a bit too heavy with her praise as he left the court room with the Indian lady whose interest was placed more on what expenses she might receive for her attendance. Bergamot seemed not to take issue with the comments, as Fish took her to the fees office for her to make her claim, knowing she was only entitled to a fixed amount whereas he suspected she thought she was on to some kind of klondike. He thanked her for assistance as a rather deflated witness left the building.

"I swear by almighty god to tell the truth, the whole truth and nothing but the truth, Detective Constable Champion, Central London Pickpocket Squad based at Baker Street Police Station." He placed the card with the oath on it, and the bible held in his right hand, on the shelf underneath the witness box lectern. On invite from the Prosecution barrister he commenced giving his evidence 'in chief', Smythe, knowing the officer had a wealth of court room experience, preferred to let the officer give his evidence without interruption or qualification. Once finished, Mario Bergamot rose to his feet to commence his forensic cross-examination of the officers. However, he was stopped in his tracks by the Recorder who declared a ten-minute comfort break before what would obviously be a roasting of the officer commenced.

'Normal service' resumed with Dave rising to his feet. In answer to Mario's question about Dave's experience he confirmed he'd been in the force some ten years, the last couple being in CID attached to the Dip Squad, and yes, he knew D/C Fish well, they had been involved together in many arrests and trials in the past.

"I put it to you officer, you were mistaken in what you saw. The charming lady we have just heard from was simply a convenient foil, to give the allegation of attempt theft greater credence. She was no more a victim of crime than my client had been, of committing it?"

"No your Honour, conscious to direct his answers through the judge avoiding might turn into a slanging match between the two of them. "What you suggest is '*void ab initio*' ", said Dave trying to sound intelligent with his newly learnt Latin.

It cut no ice with Mario, who was at great pains to explain to the bemused jury what Dave's expression meant in the hope that using the quote might backfire.

"Very impressive, officer. Now we all know that you reject my suggestion by telling the court that I'm wrong from the start. It is of course very encouraging to learn that our police officers are expanding their knowledge base. Do you know any other Latin?"

Madam Recorder sensing his cross-examination would descend into ridicule, stared at Mario as if to say '*don't push it*'.

"Yes sir, probably more pertinent to the evidence I've just given, '*post hoc ergo propter hoc*'. Which, as you doubtless know, means because one event happened after another, it happened because of it. It summarises your clients actions in the lead up to his attempt theft and then his subsequent arrest because of it."

Some jury members smirked at the barrister being played at his own game. Bergamot could no longer resist. He'd indicated to the judge during the earlier comfort break before the jury were summoned from their room, that he would be alleging the officer was lying and accepted that Harrison's previous convictions would be exposed for the jury to consider when finally making their decision.

"Officer I put it to you that you are not so much mistaken, as lying in your evidence. You have indulged in supporting your colleague's attitude towards Mr. Harrison. You know they are not the best of friends, if I can use such a term. It's fair to say neither will be on each other's Christmas card list. In short Detective Constable Fish has hatched a vendetta on my client, and you have chosen to sing from the same hymn sheet of perjury as him. What do you say to that?"

Champion was a little surprised that there was no intervention from the learned Judge, so he went back the attack to level up the score.

"Sir in all my years as a police officer wanting to serve my public and the victims of crime, I have never been subject to such vitriolic abuse by someone who I believed to be an honourable counsel for their client, but your suggestions are a bridge too far. My evidence told of Harrison 'shaping' up behind that poor Indian lady struggling to board the train unfettered, while he desperately tried to relieve her of her personal possessions. One suspects the prize would've been her purse or wallet, had we not intervened and arrested him. I am certain in what I saw; your client is a thief, and this is another instance of his 'trade'."

Mario sensed he wasn't going get any further with his cross-examination save to say, "Well Officer, that appears to be where we will have to disagree. You may not like the tone of my cross-examination, but I'm sure you appreciate I act on my clients instructions."

This final postscript together with Stephen Smythe making the point with the officer that he'd taken the oath to tell the truth and had indeed done so. This appeared to reduce the jury's apparent indignation at Bergamots' tirade. He needed to keep them on side at least. Madam Recorder thanked the officer and released him from court.

"I do solemnly, sincerely and truly declare and affirm that the evidence I shall give shall be the truth the whole truth and nothing but the truth. Detective Constable Alan Fish , Central London Pickpocket Squad at Baker Street Police Station."

Al had the devil in him, the ten pound bet with Champion was too much to resist and so he became an atheist for the trial of Harrison. That said, who could forecast what his next oath would be, perhaps smashing a plate on the floor? Not often seen, admittedly, but known in some oaths.

Once more Stephen Smythe stood, preferring Al to give his evidence without interruption. He was, however, aware of an attack to be later launched by Mario, but the gentleman's agreement between the barristers meant they alone had the knowledge of what was to come.

"Well all good things must come an end Officer." , as Mario rose to his feet to commence cross examination. "How long have you known D/C Champion?

Fish told him he thinks it's in the order of a couple of years they had been on the squad together.

"So I assume you've been involved in these kind of arrests and trials similar to that being faced by my client today. Would that be true officer?"

"Yes, your honour.", directing his response through Madam Recorder.

"Now officer, I suggest there is a bond between you and Champion, as with other members of the squad. A sort of musketeer code, where you back each other up, say, by witnessing events to assist your colleagues despite not seeing a thing. This succeeds in simply over-egging the pudding, but the result is that whenever a defendant appears at court, the dice so to speak, are loaded against him. It's always two against one, despite the fact that one of you might not see any criminal behaviour whatsoever. Am I making myself clear officer?"

The judge, tiring of what seemed a closing statement as opposed to a question, brought Mario to heel, directing him to ask his question.

"Officer, I'm not going to waste any more of the courts time, you're a liar. You have colluded with Champion to create this fictitious charge on my client.

"No sir, that is not correct. That poor Indian woman struggling with her young child was trying to board the train when the defendant targeted her for the purposes of stealing from her. Fortunately we were there to stop him in his tracks, and prevent more misery for another member of the travelling public."

"D/C Fish, now, that isn't the reason is it? You're involved in another case with Mr. Harrison, where on that occasion you find yourself the only witness to his alleged crime of attempt theft. However, before that case could be committed to Crown Court, you threatened my client with arrest for any reason if you saw him again. Something about a crystal ball. And then fortune favoured you when in the company of Champion you see the defendant again. So you were able to execute your threat. Is it ringing any bells, officer?"

"No, your honour, I swore to tell the the truth at the beginning of my evidence and have done so. The events as I have described occurred in the manner which I described. I refute any imputation on my reputation. I have not lied at all. I may have been guilty of using shall we say 'industrial' language to your client when I saw him at Clerkenwell Magistrates court, but did not threaten him. His attitude to me was both abusive and offensive. I simply gave as good as I got."

Mario turned towards the rear of the court as his solicitors clerk entered with a micro cassette tape recorder on a small tray. He placed it on the lectern where Mario stood, to a quizzical silence from the judge and the jury. Al could feel the blood draining from his face as he tried to create an air of casual indifference to its arrival, rehearsing in his mind what the guv'nor had said, and how he was going was going to dig himself out of the problem should it be played.

"What would you say officer if I were to play the tape recorder you see before you, containing your threats delivered to my client?"

Madam Recorder intervened, calling for the jury to leave to their deliberating room as well as Fish to leave the court room, while she dealt with what could be a point of law. Mario made the point that the tape recording went to suggest his instructions that the second arrest only came about because Fish had threatened Harrison with further arrest if he came across him. Having enquired what happened to the first case committed from Clerkenwell Magistrate's Court court, it apparently been leap-frogged by this second case and was still outstanding. Accepting Mario's explanation and an assurance would be restricted to ask the officer to confirm what was on the recording, the proceedings resumed the jury being recalled.

Al re-entered the bear pit waiting for an interrogation over the contents of the tape recording, as Mario launched his next attack,

"Officer, you've doubtless observed this micro cassette tape recorder being brought in by those instructing me. I put it to you officer the contents of the tape will show you to be a liar. You threatened my client on many occasions as to what would happen if you were to come across him again. I have no doubt you remember that?"

Fish took a mouthful of water supplied by the court usher before responding. "Sir, I don't recall that at all. The evidence I have given in this case is the truth, the whole truth and nothing but the truth."

Mario stood looking at the cassette recorder but made

no move to start playing it. Instead he said, "I put it to you officer you said, words to the effect that you had a crystal ball and you threatened him with arrest every time you saw him."

Al thought *'Bingo, there's fuck all on the tape. If he had it he'd play it, now he's said words to the effect, I don't reckon he's got it'.* "No sir, I don't recall that at all."

Mario looked towards Madam Recorder, said, "Due to the lateness of the hour, may this be an appropriate time to adjourn, your Honour?"

She looked across to see the clock on the wall above the jury was just approaching four o'clock. "Yes that seems appropriate. Will you be back here tomorrow morning, officer, to complete your cross-examination?"

Before Al had a chance to respond, Stephen Smythe rose to his feet, "Your Honour, in the recess I had the opportunity to speak with those representing the crown. I understand this officer is in difficulties attending this hearing tomorrow due to a personal matter which he is unable to break."

She looked across at Al who was doing his best to put on a sorrowful face in confirmation of his barristers plea. "Is that correct officer? Is your commitment in the morning or afternoon?"

Al said, "It's all day, your Honour. My wife has to go to hospital and I have to look after my two young children for the day."

He knew it was crap, but he was still just about married albeit estranged, the children situation was a bit more of a stretch! Still, he felt he was up against it, and this was nothing to do with the case, if he was investigated he'd claim what he'd just said wasn't under oath therefore not perjury. At least he hoped so!

Madam didn't leave it there though. "What is the nature of your wife's medical appointment?"

Fish as quick as a flash said, "It's gynaecological, your Honour."

She didn't pursue any further leaving it to Mario to address her with a response. Smythe remained seated while Mario retreated to the rear of the court to take instructions from Harrison in the dock.

On returning to his position, the tape recorder still in front of him he said, "In light of the instructions I've just received, I have no further questions for this witness, your Honour."

Smythe leapt to his feet to confirm that was the case for the crown, and sought Al's release, which Madam Recorder duly obliged. Al walked with a renewed air of invincibility towards the rear of the court doors, where three of Harrison's pals were sat waiting for the aborted big reveal.

One of their number looked at Al as he passed and said to him, "Oh you're fucking good man," in a low tone so as not to be heard by the jury.

With that the case was adjourned to the following day, to learn if Harrison was going to give evidence, otherwise the case would go to closing speeches. Fish lived to fight another day!

*

"Oh for fucks sake!" said Secrett as he learnt from Branch that he, Spooner and Dennison were to be investigated independently by the Chief Constable of Surrey on the direction of Inspectorate of Constabularies, on allegations of conspiracy to pervert the course of justice, unlawful arrest, and false imprisonment, levelled by the lawyers acting for D/I Trebor and his squad. Branch told the three officers that they'd each have to be interviewed probably at the conclusion of their investigations into the squad, but at present it was looking like the members of the Dip Squad wouldn't face any formal discipline as their indiscretions appeared minimal. Added to which, the investigation of Detective Sergeant Hunt had faltered after the only chance of a possible witness to Basil's demise had now disappeared to the other side of the world, with no chance of finding her. Boles had instructed Branch to return the case papers to Trebor for him to continue the case to Crown Court, leaving the allegations by Heath to remain live until the conclusion of the trial. In addition the appointed Chief would also be looking at Detective Inspector Walker's activities, particularly the Section 1 firearm and live bullets found, and the 'lost' property recovered that linked back to Sutton. The concern for Boles was that this was the person who first alleged criminal activity of the Dip Squad which was acted upon, but on which there was no basis for the extreme measures even given the now-dubious complaint by McMurray.

*

Day two saw Dave Champion at court with Harrison, waiting to see whether he was brave enough to enter the witness box to give his side of the story. He sat alone in the dock, no 'support group' with him today, as Mario Bergamot sat reading 'The Times' just in front of him. Stephen Smythe sat in front of Dave, reading Archbolds Criminal Pleading, the barristers bible for all matters legal. A knock on the side door announced the arrival of Madam Recorder as she swept in to assume her position in the centre chair on the bench. Finally the jury filed in from their deliberation room, seating in eager anticipation of what the events of the day would unfold. Mario rose to announce his client would not be giving evidence, and so closing speeches could commence. Prosecution counsel was brief, recounting the facts of the case together with supplying the jury with copies of Harrison's previous convictions of dishonesty and violence running into two pages, totalling thirteen convictions. There was little Mario was able to say that would minimise his clients perilous position. Madam Recorder Vickers QC addressed the jury on the law, stressing their need to examine the the evidence, then sent them out to consider their verdict.

Champion told me they were only out for about ten minutes, returning to give a unanimous verdict of guilty. Harrison realised he'd been beaten by better story tellers, allegedly, reinforcing the adage one should never let the truth spoil a good story! His reward, without hesitation was to be given two years imprisonment. You may be wondering what happened to the first arrest involving Fish on his own. It came up at Inner London Crown Court about three weeks later. Harrison was produced from Brixton Prison as he was still awaiting allocation of a prison to serve the rest of his sentence. He opted to plead guilty to the one count on the indictment, in the hope he'd get no further length of imprisonment which is exactly what happened. He was given another twelve months imprisonment which was to run concurrent with that already imposed. It simply meant he'd cleared the 'sheet' and would just do the two years less remission of course!

17

LOS CHILEANOS

Well here I am at those hallowed halls of justice, the Central Criminal Court, known more often as the 'Old Bailey'. Built on the site of Newgate Prison, home to many bad debtors in the past. All of you with credit cards, beware — at the moment, just a genteel civil debt, but if the banking worm turns… well who knows? The entrance to this edifice is through the revolving doors in the more modern part of the building, in the street of the same name. In response to the provisional IRA parking a huge firework display in the form of a car bomb, entry has become conditional on routine searches of clothing together with x-ray of whatever bags you propose entering with. Interestingly the police officers just regard it as a new way of life keeping everyone safe, whereas the briefs and barristers on the other hand seem to regard it as an invasion of their privacy. Twats taking client privilege too bloody far. Anyway if you needed a constant reminder, look up to your right as you walk up the broad staircase to the the main circulating area. There's a piece of jagged glass dug deep into the plaster high up in the wall, testimony to the power and devastation of explosions, courtesy of those chicken shits from across the water. Hence the heavy net curtains on all outside windows —in an effort to curtail the effects of any future big bangs. As Gerry Adams is often quoted, 'We only have to be lucky once, you have to be lucky all the time!'.

Moving on, the court lists are on the board to the left at the top of the stairs. Excuse me while look to see where my team and I will be performing, for today is the first day of the Chilean trial, or Los Chileanos as we know it.

Bob Trebor made his way up another set of stairs to the Police room to confirm he was the officer in the case and see if his counsel had shown its face yet. They'd been allocated Court One, usually reserved for more serious events than theirs. '*Clearly not enough murders being committed*', Bob's jaundiced mind thought. So he could keep all the squad together he'd arranged for an adjacent room to be available, so they could relax before their individual roastings at the hands of the defence briefs, as well as somewhere to have their teas and coffees away from public gaze, and one of the chaps could keep the key so it could be locked for the duration of the trial. It meant they had somewhere to securely store exhibits not yet tendered to the court proceedings, and just as importantly, indulge in several games of Trivial Pursuit during periods of boredom!

The trial in front of theirs was running late so it meant the South American stars had been put back to not before twelve. This wasn't unusual, although the courts would do their best not to waste time, citing their mantra of costs to the public purse. Pretty much all the squad was going to be required to give evidence at some stage in this trial and slowly but surely they each appeared in the room Bob had acquired. Farmer and Champion arrived with all the prisoner property bags and dumped them unceremoniously on the table next to where Hazel was sat. Then came Fish and Conroy to complement the 'guest list'.

Hazel said, "Guess what, I've just bumped into Mario Bergamot on the stairs. Apparently he's defending in our trial. When he saw me, he greeted me like a long-lost friend. He asked how we all are, and then said, 'I still laugh to myself the last time we did battle. You're the only officer I've ever known to call himself a liar and then blame me for it!' Naturally I told him I had no idea what he was referring to. We laughed". Whereupon the assembled 'usual suspects' of the team, did so also.

Bob said, "If you remember rightly, Paul, it was our 'double act. How many trials have we done where I go in first, talking posh, as if I've got a public-school background, then you go in like the working-class man. The briefs fell for it every time; they'd say I must be mistaken, not wanting to reveal their shit of a clients previous convictions, then in cross examination you'd accuse the brief of him calling you a liar. Usually throws them into a panic as they'd try and rescue the fight, away from the great reveal. Fucked them every time."

The squad laughed with Bob at this, among many stunts they pulled to get a conviction, but reasoned it was no different to those pulled by defence briefs; after all they had a head start with the assumption of innocence. All the boys were doing was trying to even up the score.

Bob's commitment to the hearing was essentially to tie up all the loose ends around the connections between the various thieves whether through sequential numbers on the various denominations of cash, or travel tickets on ferries, foreign travel tickets or Underground tickets. In addition, he'd take care of the question of the forged passports or travel documents or I/D cards. This left the boys free to take care of the surveillance of the various overt acts of thieving, arrests, and interviews where they were pertinent to their crimes. He'd previously told them that any difficult questions about procedure or strategy of the entire operation should be responded to they either didn't know or they were decisions for Detective Inspector Trebor, leaving Bob to tidy up any conundrums. They just needed to focus on the crimes themselves, and not stray from that. As far as Dangerfield's evidence was concerned, they should make no comment on it save to express their appreciation of such a public spirited citizen.

Ian Playton knocked and entered through the half-opened door to the Squad's new office for the period of the trial. Bob knew he was going to be prosecution counsel for the event after the vaguely disinterested head of chambers pulled out claiming he had a very nasty GBH to prosecute at Maidstone Crown Court. Ian had managed to have a junior counsel granted in the form of Allegra Cummings. Fish's radar immediately went on 'red alert' as the attractive blond twenty something smiled at the assembled squad, each having a different take on her presence, but doubtless hoping they'd be able to impress. *They flatter themselves* Bob thought. *No chance*! The reason for the junior, Ian outlined, was because there were going to be seven barristers against them, one for each of the defendants. Bob went on to explain to his squad knowing Ian was already aware, that although ordinarily the citing of previous convictions from other countries was not allowed in English courts, despite the Chilean embassies' intransigence in assisting the police with enquiries on their fellow citizens, he'd generated an enquiry for foreign convictions of the same through Interpol. That was some months ago but still no response. So as it stood only three of them officially had previous convictions for theft in the UK which could be mentioned, at the conclusion if convicted. It was madness, and seemed to offend common sense, but there it was.

Just then the tannoy announced all parties in the case of Salazar and others attend Court One. Bob, Ian and Allegra entered the court room into what looked like a barristers' convention, as they huddled together, *doubtless plotting my downfall* thought Bob. The familiar knock on the bench door announced the arrival of the Common Serjeant of London, Lord Williamson. The title is accorded to the second most senior judge of the Old Bailey and an ancient British legal title dating back to 1291. The Chileans were prompted to stand by the two dock officers appointed to ensure no misbehaviour or escape on their account. The seven barristers sat in line on the front bench looking like a row of ducks at a shooting gallery, after the judge had sat down and cast a roving eye around his scene of operation. Ian Playton remained standing to the left end of the front row with Allegra seated in the second row behind, and Bob seated behind her.

"Good morning, my Lord. I appear for the prosecution in this case and my colleague Miss Cummings is my junior in this case, due to the multiplicity of defendants and that various counts they face. To assist my Lord, counsel sat on the bench to my right each represent one of the defendants. At present a number of proposals have been made to those representing that some of the evidence may be formally admitted such as that evidence pertaining to the forged or stolen passports, however, at present no such admissions have been forthcoming."

"Yes thank you Mr. Playton, I want to hear from each of the defence counsel."

In turn they stood to plead their case for representing their individual clients, not least because their clients faced different substantive offences, albeit they were all roped in on an all-embracing conspiracy to steal within the jurisdiction of the Central Criminal Court. Williamson asked, "Why should each of them be represented separately, particularly as there doesn't appear to be any conflict of interest where the events leading to arrest were on separate dates?"

Again the the seven leapt to their feet to justify their position, accepting what the judge had said, but claiming the conflict could rest with the items found on them which linked them to others in the group. His argument was simply the property found was fact and nothing more, and in view of their insistence on each representing their client who was on legal aid, as a saving on the public purse he would only agree to half their fees for the appearance. The deflated egos sat dumbstruck they wouldn't receive all their remuneration. Bob chuckled quietly to himself at the rebuff, having been told Lord Williamson had been a tough defence barrister and doubtless the scourge of many a detective in earlier years. In fact, he'd learnt that he'd been junior counsel in a couple of gangland murder trials back in the sixties, including the Krays and the Richardsons.

Ian Playton sought permission from the trial judge for Bob to remain in court for the duration of the trial as he was the officer in the case. Williamson had no hesitation in granting the request. The court clerk swung into action requesting the court ushers to produce some twenty prospective jurors who had been waiting in eager anticipation outside court, believing they'd probably have a juicy murder or similar as they were being called for duty in 'number one court'. Before proceedings could get under way, due to some of the defendants insisting they were unable to understand the English language, even less the course of the legal process, an interpreter took up her position adjacent to the stenographer just below where the judge sat high on the bench. Bob ensured his favourite for the job, Fiona the Spanish interpreter was available for the whole trial, and so she sat, speaking in a low voice into a microphone to the seven defendants who sat somewhat incongruously, with headphones on like apprentice disc jockeys. There were only a couple of objections to the presence of two of the prospective jurors, Bob assuming they looked too conservative for such a trial, and so the make-up was seven women and five men. With that, lunch time beckoned. Bob returned to the squads' room to bring them up to speed on events thus far.

*

"I have been appointed by Her Majesty's Inspectorate of Constabulary to investigate an allegation that you, together with three of your junior officers, Detective Chief Inspector Spooner, Detective Inspector Secrett and Detective Sergeant Dennison, conspired together to pervert the course of justice. Additionally there is an allegation that you allowed another officer, Detective Inspector Walker to handle stolen goods, namely a large quantity of wallets and purses reportedly stolen from passengers on the Underground, with a man named Trevor Jones, also known as Sutton, who you caused to be interviewed on two occasions in Pentonville Prison. In addition, he possessed a Section One firearm together with ammunition without a Firearms licence, found in his office drawer, received from Sutton, which, following forensic examination has shown to have been used in two armed robberies on south London building societies. You are not obliged to say anything unless you wish to do so, but what you say may be put into writing and given in evidence."

The Chief then waited for his staff officer to complete the opening diatribe in writing, before waiting for a response from Maurice Branch as they sat across the desk from each other in Bole's office, the scene for all four interviews. None was forthcoming. Then this set the course of the interview in that whatever he was questioned, no reply would be the stock answer.

The Chief went though the details of the meetings with Sutton, how he alleged corruption against the Central London Pickpocket Squad, and whether he felt what was being said was at all credible. He went on to quiz him about his mindset behind the raid that occurred following his sanction, given that no statement had been obtained from Sutton at that stage. Branch smiled arrogantly at the

Chief, minimising his exposure to continued questioning, knowing his entitlement to remain silent as with any suspect interviewed for a criminal offence. The interview went on through the arrest of McMurray and even with the allegation of corruption of the squad again, no statement was taken either by Spooner or Secrett prior to the same raid, suggesting a familiar pattern was emerging. Additionally he asked why McMurray hadn't been taken to the local police station as he'd been arrested by Detective Sergeant Dennison but had inexplicably been removed to headquarters for his allegation to be made. Again, silence from Branch.

"Mr. Branch, would it surprise you to learn that when I interviewed Sutton, he confined his allegation to that of theft against only one officer, D/C Conroy, and even then he wasn't sure that a theft had occurred. He mentioned this to Detective Inspector Walker who in turn spoke with either you or one of your number, so that became the basis of your tasking Secrett and Dennison to establish if there was any truth in what Sutton was saying. This was followed by Secrett acting like a loose cannon, probably together with Spooner, in re-interviewing Sutton and later telling him he'd no longer be prosecuted. Then by good fortune some might naively say, McMurray is arrested by chance by Dennison, enabling him then to make his allegations of 'fit up' and corruption by the squad. Do you want to comment on what I've just described? Is there anything you'd want to correct or clarify, because it seems to me that it was thought irrefutable the Dip Squad were corrupt and the basics of obtaining complainants statements could be an afterthought. The problem is, apart from the question in relation, Hunt, the only evidence one has of criminality is against Walker. But you and your team have tried to smear the Dip Squad with innuendos and imputations which are of a minimal nature. Correct me if I'm wrong?" asserted the Chief.

Branch remained steadfastly silent. He realised it didn't look good as a backdrop to the raid, but trying verify his reasons behind the extreme decision to raid wouldn't come from his lips, particularly as it looked as if that 'treacherous bastard' Boles was going to throw him and the other three to the wolves. Promotion in preference to 'esprit de corps' was the Boles way out of the difficulty. The Chief continued with how it was that Walker had a gun and ammunition used in a couple of robberies, without any authority whatsoever, and lastly the rather 'quaint' way in which property subject of a variety of dippings, via Sutton, was reintroduced into a lost property system which ultimately find themselves back to their rightful owner. Finally he made reference to the mess, which, had they acted earlier meant the suspected manslaughter by Hunt may have been resolved, commenting he'd never known such a shambolic way to run a department. Tiring of the 'no comment' interview and conscious his staff officer was tiring of being the 'scribe' of the contemporaneous notes, he brought the interview to a close, inviting Branch to sign the notes as a true record. Branch obliged.

The next interview commenced at two o'clock with Spooner, as the afternoon sun traced its presence on the plush carpet of Boles office. The four suspected conspirators had previously got together to try and operate a unified approach but as none trusted the others in the group, it seemed likely one of them would run for cover, trying to dump the others in their wake. At this point though Spooner maintained exactly the same attitude as Branch. The same questions were levelled at him surrounding the events leading to the raid, the interviews of Sutton, the McMurray arrest and subsequent allegation of corruption, but the Chiefs main focus was on his slowness at following up the interview of the Knightsbridge court list office assistant, which if he'd acted sooner might resolve the question of Hunts guilt one way or the other. He had no answer and consequently gave a 'no comment' response. The interview was terminated early much to the relief of his staff officer whose hand was beginning to ache from contemporaneous note taking, and as it was quite apparent this would be the strategy of all four. Undeterred the Chief had been tasked to do a job and do a job he would! He interviewed Secrett and Dennison the following day, gaining the same response as the first two. His annoyance at their intransigence and were to his mind, clearly colluding to hide the truth on the various matters. He told each of them they'd be report to the Director of Public Prosecutions for being involved in acts tending to pervert the course of justice. That said none of the four were suspended from duty, particularly as the decision might take some time, and he was in no mind to give them 'gardening leave' for an extended period.

*

Ian Playton lead each of the officers through their evidence-in-chief before the respective defence counsels were let loose in cross examination. What became immediately apparent to Bob was they had obviously agreed a strategy in an effort to destabilise the professional manner in which the squad gave their evidence. So barrister one would go through the evidence in detail, then barrister two would have no questions, likewise three, then barrister four would jump to his feet to ask most important questions regarding his client, but would then pick up pieces of the jigsaw pertaining to defendants two and three. When they were unable to find a chink in the Dip Squad armour, they'd then get nasty alleging the officers were lying, something they could do with impunity, or so they believed, as their clients had little or no form in the UK. The barrister whack-a-mole roulette went on with each of the officers, deftly avoiding any difficult questions by claiming they weren't the officer in the case but Detective Inspector Trebor would have the answers.

Paul Hazel having given his evidence, stood waiting for his roasting under light in the canopy over the witness box, something peculiar to only that court room. And so it fell to Mario Bergamot to test the veracity of Paul's evidence.

"I must firstly congratulate you officer on the manner in which you gave your evidence in relation to my client. I was particularly impressed and indeed the court must have been, with your efforts to communicate with him in his native tongue. Remind me, what was it you said to him?"

Paul said, "It was at one of the earlier remands at Bow Street Magistrates Court Sir. He looked a little confused and so I tried to confirm with him why he would be in custody awaiting his trial here today. I simply said, *ladron* to which he immediately hung his head and said *si.* "

"Thank you Officer, very impressive, can you tell the court again what was meant by that?", Mario looking across at the jury with a raised eyebrows.

Paul responded saying, "I told him he was at court for being a thief. He agreed saying yes."

"It seems you have a good grasp of the Spanish language. What other Spanish do you know?"

Paul quizzically said, "*Dos cervezas, por favor?*" and was greeted by muffled laughter from a number of the jury members, at which point Mario announced he had no further questions for the officer, and so he was formally released by the Common Serjeant.

Next to give evidence was John Conroy. He had been involved in arrests with the squad, had secured the evidence of Mr. Dangerfield the member of public witnessing events, who with his sense of civic duty, had made statements regarding the Chileans' nefarious activities. In addition John had arrested the final two thieves on his own, for which Bob had commended John's singular actions. They had been linked to the other five through the continued cross pollination of sequentially numbered bank notes and travel tickets, so were connected into the conspiracies to steal, but the actual count of attempted theft from a person unknown stood alone on the indictment with only John's evidence to be challenged by the defence barristers.

Having given his evidence in chief, Ian Playton requested John remain there under the light of the witness box, for defence to challenge the veracity of what he'd just said.

"Officer, I appear for Mr. Caro. I've just had a note passed from him, the content of which suggests he's never

seen you before in his life. How do you account for that?",
said the diminutive figure more suited to a position with
Snow White.

"I can't account for his lack of memory, sir, The evidence
I've given is the evidence pertaining to your client. I'm not
sure how I can help you further.", explained a non committal
John.

"Let's try another way then, officer. Would it be fair to
say, you are a person of corpulent frame?"

A confounded John who'd not heard of the word before
said, "Do you mean I'm fat? I suppose that's true yes. But I
don't know why you want to insult me, when all I've tried to
do is tell the truth about your client."

"I'm simply trying to ensure the correct identification of
you. That being the case I suggest the evidence you've given
is a tissue of lies. Brothers Grimm would be proud of such
a narrative."

Realising he was out of his depth, not being well read
simply said, "No sir. What I have said is the truth."

Mario rose to his feet, "Officer, just so a distinction is
drawn, I'm not suggesting the same. I say your involvement
with my client was a simple case of mistaken identification."

John, gaining in confidence that perhaps the whole
world wasn't against him firmly stuck to the script,
something which had been well rehearsed, not only at the
time of writing their 'arrest notes' but also visiting the scene
prior to giving evidence. So John was released from the box.

*Good man. Defence can't break into us. The trial has been
dragging on for a couple of weeks now but I think the jury are
right with us. I've been in the courtroom each day sorting out*

whatever exhibits prosecution — or more often than not, the defence want to have a look at. I've given my evidence which went well, stuffed the defence. I gave it all from memory, which meant they couldn't ask to look at my pocket book. They were more preoccupied with that, than anything to do with them suggesting they'd been fitted up. The very idea! Deep joy! There was only one problem which would've screwed me. I could see where the line of questioning was going with barrister three. He set me up with a series of questions about times the defendants were in and out of the cells. My answer would have dropped me in the shit if I'd been wrong, it would suggest I'd been lying, and you know I don't do that. So I needed to get back to the nick to check the custody records so when it came to barrister five who was going to ask me the killer question, I'd have an answer which I knew was correct even if they asked for all the records to be seen at court. Luckily Lord Williamson declared it was time for lunch. On return at two, I advised my barrister I had a migraine, which I'm sure you'd accept I had! The court were told, the judge expressed a sympathetic ear, confirming he too suffered with them. Bingo! He adjourned the hearing to the following morning and wished me well. Problem solved. My examination of the various prisoner records enabled me to return the following day and knock them out the park, end of allegation of perjury!

Oh yes meant to tell you, the prison officers who bring them to court each day told me that one of the defendants kept on insisting to have his clothes back ready for the trial and another one wanted his shoes. So before they obliged with the request they searched the clothing a bit more thoroughly. They found in the pair of shoes one had a hollowed out heel and neatly folded away was five one hundred US dollar bills. And it just goes to show what extent they'll go to — in the zip fly of one of the pair trousers, another hundred dollar bill sewn in. Now that's what I call professional thieves. Secreting some of their stolen money in case they need it inside or to bribe bent coppers, well I'm happy to say, not us! We love just nicking them.

Next up, Mr. Dangerfield.

"Mr. Trebor, we've got our star witness next, Mr. Dangerfield, I assume he's here is he? I guess he's the chap outside, is he?"

"Yes, Mr. Playton, the guy looking like he's just stepped out of a Saville Row window. In answer to your next question, yes, he's read through his evidence. He's very keen to do the right thing. He should come over well to the jury."

"Can you do a PNC check on him? Obviously we want him whiter than white don't we."

Bob assured Ian he'd get it done right away before the trial kicked off again at ten thirty, with Bob finishing off his cross-examination. Dave Champion immediately started dialling the enquiry from their police room, while Bob answered the call to the witness box.

Replacing the receiver, Dave said, "Holy shit, this is a problem. He's got form John", John was immediately galvanised to attention by this revelation, fearing perhaps he should've done a check for previous convictions at the time he took his statements.

Looking at the sheet of rough notes John said, "What are they for? We're going to have tell the guv'nor when he comes out. Fuck me. Four of them, no wonder he saw what he saw on the Underground."

The door opened with Bob entering to see two of his squad looking very sheepish, the paper with the details now firmly pressed back into Dave's hand. He gave him the news about their pillar of society, that apparently he'd been nicked and fined four times after pleading guilty, for 'bustling' on the London Underground. In layman's terms this meant he'd indecently assaulted females, probably by pushing up closely behind them, probably during the time they were boarding the train. Bob demanded someone make him a coffee while he deliberated in his mind how this little bombshell could be delivered with the least damage to a prosecution which to his mind, was going well, despite three days in the witness box mopping up all the questions the boys were unable to answer.

"Right, no problem. I can't see any offences of dishonesty there. I'll have him in. You lads go out, needs to be just me. Fetch him in will you John?", said Bob.

Dangerfield entered the room with a buoyant air, ready to give his evidence. He initially denied his 'form'. Bob insisted it must be right unless there were two people with the same details. Eventually he relented telling Bob he hadn't done anything like that for years. It was a moment of weakness when he was going through a difficult time with his ex-wife, which ended in divorce. He figured the best way was to simply put his hands up, so to speak, and take the fines.

"Right here's the way we'll do this. I'll have to speak with our prosecution counsel and I'll tell him you have no previous convictions for dishonesty or violence, Okay? So when you get in the witness box, I expect our barrister will ask if you have any previous convictions for dishonesty, to which you can answer none. With any luck the defence won't push any further, okay?", said Bob.

Dangerfield went to great lengths to apologise to Bob, who brushed the 'little local difficulty' away like an irritating fly. Ian Playton entered, asking if all was ready to go with Mr. Dangerfield as he'd be on next once the court was sitting. Dangerfield left the two of them in consultation. Bob was able to confirm he had no previous for dishonesty or violence, which Ian was happy to accept. So the gentleman doing his civic duty came up to proof in his evidence in chief. None of the defence barristers dared to challenge his version of events except to suggest he was perhaps mistaken in what he had seen, and perhaps their respective defendants actions were simply borne out of innocent tourist confusion and nothing more. He fought back in assertive tones, declaring he wasn't for a moment mistaken in what he'd seen. They were professional thieves. That closed the prosecutions case.

18

WELL, WELL, WELL

We seem to be getting somewhere now. I've had the case papers back on Heath, you'll remember I'm sure, the dip who had breached his bail conditions by being on the underground system at Knightsbridge. When Detective Sergeant Hunt, (rhymes with …) and Basil Chakrabati tried to nick him for that and also trying to dip Basil on the escalators, he became violent, lashed out and Basil took a fall to the bottom and he escaped. At least that's what Hunt's evidence is. Basil was hospitalised but to mine and everyone else's astonishment, he contracted a thing called sepsis. I'd never heard of it, but basically there was no way back for the poor bastard, and he died.

Hunt is still suspended, pending the outcome of the trial which kicks off today at Knightsbridge Crown Court. Obviously he can't be officer in the case so I've told my other Detective Sergeant, Brian Kent to cover the case for me. I know Complaints Investigation Bureau will send someone to sit at the back of the court and keep a watching brief so let's see what happens. They take no part in the proceedings, just sit there looking menacing, and that happens in any trial where the defendant has made a complaint, prior to the date of the trial, usually of perjury. Wankers! Brian will give me the heads up on how it's going.

Hunt will still have to attend to give evidence but we'll wait and see what dramas unfold.

"Good morning sir, I'm Detective Sergeant Kent, I'm the officer in the case. I'm in place of Detective Sergeant Hunt, who is suspended from duty on allegations arising out of this arrest and is also being investigated together with his fellow officers on other unconnected matters."

The prosecution barrister Mr. Donald Thwaites, was well aware of the challenges there may be in relation to the trial when he held the case conference with Bob in the previous week. They made their way to court six down in the basement of the building, where defence counsel, Mr David Farmington, was waiting to negotiate with his opposite number.

"Guilty plea?", asked Donald to Farmington whose focus had been to the flimsy evidence against his client.

"I've spoken with Mr. Heath, and he's firmly of the opinion he's not guilty of attempt murder or manslaughter of the officer, and from what I've seen of the evidence I would have to agree with that. I think the breach of bail conditions doesn't really take us very far as his explanation will be he was just passing through the station, to avoid negotiating the street above. So really, he has a reasonable explanation for that. I think if he were to plead guilty to the attempt theft and if he accepts he may have inadvertently pushed the officer, say a section 47 assault occasioning actual bodily harm, accepting the officer may have slipped and fallen down the escalator, or at most a section 20 assault: grievous bodily harm no intent to cause same, both of which have the same maximum imprisonment of five years. We may have a short day. I would of course have to speak with Mr. Heath on whatever you decide on."

Thwaites looked to Detective Sergeant Kent for his thoughts. Given that it seemed like quite a downgrade from what they'd started out with he told him he'd have to seek guidance from a senior officer before making any form of agreement to the plea proposal. A phone call from the police room to Bob was Brian's first mission.

"Hello guv, Brian here. I think we're being given a bit of a gift from Heath. I reckon he thinks if Jim sticks to his script he runs the chance of getting potted for at least a manslaughter. I mean, I never rated it as murder or an attempt, not from a strictly legal basis, but what do think of a deal of an assault and the attempt theft? What do you reckon?"

Bob leant back in his captains chair in his office, searching the aquarium and the fish for inspiration. He asked if Brian was on his own, and that nobody was listening to their conversation, which he was happy to confirm. Bob thought about the ramifications of Errol's offer of a plea as it might certainly get Hunt out of a hole, but having said that, he'd read through the evidence such as it was, including Penny from the court list office which didn't take the case any nearer to either supporting or refuting Hunts account and the late Basil's statement, which was more akin to a dying declaration. Of course he didn't know that Hunt in his desperation, had forged his signature, following his ejection from his bedside by the nursing staff. So only Hunt knew of the stunt he pulled. The post mortem statement confined itself to confirming that Basil died from sepsis, noting he only displayed superficial flesh injuries, none of which were life-threatening or contributing to his death. When looking at the photocopies of the statements, Bob, who's mindset was more on ensuring the apparent integrity of the squad, searched for a 'get out of jail free' card which would satisfy the prosecution barrister, the judge, and probably more importantly to avoid a witch hunt by those tasked with fitting up, as he saw it — a member of his team. Whatever was decided, it needed to look like both prosecution and defence counsel had come to the agreement, without any pressure from the police, thereby ensuring any subsequent review would focus on their decision. Bob felt this would mean they'd be home and dry. Hunt would still be wrapped up in the general allegations of corruption against the squad but at least he wouldn't be nicked for Basil's demise. Bobs surmise was that Hunt would have to live with himself for his idiotic and terminal actions that day, doubting he would've ever wanted or foreseen this outcome. *He'll have to live with his own subjective test on Basil's fatality* he thought to himself, as he took stock of his considered opinion and related it to Detective Sergeant Kent. He finished the call accepting that a plea to attempt theft and an assault occasioning actual bodily harm might be the best that could be hoped for, impressing on Brian the constant need to save the public purse — in other words, tax payers money — the alternative of a 'not guilty' trial lasting days if not weeks, being the justification for taking the plea.

Right, I'll leave Brian with that. He told me that Hunt had turned up to give his evidence. I instructed him not to appear to get too close to him, remembering that the idiot from complaints would be watching for tricks. He did say though that the defence barrister usually prosecutes so he didn't think he would have much time for Errol Heath, just going through the motions of doing his best for his client.

My Commander has just called wanting me to pop across to his office to speak with him. See you later.

Bob knocked on the outer door to his guv'nor's office, and as anticipated he secretary stood waiting like a terracotta warrior, guarding her leader, saying "Hello Bob, Mr Brown is expecting you."

She knocked on Ed Browns door, announcing Bobs presence, and was guided in. The usual invitation for a 'drink' was gratefully accepted by Bob as the guv'nor poured two 'gentlemen's measures' of Scotch, hiding the bottle back behind the *Stones Justices' Manuals* on the top shelf of his book cabinet.

"I'm not sure if you were aware, but I took issue with Mr. Boles over the course of action they took and the subsequent raid. Read this. Bear in mind there's still more to come, I'll fill you in afterwards."

Bob took hold of the guv'nor's papers vowing to himself to read them calmly, the generous slug of whisky hoping to help. Within the body Boles declared that 'it's essential when complaint is made that it is investigated in the interests of the subject of the complaint as it is to protect the rights of the complainant'. *That's rich,* thought Bob. It went on to say Boles was challenged on the motive for the extreme raid when Sutton only made an allegation of theft against Dc Conroy and nobody else, albeit he made a scattergun allegation that all the squad are corrupt and on the take, without citing anything in detail. The decision to raid the entire squad was taken following the first specific allegation made by McMurray, following the arrest by Detective Sergeant Dennison, and not to advise any senior officers on L Division was to ensure confidentiality of the operation and not out of mistrust of senior management. Furthermore, no inference of malpractice in the manner in which Superintendent Lyle or his junior officers carried out their visit, having satisfied themselves it was clearly necessary to act swiftly. This was also why no statement of complaint had been taken from McMurray prior to their raid. Ed Brown challenged the validity of Detective Inspector Walker continuing to remain unsuspended given he'd quite clearly committed criminal offences relative to the firearm and ammunition found in his personal property. Boles response was to suggest that as the members of the Dip Squad hadn't been suspended he saw no reason to deviate from the practice of keeping officers at work, albeit in a restrictive capacity, rather than allowing them to languish on gardening leave at home. The redness in Bobs face was discernible to the guv'nor, not borne out of any refill of the scotch; simply this was some kind of jealous reprisal against him. There was a constant reminder of envy by those not working on L Division at the semi autonomous financial independence the Division enjoyed, and as a result funding to police the underground network was not challenged to the extent as that elsewhere in the force. Reading between the lines of what Bob had just read the was considerable effort by Boles and his cohorts to even up the score, made easier by Dennison's efforts to over egg the pudding with the 'pseudo' arrest of McMurray and then a complete deviation from practice by taking him to headquarters to make his allegations instead of going to a local nick to be processed, and to pressurise Ed Brown into subservience. *The whole thing stinks,* Bob thought to himself as he gave the report back to Ed Brown.

"What you might like to know also Bob, of course I haven't told you, but Mr. Branch together with Spooner, Secrett and Dennison have been investigated and interviewed by an outside Chief Constable directed by Her Majesties Inspectorate of Constabularies. I've seen papers that suggest all four are guilty of at least malfeasance of public office and or corruption. In fact the expression he used was to say 'its difficult to distinguish whether this whole investigation was complete incompetence by those involved, or corruption'. I appreciate you and your team have a few irons in the fire so to speak, but what I have just told you remains between you and me for the moment until someone else makes public. Okay?"

Bob appreciated what the boss was saying as he thanked him for his continued support, behind the scenes as he took the last swig of scotch and left his office.

So there we have it. Sutton alleges he's lost a fiver when he's nicked by Conroy but then didn't want to pursue it at the time. Then he whinges to that idiot Walker who obviously spoke with Branch. Dennison, by virtue of his dubious experience in nicking dips in the past teams up with Secrett to investigate what Sutton has said while on remand in prison. But Dennison has a problem: the possible discovery of his own corruption. Luckily for Dennison, Secrett can't bring himself to believe Dennison has ever been on the take from dips and so the convenient arrest of McMurray occurs. His more recent allegation of Dip Squad corruption justifies the raid and the subsequent investigation. No statement is taken from McMurray until after the raid, a basic mistake also made by Lyle who trusted Branch and his merry heroes. Then those investigators try to repair their mistake by finding enough of a smear on the squad to justify their actions. Meantime Walker gets turned over on the suspicion of his connection with Sutton and not only do they uncover the lost property scam but more importantly the unlawful possession of the gun and ammunition. What a monumental fuck up!

*

ADVICE

1. I have been asked to advise a number of individuals about the various claims they have arising from allegations made against them in the course of carrying out their duties as Police Officers.

2. A generally issued writ was issued seeking damages for false imprisonment and misfeasance in a public office. It was served but no Statement of Claim has yet been served.

3. I am conscious that very little has been achieved in the terms of moving these claims forward. I have discussed the position with Instructing Solicitors and we have agreed that I should advise on merits and quantum and draft a Statement of Claim which can then be refined and improved in conference.

4. First I propose to advise on the several matters of general law. I shall then turn to the specific incident and advise on the merits of the claims and the quantum of damages that the clients might recover.

5. This is a very straightforward case which has become bogged down in pursuing red herrings. Whilst I have every sympathy for the clients experience in confronting totally groundless allegations of misconduct, I do not believe it's helpful to incur immense costs because we have lost grip on what the case is about and what can be achieved in pursuing litigation.

6. The clients must appreciate at the outset the limited nature of the legal claims they can bring. Their complaint is of course that they were subject to detention, and emotional distress as a result of investigations into groundless complaints made by criminals with many previous convictions.

7. The clients are not entitled to any damages from the Police simply because they were subjected to discipline proceedings. I take the view that the clients could sue for breach of contract, defamation and/or misfeasance in a public office.

8. There is a term implied into every contract of employment that an employer is obliged not to undermine the trust and confidence his employees have in him as employer.

Consequently, it has been said in the decided cases that an employer cannot without reasonable and probable cause to conduct themselves in a manner calculated to destroy or damage the relationship of trust and confidence between employer and employee.

9. It will be a breach of that implied term if an employer falsely and without reasonable cause accuses an employee of theft, or undermines a supervisor by upbraiding him in front of his subordinates, or failing to treat a longstanding employee with dignity and consideration.

10. A claim for wrongful arrest or false imprisonment only relates to the detention the clients were subjected to when disciplinary proceedings were first launched. In order for such a claim to arise, the clients must show that they were prevented from exercising their liberty. The proper defendant for such proceedings is that of Branch.

11. However, the following defences are available to the claim for false imprisonment made by the clients;

    A. That the officers consented to the detention and they were not in fact detained against their will.

    B. That there were reasonable grounds for detaining them ; and

    C. They were given grounds for their arrest as required by law.

> Whenever the police arrest or detain someone there is a burden on them to justify their actions.

12. In my opinion the principal defence that will be raised in this case is that the clients consented to the detention. This might explain the police's inability to identify the nature of the clients claims from correspondence with instructing solicitors. The prospective defendants would have to prove that in all circumstances the clients consented to detention, which course they didn't.

13. Finally, an arrest will be unlawful if the person arrested is not given the grounds for his arrest. Now a statutory obligation under section 28 Police and Criminal Evidence Act, previously the case of Christie v Lechinsky (1947). In the incident it appears some of the officers may have been told they were being investigated on allegations of corruption against the pickpocket squad but the issue for determination is whether the clients were given sufficient information to constitute being provided with the proper grounds for their arrest.

14. The police are obliged to do more than simply assert the bare grounds for arrest. In Christie v Lechinsky, it is clear that one of the reasons why an an arrested person is entitled to be informed of the grounds for his arrest is order that he may be able to give more than

a bare and unconvincing denial if he is in fact innocent. To tell a man that he is arrested for murder without any details of who he is said to have murdered and when and where, puts the citizen in a very difficult position that all he can say is 'No I did not'. That is not likely to be convincing to anybody. On the other hand, the more detail he is given the better the opportunity to give a convincing answer and therefore, the better his chances of being speedily released from arrest.

15. In my view, the information given by those investigating, was so general and vague in nature that it did not provide the clients with sufficient to attempt to rebut the accusation. In any event, it would seem the allegation by Sutton was strictly speaking only against Conroy, so that it is difficult to see how a generalised allegation of corruption can satisfy the requirement to provide all the clients with proper grounds for their arrest.

16. I take the view that the only realistic causes for action for the clients are that of arrest, false imprisonment and breach of contract. I believe the most important question to be tried is whether the clients were in fact imprisoned. I take the view that evidence provided by the clients themselves mean that there are good prospects of proving that they did not consent to their detention.

17. Finally I would advise that the clients have good prospects of showing that the investigating officers failed to provide them with proper grounds for their detention. The real issue is whether they were ever arrested in the first place and the clients have good prospects of succeeding on that issue. They also have an arguable case in breaches of contract, and misfeasance of public office.

STATEMENT OF CLAIM

1. At about 8am Detective Inspector Trebor, the first plaintiff arrived at Baker Street Police Station and went to the corridor where the Pickpocket Squad worked, when he was approached by Detective Superintendent Branch and acting Detective Chief Inspector Secrett and was told they had been asked by deputy Chief Constable Boles to investigate allegations of corruption in the pickpocket squad and that was all he could say at the moment.

2. The first plaintiff was taken against his will to his own office. He was prevented from touching anything in the office or in or on his desk, prevented from using the telephone or receiving telephone calls. He could only go to the toilet when escorted and he was prevented from speaking to anyone other that Branch and Secrett. He was then interviewed by the

said officers, and cautioned he need not say anything as with any criminal investigation. He refused to answer any further questions until a senior officer from his own L Division was present. He was prevented from leaving his office while waiting until someone appointed by Commander Browns office would attend.

3. He remained in his office believing he'd be taken to a central police station for processing. He was detained against his will until he was released at midday, without being taken from the office.

4. By reason of the matters aforesaid the first plaintiff was unlawfully detained and has sustained loss, damage, inconvenience, distress, loss to reputation and deprivation of his liberty.

5. Further, by reason of the matters aforesaid, the first plaintiff is entitled to exemplary damages.

6. Further, by reason of the matters aforesaid, the first plaintiff is entitled to aggravated damages.

7. By reason of the breach of contract as aforesaid the first plaintiff has sustained loss, damage and expense.

So now you know broadly that we are suing the job and my statement of claim, which I've tried to consolidate for easier reading. It will be served on Boles and his merry band in the next couple of days.

I was arrested by Branch and his cohorts the day after the squad members had been nicked. It wasn't until after I'd been released I was able to find out what had happened to them.

They gave a similar story to my experience. Each officer was nicked, not told the details but given a short interview in isolation, none of these were voluntary. Paul Hazel tried to get his Police Federation representative to be present but was prevented from doing so. Dave Champion was due at court that morning, and because the officers refused to remove the female officer who was part of their team, he had to change in front of her. She joked that she'd seen a mans cock before and not to worry. Various members tried to illicit if they were under arrest but were not given an answer. They just kept repeating they were investigating an allegation of corruption against the pickpocket squad but refused to say more. I'm told we're entitled to interest on our claim pursuant of section 35A of the Supreme Court Act 1981, and at such a rate as the Court thinks fit. In summary we are each claiming damages and interest.

So now it's war!!

One funny thing the boys told me was that at the end of their raid, Branch told them to carry on with their duties. John Conroy tried to create an impression of indifference, by sitting at his desk and reading the Sun newspaper. Branch said, "Right carry on with your duties." John without looking said, "I am." With that they left. Good man, fuck 'em. Right, back to the Old Bailey to see how we're doing.

19

JURY'S OUT

Ian Playton assured the attentive jury that this was a straightforward case where they had heard from various members of the Central London Pickpocket Squad give evidence about entirely separate incidents where they say they witnessed the various defendants in the act of stealing from members of the public using the Underground system.

"You will recall members of the jury, how this whole case started. One of the officers had utilised the police intelligence gathering network to establish that the number of thefts from the person, or 'dippings' as you've heard it referred to by some defence counsel, had been reported on transport infrastructure namely Heathrow and Gatwick airports. The modus operandi by those arrested was to infiltrate into dense crowds milling around the termini, then by subterfuge create any one of a number of distractions, diversions or block a passenger's intended path whereby the thief would strike before making good their escape with some or all of the target victim's property. As you heard Detective Inspector Trebor explain, none of the arrests of both Chileans and Colombians appear to have any connection to the seven defendants before you, save to say the methodology is strikingly similar."

"Following those arrests, the officers you have heard from organised covert surveillance on the Underground network following reports of similar incidents coming to their notice. It seemed some of the officers were very quickly rewarded for their hunch when they saw the first three defendants attempting to steal from members of the public. Their suspicions and subsequent arrests were reinforced when a member of the public, Mr. Dangerfield, who you have also heard from, stepped forward. In a public-spirited fashion, he told them not only what he had just witnessed, concurring in what the offices had seen, but as a regular traveller on the Underground he gave them details of earlier incidents on previous days."

"The first three were charged at the police station with the substantive offences, together with a broader charge of conspiring to steal, in the jurisdiction of this court. In other words, the Central Criminal Court is all-embracing across England and Wales and therefore the highest criminal court which has that jurisdiction. A full record of their property was recorded by the officers together where it was suspected, the forged travel documents in their possession. In an effort to halt the tide of these crimes, the officers, together with other members of the squad resolved to conduct further operations. You then heard that Mr. Dangerfield, again in that continued public spirit, volunteered his assistance once more."

"The next two defendants as they appear in the dock were arrested within that same week, and you know that

Mr. Dangerfield identified them as being involved in thefts or attempted thefts on previous occasions. The same diligent recording of their property including their cash, occurred, something I shall come on to. As with the first three, they were charged with similar offences together with the conspiracy to steal, but separately to the first three. Then lastly, you heard from Detective Constable Conroy, relative to defendants six and seven. Their arrests came about, you heard, when the officer was on his way to court to deal with a remand on another entirely unconnected theft from the person. To his credit, either bravely or some might erring on the side of caution, he stepped in and stopped the commission of their theft. A passing member of Underground staff came to his assistance, who while not witnessing a crime, ensured the officer was able to safely take them in custody to the police station."

"You'll see from the copy of the indictment front you, the various members of this group were in possession of either forged passports, or identity cards, we say, to enable them to avoid revealing their true identities and continue engaging in multiple thefts across Europe, their true identities the prosecution say, we now have. You have heard of many statements, which have been served on the various defence counsel and have been formally admitted which revolve around the travel documents. Now we come to the conspiracy to steal within the jurisdiction of this court, which includes all seven of the defendants."

"The last witness you heard from Detective Inspector Trebor, whom you have seen in the court throughout the duration of this trial. There is nothing particularly unusual about that as he is the officer in charge of this case and his presence doesn't prejudice or conflict, with the other officers having given evidence. His evidence spoke of the various connections between each of the defendants. First we have Bank of England currencies where the defendants are connected through sequentially numbered notes. Add that to travel tickets which also suggest that various defendants are known to each other. Plus, some had concealed either identification documents on their person or had concealed high value foreign currency in shoes or in the fly of their trousers, all of which we say, goes toward their dishonest intentions. In the round, we say these are all contributory factors in the conspiracy count. I don't intend to take up any more of your time, you will of course have all these exhibits with you, when you come to make your deliberations when you retire to the jury room."

Now it was the turn of the seven defence barristers. In summary their only defence was that somehow the detectives in this case had developed their own conspiracy to link them all together in common purpose of thieving, whereas they declared that none of them were known to each other.

The very idea!

It quickly became clear their lawyers hearts weren't in it, whether it was because the squad had done their homework so well and there was no getting through the wall of the alleged fit-up and they weren't the hapless lost tourists they tried to portray, or because the judge had warned them at the outset they'd only receive half their fee because he failed to see how two defendants couldn't be represented by one barrister where there was no evidential conflict of interest.

Either way they each gave lacklustre performance on behalf of their respective clients.

I'm going to sit out the judges summing up and go for a coffee in the police room. You'll never believe it, you remember I tried to get the seven's previous convictions through the embassy and the diplomatic attaché wouldn't play ball. After that I put in a request through Interpol at the 'Yard' for all previous convictions worldwide. Imagine my surprise when I learnt what I got in return. These are hot off the press as we speak! Just as the jury are about to be sent out to decide, I find that two of the seven have 'form' for murder and terrorist related offences in Santiago, Chile a few years back, another three have convictions in Athens, Paris, Rome and Madrid. Now I'll need to get these previous convictions typed up with a view to seeing if the judge will accept them being mentioned at the conclusion of the trial.

*

Detective Sergeant Kent sat at rear of the court at Knightsbridge as Donald Thwaites outlined how he and the learned Mr. Farmington had reached an agreement that the trial of Heath could be dealt with by way of a plea of 'guilty' to a lesser charge — a Section 47 assault and an attempt theft. This, the judge emphasised appeared entirely appropriate in all the circumstances, and saved the public purse a lengthy trial. The judge warmed to Thwaites summary of the case, reflecting it appeared overkill in common mans parlance, to have added murder alternative manslaughter, when the evidence didn't support such a serious view. Heath accepting that he assaulted Basil when the evidence surrounding the incident suggests he couldn't possibly have foreseen the consequence of his actions, particularly as it would appear Basil slipped and fell down the escalator rather than being pushed by the defendant. Thwaites mentioned the missing witness who may well have provided more of a glimpse into the assault, told the court that despite knowing she had gone to Australia, he had no further details as to her whereabouts which he lamented was a most unfortunate oversight by the Police, who perhaps should have acted earlier to secure her evidence. *That fucks Spooner*, Brian thought to himself, who imagined Detective Sergeant Hunt would also happy with the negative slight against the investigating officer.

The two remaining counts of attempted theft from the person and a section 47 assault occasioning actual bodily arm were put to Heath by the clerk of the court. The third count relating to his breach of bail, being on the Underground system was allowed to rest on file. Heath appeared relieved to plead guilty to the two counts against him.

"Heath, I have read the pre-trial reports and I have heard from counsel representing you. When it comes to committing offences of dishonesty with or without violence it suggests you are a recidivist of the worse kind. You have been given chances to improve in the past but it seems with no discernible change in you behaviour, treating prison as an occupational hazard. It is with that in mind that I'm sure you will not be surprised that intend to impose a considerable term of imprisonment."

Heath clenched his fists underneath his thighs as he awaited his fate.

"You need to learn that this kind of thieving impacts great misery on your victims, often leaving them stranded and inconvenienced for some considerable time. Also, assaulting any officer in a bid to escape your arrest will not be tolerated by this or any other court. You will go to prison for three years, counts one and two to run concurrently. Take him down."

Brian Kent rose to his feet as he judge swept out towards his robing room, giving the officer a chance to thank Donald Thwaites for such a quick result. He then left to find Hunt in the police room, indulging in his fourth coffee of the day. The officer from Complaints and Discipline, slunk away from the court building without speaking to either officer.

"Hello guv, Brian here down at Knightsbridge. Yeah yeah, all fine, plea to the attempt and a section 47. I don't think we could've got any more of it out of it to be honest. Yes, he knows guv, he's like a dog with two cocks. Great relief. Okay guv, I'll tell him to go straight home, and stay there until he hears from you some time tomorrow. Okay, I'll see you later back at the office."

Well there you are. In all honesty I don't think we could've got any more out of it. Heath was only charged with serious offences because of Basil's death. That was more about Basil's wife believing we were going for broke, but without any direct evidence it would be impossible to make it stick. At least this way it's the barristers who have come up with the resolution and not us. So we can't be criticised for backing off. I got one the lads to type up the foreign previous convictions aka 'precons', in anticipation the judge will be with our proposal to cite them at the conclusion before sentencing, just to give a fuller picture of their 'form'. The jury is still out deliberating, but to be fair they've got a fair few counts to consider.

Well that's close of play for today. The Common Serjeant has sent them home for the night, not wanting to rush their deliberations. It's not unusual on a trial of this nature which has been some weeks in its process and the number of counts on the indictment to consider. In my experience, although they might have reached decisions on a few, the judge won't give a majority verdict direction probably until mid-morning tomorrow.

Oh yes, I didn't tell you did I. There was a half day in this trial, and was called over to the big house to receive my notice of what I was being investigated for following those bent bastards doing their raid. It ran to five pages, none of which was actually alleging that I had committed any internal disciplinary offences. The whole lot was about me allowing — or I guess, enabling — officers of my squad to do wrong things. There is one bit though that did make me laugh out loud when I read through it. Remember, all the members of my squad had received their notices some weeks before, except me. When I was called up I was given the police caution, served with the notice but not interviewed, and I never have been. But getting back to my reason for such hilarity: you'll recall John Conroy is a practical joker who had a small starting gun together with caps concealed in his top drawer. On occasions when the office was quiet and everyone was grafting on paperwork, he'd let the bloody thing off, incurring the wrath of the boys, who would retaliate with anything that wasn't nailed down, throwing it in his direction.

So when we were subjected to our unlawful incarceration and searched, they found John's cap gun. In fact it was referred to as that in his notice. Not wanting to miss a trick and up the *ante, when it came to my notice, it seems I had allowed John to have an imitation firearm together with ammunition! Surely they were mixing me up with Walker. What a bunch of twats! Right, I've told the lads to get away back to the office, in the anticipation of a liquid debrief later at the Allsop Arms, just round the corner from the nick. In the meantime Conroy and I will tidy up the exhibits, lock up our room and retire to Snow Hill Police Station to their bar down in the basement of this fine City of London Police Station.*

Bob and John made their weary way, all of five minutes, past the ever open doors of the Magpie and Stump pub opposite the Bailey, to Snow Hill nick the other side of Holborn viaduct. As they past Holy St. Sepulchre church to their left Bob imparted a little bit of local knowledge in that it was the venue of his mum and dads wedding. Conroy cheekily asked if Bob had been a page boy on the day, to which he got a swift clip round the back of the head, the riposte that carnal gymnastics in their day was not so procedural, and the demand that the first beers were on John. They entered what almost looked like a multi-storey cottage with its lead light windows, and passing the duty sergeant at the front desk they descended down to the basement finding the ever open bar at the rear of the nick. It was an ever present mystery to Bob that the bar staff, that usually one person was drawn from the late turn patrol shift at the police station. So his or her late turn duty would be in the bar serving and clearing up. One proviso — they could remove their ties and epaulets! This was the case at Bishopsgate and Wood Street police stations as well. *I know they're in the pocket of the City Fathers, the movers and shakers in the City of London financial district, but is this really police work? Stretching it a bit,* thought Bob.

"Cheers John, need this. Nice pint of chilly lager! Oh. I didn't tell you did I, you remember last week I got called over to the dream factory to get my notice of investigation from that corrupt bastard Spooner? I've got it with me. It seems they are trying to blame me for allowing you all to be naughty boys. But when you look at it closely…well, I'll let you have a look," and with that Bob fished it out of his inside jacket pocket. Conroy opened the document going into a number of pages and began reading intently as Bob continued savouring his pint.

'Complaints Investigation Bureau:

'Detective Inspector TREBOR, I have been appointed to investigate a complaint which been received from Trevor Sutton a person arrested by Detective Constable CONROY.

'Between diverse dates, you were the Detective Inspector in charge of the Central London Pickpocket Squad at Baker Street Police Station.

'Officers from the Complaints Investigation Bureau visited your offices, searched desks and seized a number of items, namely pocket books, incident report books — both used and unused, case papers in the case of Sutton within a Case History folder, crime reports and messages which may have a bearing on Sutton's activities. They also seized an imitation firearm and ammunition from D.C. CONROY'S desk. There was no trace of a pocket book register which would be utilised in the lawful consecutive issue of the aforementioned pocket books.

'You were seen in your office and you were asked about Force and office procedures. You declined to fully co-operate with answering those questions, so your Commander BROWN was advised.

'You were found to be in possession of three used pocket books all of which have been returned to you together with two Incident Report Books which likewise have been returned to for outstanding court trials. Other seized pocket books and incident report books have been returned to respective officers for their use in court cases. You failed to maintain a pocket book register ensuring the supervised issue and return of such documents, and an efficient system for storing them once used.

'Your official diary was made up to the day before the visit by officers. Therefore your diary was not up to date. You visited Snow Hill Police Station in connection with the prisoner SUTTON. You've not shown that in your diary. You are therefore in breach of Force Standing Orders.

'You have failed to ensure that Detective Constable CONROY properly and efficiently dealt with the investigation of the case against Trevor SUTTON.

'YOU ARE NOT OBLIGED TO SAY ANYTHING CONCERNING THE MATTER BUT YOU MAY, IF YOU SO DESIRE, MAKE A WRITTEN OR ORAL STATEMENT IN ACCORDANCE WITH THE REGULATIONS. I MUST, HOWEVER, WARN YOU THAT ANY SUCH STATEMENT MAY BE USED IN ANY SUBSEQUENT DISCIPLINARY PROCEEDINGS. THE FACT THAT THIS NOTICE HAS BEEN SERVED UPON YOU DOES NOT NECESSARILY MEAN THAT

DISCIPLINARY ACTION WILL BE TAKEN. THE INTENTION IS TO INFORM YOU OF MATTERS UNDER INVESTIGATION AND, THEREFORE, TO SAFEGUARD YOUR OWN INTERESTS.'

Conroy's eyes glazed over as he searched for the 'wheat from the chaff', but frustratingly none seemed to be forthcoming.

"This is bollocks guv. What is it you've supposed to have done wrong — come to that, what is it any of us are supposed to have done wrong? All the pocket books and I.R.B.s have been returned to us now, so they must be satisfied there's fuck-all in those. We've been getting the prosecution files back from those little shits Spooner and Secrett, so our court work is continuing. Do yo know what happened to the register guv? They must've had it away 'cos they thought they'd got us, but now they can't return it and make themselves look bad. Your diary was out of date by a day, not exactly a hanging offence is it? And why would you include a quick look through the wicket gate in your diary? You wouldn't know the the importance of it at the time would you? It was about identification, and you didn't. He's a dip who's a liar — well, what a surprise, they all are! They're fucking thieves. Then to say my cap gun has turned into an imitation firearm on your notice is just ridiculous. They're on the run, guv, they're laying it all off onto Sutton, and for you there was nothing to supervise, everything we could do had been done. But the biggest omission is McMurray. Not one fucking mention, in any of our notices. I reckon they're going to trump up some bollocks just to pot us for something. You've got to ask why they thought it appropriate to serve your notice on you half way through a complicated trial? They're trying to break you and divide and rule. I can tell you, guv, we're solid behind you, fuck them. Let's just sue the bastards' arses off for this. We ain't bent and they know it."

Bob thanked John for his response to reading the allegations and the laughable manner in which the investigators, clearly struggling to justify their over exuberant raid, had failed to find anything substantial or criminal against any of them. One concern was the disappearance of the pocket book register, which again would kick their allegations of corruption into the long grass. But the biggest was the allegation was that 'created' courtesy of Detective Sergeant Dennison. *Obviously the investigators can't make up their minds which villains allegations to hang their hat on,* thought Bob.

"Right come on John I want to get back to the nick. Brian Kent and possibly Jim Hunt have gone back from Knightsbridge but I hope Jim took the hint and just went home. I want to nip round to the Allsop to see the landlady," said Bob.

"You're not giving her one are you guv?"

"Twat. No, I want her to rope off part off the boozer for tomorrow night after — with any luck — we've got a good result from the Chilean trial. I'm going to ask her to put on some grub for the team. I expect a few from general CID will pitch up as well."

John agreed and told the guv'nor he thought it was a good idea after all the stress they'd been through.

20

DECISIONS, DECISIONS!

Bob woke to find he was in a bedroom he didn't recognise. The excess of Budweiser on drought last night had clearly affected his judgement as the tell tale signs of floral wallpaper, curling tongs on the dressing table, and furry toys scattered around the floor, he quickly realised he was in the landlady's bedroom. How he got there was a mystery to him, as he regained consciousness hoping he'd not been violated by the voluptuous host. She was missing albeit he could hear her dulcet tones of urgent ablutions coming from the en-suite at the foot of the bed.

After about five minutes she emerged, her body dry and as naked as Botticelli's Venus, without the clam shell, of course.

"Good morning stud. Would you like some breakfast before send you on your way?", she said with a knowing smile.

It seems things went a bit further than expected, thought Bob as he tried to feign such an encounter as purely routine. He tried to engage in polite banter as she assured him their secret was safe with her. Nobody had witnessed his overnight proposition and consequently could remain between them. A full English settled his digestive system and with a quick peck on the cheek, he left via the side gate to the establishment, knowing two or three of his squad had overnighted there before and wondering where he fitted into her hierarchy of suitors.

His battle-weary suit had lost the sharpness he was known for. He called into a small outfitters just off Baker Street which sold shirts and ties. Five minutes in the changing room, to acquire a new shirt and paisley tie, then into the dry cleaners next door where Mo pressed Bob's jacket and trousers. He appeared a different, smarter man, hoping to avoid any squad interrogation as he entered the nick. To his surprise nobody noticed. He breathed a sigh of relief, feeding his fish as he listened to George Michael vowing never to dance again, *'guilty feet have got no rhythm'*. A visit to the office saw Paul Hazel being told to join the guv'nor for a trip to the Old Bailey and for Al Fish to come to the court in time for one o'clock lunch, when hopefully Bob says they should have a result for the trial. Brian Kent put his head round the corner confirming the guv'nor was happy to chat.

"Guv, I know you're off down to court shortly but you know we had that plea from Heath and he's been weighed off. Jim went home as you suggested as he's still suspended, does the result have any bearing on him coming back to work because he's just in the same boat as us now isn't he?"

"Leave it with me Brian. Obviously because they had an observer in court, the powers that be will know the case is dealt with. Tell Jim just to stay at home for the time being until he hears from me. If we get a result on the Chileans today, I've organised a bit of a do round at the Allsop Arms this evening. As he is suspended, Jim can't enter any police premises, but that doesn't extend to the pub, so can I leave it to you to convince him? If he wants to come tonight we'd all be pleased to see him, no problem, okay? Now, I want you to crack on with the forged Amex job today, see how we can progress that over the next week or so, will you?"

Brian confirmed he'd let Jim know the position and would press on with getting 'control' statements from American Express about suspect defects of the forged traveller's cheques and the genuine article together with the printing processes involved. With that, he made favourable noises about the aquarium as he, left and Paul Hazel entered.

Just so you know what control statements are — they're basically procedural, seen through rose-tinted glasses. What should happen, say, with a traveller's cheque? How it's printed, who prints it, where it's printed, what security markers are there to ensure integrity of the item? And so on. Right I'm off to the Bailey.

Bob and Paul negotiated the revolving door and security checks before they scaled the wide staircase to the mezzanine floor of the Central Criminal Court. As they did, a familiar face was descending at the same time — and was someone Bob recognised from his days in the Police cadets years earlier. Bob stopped midway while Paul pressed on to the police room.

"Bloody hell Terry Cross, as I live and breathe. Hello mate how many years has it been?"

said Bob as he watched clearly troubled Terry walking towards him.

They had been room mates when all the Hendon cadets were relocated down to Grosvenor Hall, just outside

Ashford in Kent, for the second phase of their training. The pair spent a whole year there before relocating back into London, into one of four 'Section houses'.

"Can't stop right now, Terry, I've got a jury just about to come back in with verdicts, but how about a coffee afterwards? Where's your trial? I'll come and dig you out?"

"Hello Bob, I'm not in a trial, I *am* the trial. I was nicked on the 'Countryman' enquiry. There's four of us, and it don't look good. If I get a result I'll get in touch with you, mate. Do yourself a favour, don't approach me in this place. The fuckers are tailing me everywhere and I guarantee they're filming and taping, trying to break us. They haven't yet."

Terry gave him some detail of how he'd become a scalp in their enquiry, warranting an appearance at the 'Bailey'. Bob took the hint, understanding what is was like to be under the microscope even if you'd done nothing wrong. He rejoined Paul outside court one, was obviously deep in thought but Paul didn't want to ask further.

*

The familiar sound of Boles voice on Branch's intercom demanded his attendance for a brief chat in his office. Maurice confirmed his compliance with a sigh to himself as he finished his cup of Earl Grey tea.

"Ah. Come in Maurice, sit yourself down,". as the double tap on the guv'nor's door announced his presence. He sat uneasily opposite his boss, who he viewed with considerable scepticism, about to be confirmed.

"Now, I've had the opportunity to review where we are with this whole Dip Squad debacle. You've not informed me of anything further revealed from, I assume, the earnest investigations by Spooner, Secrett or Dennison. As we now know, the trial of the dip Heath led to a guilty plea, accepted by prosecution counsel in the case. I've read counsel's summary after the trial and unfortunately I have to concede pleas are the best we could have hoped for. So now I have to decide what to do about Hunts continued suspension. I think he needs to be returned to duty but still under investigation for the general allegations of corruption. I shall instruct Commander Brown to have him in to do that immediately, so we can start killing off this unholy mess. Do you have any views on that course of action?"

Branch remained steadfastly quiet, believing that Boles was working his own 'get out of jail free' card. Without any update on him being reported to the Director of Public Prosecutions together with the other 'three musketeers' he saw no reason to align himself with anything Boles suggested, not trusting him for moment.

"Well I thought you might have something to say Maurice. I realise your business hasn't been resolved yet, but I'm confident it will eventually come back, 'not in the public interest to proceed', and it will be expected that some kind of disciplinary sanction be exercised, I would imagine. I'm anticipating that if I call each of the squad members in, individually, and give them 'words of guidance' it might diffuse their intent on legal action against the Force. It's bloody annoying the Police Federation saw fit to financially support them in their quest to have us investigated, and to that end they seem to have succeeded! What their ultimate goal is, I know not. But the threat of adverse publicity has to be kept to a minimum for obvious reasons. I must say, Maurice, I think the whole enquiry could have been dealt with in a more arbitrary fashion. They're bent, I know it, you know it, and they're thumbing their noses at us because our hard evidence wasn't hard enough. Needless to say, it's been complicated by that idiot of a Detective Inspector Walker and his impromptu property store, and of course the gun! I'm going to leave that aspect to CIB2 to sort out. That can be left as a separate internal discipline enquiry and they're happy to deal with that, as it appears the gun features in a couple of robberies elsewhere in London. Of course, they'll have to put Sutton through the mill, so to speak, as he's the one who palmed it to Walker in the first place."

Branch resolved to remain completely silent by nodding and agreeing with Boles when he felt comfortable to do so. His attitude was to come over as an admirer of the guv'nor's superior intellect and readily accepting whatever his strategy was. At the same time thinking, *Fuck him, he's not having me over!* Sensing the meeting was over he asked to be excused, so he could get on with other matters arising that day. Boles waved him away in his usual dismissive manner.

*

Having ignored the various defence barristers arriving in court one as they tried cheerfully engaging Bob in conversation as to say, 'All is forgiven, you're not really a lying bastard, it's just my job', he greeted Mr. Playton. His junior counsel was no longer needed or present as she was on another case from chambers, sadly to the disappointment of the lads doubtless, but that's life's rich tapestry. He confirmed all was ready in relation to each of the defendants' previous convictions and antecedent history, in readiness for guilty verdicts from a jury who appeared to be attentive and with them on what the prosecution was driving at. But juries in Bob and Ian's experience can be a fickle and mystifying group at times, either asking unforeseen questions of the judge or just returning completely bizarre verdicts, so an open mind is always required. Never read anything into the length of time they spend deliberating, the only time this can be speculated is if the judge enquires if they are near a verdict or gives them a majority verdict direction. Knowing the jury would be reconvening in their jury room to consider their deliberations, Bob excused himself, leaving Playton to go into a huddle with the other barristers. *Probably discussing what trials they coming up next, fucking egoists* thought Bob.

"Come on Paul, lets go for a coffee in the canteen while we've got the chance,". And they did just that.

Not sure if he should ask, Paul said, "Guv, that mate you bumped into on the stairs, is he on trial here? What the fuck has he done?"

"Paul, put it this way. He's been captured — not on the take, he's not bent like that. His dad is a 'Jack Reagan' on the squad and I think he wants to emulate him. The only problem is, the crew he was working with had tucked up a blagger with a sawn-off shotgun, which he said in his evidence at the original trial, he'd found. What he didn't know was that it had been in prisoners property from another job. Surprise

surprise, the shooter was then found in the boot of the blaggers motor. It was submitted for forensic examination as you would expect, but then a monster allegation then grew. First the blagger was claiming fit-up, but worse still, the shooter had been through forensics before and was covered in fingerprint dust as well. 'Countryman' weren't even after them, but it was a gift. Gave them a 'starter for ten'. They were actually brought in to look at a series of blaggings in the City of London where senior officer involvement was suspected. It's a shame, just trying to put away the bad guys like we all do. He's a good bloke, I was in the Cadets with him, good little wrestler too. Hope he can fight his way out of it, he doesn't deserve this. That 'Countryman' team is a load of 'carrot crunchers' from the sticks. I'm told they know nothing about working in London; it's a different beast altogether. If they have one robbery a year they'd be mortified if they had a second which would then increase their crime rate by fifty per cent. Bad for their stats. Anyway, their briefs are putting up a fight before the trial even gets under way, on an abuse of process. I don't know much about it, but it seems prosecution didn't exactly play fair in the lead up to the trial, withholding all sorts of evidence. So I guess we haven't got the monopoly on being investigated by arseholes."

Paul nodded in agreement, mindful of those words he'd heard the guv'nor use so many times, 'failing to plan is planning to fail'. As they finished their coffee, the tannoy announced everyone to return to Court One. They arrived to see Ian Playton tell them the jury had reached decisions on the counts and would be back in shortly.

The clerk of the court rose to his feet to address the jury while the Common Serjeant shuffled his red books full of his copious notes taken throughout the trial.

"Members of the jury, have you reached a decision on each of the counts on which you are all agreed?"

The middle aged man dressed in the two-piece tweed suit, with an air of country farmer about him, sat nearest to the Judges' bench, rose to his feet. "We have," he boomed across the now-crowded courtroom. The press benches waited with bated breath before rushing off to file their reports for the daily papers.

Each count read over, whether the all-encompassing conspiracies to steal or the substantive offences of theft from the person, returned a guilty verdict. Only one count returned a not guilty verdict, that of the one offence witnessed only by John Conroy. Bob sat behind his barrister, recording all the verdicts, pausing in surprise at the one case not proven. In his mind, though he thought it was a decent batting average and probably wouldn't have much, if any, impact on what the judge would give the seven South Americans.

That's odd. So one count is a not guilty for one of Johns when he was the only officer witnessing the offence and nicking the offender. Oh well. Various members of the jury keep looking across at me and giving me a knowing smile. See how it goes but I might invite them to our little post trial 'drinkies' if they're still around at the end. Right here we go — speak to you afterwards.

"Members of the jury, your duties are now fulfilled and you are free to leave the court if you so wish. However, should you wish to remain through to conclusion then you are welcome to stay for the duration," said the Common

Serjeant. There was no movement from the jury benches as they sat in eager anticipation awaiting the next episode. The judge turned on his chair to then invite prosecution counsel to reveal what was known about the convicted prisoners.

Ian Playton ran through each of the defendants asking Bob to give details of their antecedent history including their previous convictions so far as the British courts were concerned. He then sought leave of the court to reveal those worldwide convictions, and with the blessing of the judge he proceeded to do so. The various members of the jury either shook their heads in disbelief that in the ordinary course of events the convictions wouldn't be mentioned, as many nodded their heads when a truer picture of the defendants was known. The decision to find them all guilty, left them with no doubt they'd made the right decisions.

The clerk of the court stood facing the seven defendants and through the interpreter, commanded them to stand. Lord Williamson was brief in his address telling them their activities would not be tolerated in the country, and sentenced each of them to four years' imprisonment, and deportation at the the conclusion of their sentence. Their reaction was simply to turn and walk towards the stairwell leading to the stairs. Given the complexity of the case, Bob thought there might be some recognition from the judge but none was forthcoming. He simply rose and walked from the court via the chambers doorway to his right, not even acknowledging the presence of the jury. Over the duration of the trial, Bobs face had become familiar to the twelve. He wandered across to speak to them.

Craning his head over the top of the lower bench from the well of the court, he said, "Thank you for your patience throughout. The trial went on for longer than I anticipated, but I think everything having to be translated through the interpreter before being delivered to the prisoners was always going to make the process longer. But thank you for delivering the right result."

The mid twenties lady on the front row, who'd let slip when being sworn, that she was a market trader who really couldn't afford a long trial said, "Oh that's alright darlin' we knew they was wrong 'uns, you wouldn't 'ave nicked them otherwise would yer. And when we heard their form from round the world that really clinched it. We was all agreed. Thieving bastards, who do they think they are coming to our country like that? Send them home when they've done their porridge."

Bob smiled, looking across the other jury members, a demure young girl who looked like she'd just finished her 'A' levels nodded towards him. A more refined lady, obviously in her forties with silver grey hair, winked at Bob; she'd been giving him regular eye contact throughout the trial.

He parked his thoughts and said, "I don't know if you would be interested, but usually at the conclusion of a lengthy trial we usually have a few drinks, a bit of a post-mortem. If each of you don't have commitments this early evening then we'd love you all to come along to our little gathering. It's at the Allsop Arms in Baker Street, at six onwards. There'll be food and drink there. Thanks again."

As he walked back across the court to rejoin Paul in clearing up papers and exhibits, Bob extended the invite to

Ian and two of the defence counsel, one being Mario, who were cordial company and he'd known for some time, unlike the others who he thought *were shits!*

*

Paul made arrangements with the court staff to leave all their papers and prisoners property in a small locked office leading off the side of Court One assuring them they'd be collected before start of play in the court the following day. He joined Bob who went on a search for his pal standing trial. His search was short lived, as he checked the court list outside Court Four the other end of the mezzanine floor, and there was a bit of a commotion through the double part-glazed doors to the court. He deferred entering. After a couple of minutes Terry emerged with his three cohorts, jubilant and punching the air. The abuse of process argument against CIB2 and prosecution had worked. They were each found not guilty of any crime and so were free to go. Bob called for a celebratory drink. He first thought of Snow Hill Police station bar, but as they were still suspended — and with two 'observers' from CIB2 watching their every move — a more appropriate venue was sought in the form of the Cock Tavern underneath Smithfield meat market. Three or four pints later Bob told Terry he and Paul would have to leave them to it, as they were returning to the squad 'rinse' at Baker Street. Terry and his cohorts declined joining, but Terry promised he'd keep in touch.

21

THE WIND OF CHANGE

"Come in, Detective Sergeant Hunt, sit down," said Commander Brown as he acknowledged his secretary leaving and closing his office door. "Now I've been instructed by the Deputy Chief, Mr. Boles, to speak with you about your suspension from duty and the subsequent investigation following the tragic death of Detective Constable Chakrabati. As you know the suspect for the crime has now been dealt with at Crown Court and I have no intention of commenting on the case and it's evidence."

Hunt gulped as he waited for the sword of Damocles to fall, giving him an insight on his future career.

"I am advised that you are to return to duty with the complaint against you from Heath being unsubstantiated. However, you are still under investigation in relation to the Pickpocket Squad allegations of corruption. I can see you're nodding which I take to mean that you understand what I am telling you. Will you sign this document to certify that you understand it's conclusion and will return to duty? I have your warrant card here. As Commander I have decided that until such time the other investigation is complete, you will be returned to divisional duties, not working with the Squad. I believe it's ultimately in your best interest to separate you, and for you to have a period of stability. Now go over to the nick at Baker Street and report to the Divisional Detective Inspector, he's expecting you. And a personal advice from me: keep your head down. I'm sure all this business will come to an end soon, but at present the investigation remains open. Go on bugger off," as his wry smile of told of what he thought of the enquiry.

*

Bob was on a mission! He went round to the Allsop Arms to chat with the landlady on the future evening's proceedings. She showed him the finger buffet she'd created, together with a huge cream cake for those owners of a sweet tooth. She had roped off a large section at the far end for Bob's boys and friends to schmooze, the euphemism for getting pissed in a post trial celebration. Content she'd done him proud, he returned to his office to tidy up his outstanding paperwork, fiercely aware that albeit his attendance at court for the past few weeks was required, the deluge of daily correspondence continued its unrelenting march to his 'In tray', requiring his attention.

"Oh hello. No, no, I'm just sat here killing off some paperwork," said Bob with phone in one hand and stretching the cord to feed his ever hungry tropical fish at the same time, and mystified why the brief was calling.

"I've just heard you had a good result with the South American's. Well done. Someone in the chambers I use was telling me how they'd met their match jousting with the Dip

Squad. Really? Well I'm not washing my hair this evening. Lovely I'd love to. Ok I'll be there about seven."

Bloody hell, that's a turn up. I thought she'd dumped me, choosing her pisshead, kinky barrister to me. Well, as they say, one door closes, another one opens. Who am I to argue with that? I must admit I'm really pleased she's called, and who knows… one more time perhaps!

*

Locking his office door, and office lights turned off, leaving the aquarium to illuminate, Bob turned to see Paul Hazel emerging from the squad office. He shared with him the latest bombshell — as he saw it — of the brief promising to attend their 'soirée'. It pleased Paul as he knew how much the guv'nor still wanted to be with her and was lost without her. Five minutes saw them in the pub. A cheer went up as they entered. The rest of the squad, plus quite a few from general CID had commenced indulging in, as the guv'nor would say, chilly lagers. More specifically Budweiser on draft. A pint was thrust into his hand as Bob turned away from the bar to see 'twelve men good and true' also known as the jury from their trial enter through the main double doors, looking bemused as to what the evening had in mind, not being experienced in CID drinking sessions and certainly not post-trial celebrations. Bob stepped forward to welcome them, thanking for their attendance — every single one turning up! — and ensuring various members of the team took them to the bar to ply them with first drinks.

Some of the boys began eyeing up the buffet as it was ferried from the pub's kitchens. With a stern look from Bob, they were dared to touch it until he gave the signal. Their behaviour became more boisterous as the pints were disposed of. The next 'guests' to arrive were four barristers involved in the case, including Ian Playton, who perhaps unwisely had asked his betrothed to accompany him. Her presence was greeted with a succession of wolf whistles and a couple of the team barking like dogs.

The tirade prompted Ian to say to the love of his life, "Remember what I said darling? Rough and ready darling, rough and ready". She smiled at him demurely, accepting the newly proffered drinks from Al Fish. The drinks and the evenings' intoxicating atmosphere, enticed the party animals to mix flirtatiously.

Dave Champion opened up proceedings, extending the 'hand of friendship' with the twenty-something nurse from the front row of the jury. They sat on the battle-weary Chesterfield at the far end, heavily engaged in animated conversation. Bob looked across and thought, *Is this the first love affair of the evening?* Fish surreptitiously moved in on Dave's left side, blind to the nurse. Temptation got the better of him as he released his 'honourable member' and placed it in Dave's left ear. Dave turned, looked at it, turning back to the object of his desires, ignoring the attention seeking Fish as if it was a routine occurrence. To his relief 'Nursey' saw nothing. Undaunted, Fish continued circulating and saw an opportunity to express his 'manhood' when he saw Farmer with his hands clenched behind his back as he chatted to a couple of the jury. Height was no restriction as it flopped into the palm of his hand. Pete grabbed it firmly and dragged him around the pub as Fish winced in pain. Lesson learnt. He backed off and sought solace in another pint. The more middle aged juror with the long grey hair made a 'bee line' for Bob who, having seen her advances, side-stepped and engaged in casual chat with Ian Playton's girlfriend, desperately aware his brief would be turning up shortly.

The street trader cornered Paul and Conroy at the bar, as she said, "Which on of you two is going to take me home and fuck me, or have I got to play with myself again?"

Neither of the lads could be described as shrinking violets, but by the same token they weren't up for remedial sex this early in the evening, and so excused themselves from her presence. They joined in the group with Brian Kent welcoming Jim Hunt back into the fold. She saw Bob peeling away from Ian, so engaged him in post trial banter.

Bob said, "Thanks ever so much in convicting that bunch of South American bandits. There was obviously a lot to consider when there were so many counts on the indictment — confusing at times, I expect. Tell me, you found them all guilty of everything apart from the one count where John over there was the only witness, and of course, was the arresting officer. I'm just interested, what made that one so different and why?"

"Cos he's a lying fat cunt. That's why. No other reason. You all did a good job apart from the crap he came out with," she said firmly, taking Bob by surprise.

He thanked her for her efforts and frankness, moving across to where the finger buffet was still covered in cling film. Bob feeling he should mark the evening by thanking the fine efforts of his squad, tapped a knife on the side of his beer glass to draw everyone's attention.

"This is a great turnout, boys and girls, and the fact that so many who were involved in the case, are here this evening. Behind me you'll see a buffet which our gracious landlady has kindly provided for us, and rather than sending it airborne at one another, just try eating it, you sods. That said I'm reminded of something a gentleman by the name of Roy Atwell in 1915 said as a cautionary tale so here goes;

In these days of indigestion,
It is often time to question,
As to what you eat and what you leave alone,
Every microbe and bacillus,
Has a different way to kill us,
And in time will claim us for their own,
There are germs of every kind,
In every food that you will find,
In the market or upon the bill of fayre,
Drinking water's just as risky,
As the so called deadly whiskey,
And it's often a mistake to breathe the air!
So keep it clean, keep it tidy and don't get pissed.
Well not too much. Enjoy"

Bob spotted his femme fatale at the back of the room had just arrived so joined her with a drink as his 'sermon' was greeted with cheers and respectful derision.

*

Dave Champion's overtures to the young nurse appeared to strike a chord as they left the now-boisterous celebration marked with parts of the cream cake going airborne in some kind of food fight across the inebriated party. Fish had made progress with Angie Scott and indulged in heavy kissing with each other. Bob sensed this was the time for him to leave to avoid witnessing the degeneration into a Caligula-like party. The brief went with him back to his office in the Police Station which was mainly in darkness, the late turn officers out and about on patrol. Locking the door, the room remained illuminated by the aquarium.

She expressed a passing interest as they fell into each other's arms, exploring each other's bodies as she said, "Sling that in tray off your desk, I've got a much better 'in tray' for you," grinning as she leant back from the edge. He gently moved her french knickers to one side as she let out a sigh of pleasure as he teased with his cock, her wet pussy waiting in eager anticipation. Their lovemaking intensified as climax followed and the lovers re-affirmed their need for each other. As they leant back, relaxing on the office chairs he told her of his investigation which would shortly take him north of the border to catch some Scottish villains. She readily agreed to join him for the journey and anonymous residency in a central Glasgow hotel while Bob locked up the bad guys during the day. He promised to keep in touch for the impending expedition, so she could arrange her court diary in good time, before a last kiss saw them part. She went back to her flat and Bob returning to the pub to ensure behaviour hadn't deteriorated any further than when he left it.

*

"Come in Walker, sit down," said Detective Chief Superintendent Lyle, his back to the eighth-floor windows of his office in Tintagel House, a sixties' office block occupied by various Police departments on the south bank overlooking the Thames, just between Vauxhall Bridge and Lambeth Bridge.

"I have been appointed to investigate a complaint which has been received from Trevor Jones, also known as Sutton, who was arrested by Detective Constable Conroy of the Central London Pickpocket Squad at Baker Street for attempted theft. Following his arrest, Jones met you in the Wellington Arms Public House, Waterloo, and discussed his arrest by the officer with you. Contrary to Force Standing Orders, you knowingly met Jones, a prisoner on bail, at a place other than a police station. Following your meeting, you failed to report the circumstances of that meeting and the result, promptly in writing to the Operational Head of the Force. You failed to record details of the meeting with Jones in your official pocket book or in you official CID diary. Prior to this meeting you notified your Divisional Superintendent of your intended meeting —an informant, you said — but you misled your senior officer as to fact that Jones was a person known to you to be on bail for a criminal offence. During your meeting with Jones you were informed by him of an official complaint against Detective Constable Conroy of unlawful arrest and detention, theft and allegation that the officer may be trying to solicit a bribe from him. You failed to comply with Force directions on such matters and failed to notify Headquarters of the details of Jones' complaint. Furthermore, for over a year you have had an ad hoc arrangement with Jones to dispose of stolen property via the Lost Property Office at Waterloo Station. When searched, you were in possession of several wallets and purses and more seriously, a Section One Firearm as defined under the Firearms Act 1968, together with ammunition, and failed to comply with Force Instructions for the safe handling of such property. You are not obliged to say anything concerning the matter, but you may, if you so desire, make a written or oral statement concerning the matter in accordance with Discipline Regulations. I must, however, warn you that any such statement may be used in any subsequent disciplinary proceedings. Finally, the fact that this notice has been served on you does not necessarily mean that disciplinary action will be taken. The intention is to inform you of matters under investigation and, therefore, to safeguard your own interests."

Lyle then handed a copy of the silent Walker, who was clearly shocked as he sat, determined not to make any verbal reply to this formal notification. His only reaction was to say nothing and get out of there as quickly as he could. The thought of maybe having to get himself some legal representation filled him with dread, knowing he was well overdrawn at the bank as it was, and his credit cards were maxed out. He cursed his addiction to the horses, but he couldn't leave Ladbrokes alone. His doctor had put him on some new pills on the market, *beta blockers* he thought, supposed to help with controlling his heart beat, as he stepped out the front doors of the building, and headed back towards St. Thomas' Hospital and Westminster Bridge.

*

"Ah. Come in Maurice I wanted to have a word with you," said Boles as if he was greeting a long lost friend.

Branch sat on the upright chair opposite Boles and imposing desk, despite being invited towards the easy chairs and the coffee table already set with two china cups.

"No I'm fine. I wanted to speak to you too."

Boles was mystified and wondering why such irreverence for his position in the Force.

Branch wasted no time, "I've had enough I'm putting in my ticket. I've checked my figures and my pension will be enough. All this crap with the Pickpocket Squad did it. I told you we didn't have to go steaming in on a raid, particularly as we didn't have statements of complaint from Jones or McMurray. Fucking stupid. Basic rules of the game and you as officer in charge of professional standards in the Force, ignored the rules of engagement. Worse still, you tried to dump the whole shitstorm on me and the others. Now you've got them trying to cover up the mess, two dips who say at least one of your officer's is bent, you've got a squad who it seems have done very little wrong and now they're suing you. Well, guess what? I've had enough so I'm going."

Alarmed at the tirade Boles said, "Maurice, I've got the answer back on the Director of Public Prosecutions report that the Inspectorate did. You're in the clear, not in the public interest to take the case any further. Just words of guidance for each of you, which of course I give."

"I've got to the stage where I actually don't give a fuck what you say. In fact, you're mixing me up with someone who cares what you say. You've got no idea how to do the job, you're not a detective. You should've left this to me."

"May I just remind you who you're talking to, Branch. I am the Deputy Chief and as such, I am superior to you, so I'll thank you to be more courteous in your language."

Maurice 'barked' back, "You might be senior to me, but never are you superior to me. How fucking dare you? Just so you know, today is my last day. I've got plenty of annual leave and time owing to me to cover my notice, so I'm off. Bye."

With that Branch left Boles to try and comprehend what had just transpired, as a degree of panic in his own mind began to grow.

22

BEST SERVED COLD

Spooner made his way round to the Command suite to see Boles and knocking and entering said, "Good morning, sir. I've just been looking for Mr. Branch but I understand he's taken the day off. How can I help you sir?"

Boles looked up from the papers on his desk and said, "Right. I'm afraid we won't be seeing Branch anymore. He's submitted his papers for resignation. A great loss to us all, I know, but he feels he's done his time, and retirement beckons. Now that leaves us with a bit of a vacuum, which I want you to fill temporarily, and of course it follows you'll be remunerated for it. So what I want you to do is to get hold of Secrett and Dennison, and the three of you come and see me at two this afternoon, as I have the conclusion of the investigation conducted by the chief of Surrey Police. Don't ask anything because I won't tell you. Now out you go. Go on get on with it."

Two o'clock couldn't come quick enough for the three who were led into the room by Boles to the upright chairs ranged in front of his desk as he sat back into his leather chair. They resisted the temptation to speak until they were spoken to. Boles effectively outlined where they had fallen short of his expectation on professionalism, neatly sidestepping the fact that the whole mess had been driven by him in the first place. He summarised the the report and its findings, together with the decision that the whole episode — although it appeared each of them had committed offences of malfeasance in public office for which they could be successfully prosecuted — it was thought not in the public interest to proceed criminally with it, thereby ensuring the Force image was intact. It was therefore left to Boles to decide what course should be taken, the only caveat being that unbeknown to them, none of the three were to progress any further through promotion in the force. In consequence, Boles told them he would give each of them words of guidance as to their future conduct, without revealing the restriction on their advancement. This lowest form disciplinary sanction is something no officer can refuse to accept. The fact they've been given such guidance is recorded on their personal records and remains there for a period of two years, but that's as far as it goes. They're not required to sign anything and there is no right of appeal. So as far as Boles was concerned, job done!

*

Commander Ed Brown lit his familiar half Corona as his secretary left his office having delivered the mornings selection of correspondence demanding his attention and decision to his secretary. Next came the morning cup of coffee delivered by his Detective Sergeant responsible for

Special Branch liaison and Box 500 enquiries with the security services.

"There's only a couple of small things to note, sir, relating to our friends across the water and their most recent activities," said the sergeant, who enjoyed talking in riddles, albeit both knew he was referring to provisional IRA. The guv'nor's phone ringing was the cue for him to leave and leave the boss to it.

Commander Brown recognised the voice straight away, it was Boles. "Hello Commander it's the Deputy Chief here. I wanted to bring you up to date on the Pickpocket Squad enquiry together with my proposals."

Brown remained silent waiting for Boles to declare his hand. "As you are aware, this was an investigation which admittedly has taken some time, not least being complicated by extraneous matters which I needn't go into now. The result of the investigation was submitted for legal advice as to whether any of the squad had committed criminal offences, whether there was perjury, corruption or indeed malfeasance in public office, or a conspiracy to commit any of those. It is that which has taken the time which has doubtless led to the officers' perhaps understandable frustration at not getting the regular monthly updates which ordinarily the investigators would strive to achieve. Be that as it may I have decided each of the officers should receive words of guidance, including Detective Inspector Trebor,"

Ed Brown was aware of the efforts by the squad members to sue Boles and his cohorts, but resisted the temptation to say that he was aware of the impending litigation, or indeed, that he'd assist them in any way he could. His contact on the

Sunday Times did a good spread on the injustice meted out on his officers and his friendship with the editor of the Police Review, a magazine for coppers, helped in stopping the rough justice going any further. His own self-preservation was important to him, so anything he did would be covert and surreptitious; after all, he still had took work with this less than competent, dangerous idiot, although he didn't say so of course.

Boles went on, "Brown I want you to give those words of guidance, I think it's appropriate as they are under your command. Even to Trebor, although I must say his activities should be directed away from the world of pickpockets and robbers. It's not good for him or those that work for him. His trouble is that he wants to go running around arresting people and getting commendations."

The commanders response was short, "Now just hang on there, sir. He's an officer who leads by example. He commands the respect of those who work for him, and his team have been the most successful ever in combatting robberies and dippings throughout the transport infrastructure. It seems to me the only people complaining are those who have incurred the experience of being arrested by an incorruptible squad. They're an asset, not a curse. However, I will do as you direct."

Boles, silent at first, then said, "Be that as it may. Deal with it, will you Commander, as soon as possible?"

Click. The phone went dead. Ed Brown sat back in restrained astonishment, assuming he not was going to be given any papers. *What a way to run a circus,* he thought to himself.

*

I've just received a phone call from my guv'nor Ed Brown. He wants to see me this afternoon to give me words of guidance on all this crap investigation of my squad. He wants to see me first and he's going to see the rest of the team tomorrow. So after being under the microscope for so long on something which we almost daily encountered from the villains, it's come down to words of guidance!

Just so you know, we haven't been inactive. While the investigation into our 'naughtiness' continued, each of us separately submitted recorded delivery letters to Boles and the Police Committee who he's answerable to, alleging a conspiracy to pervert the course of justice, malfeasance in public office and so on. The response was to say that it was not a public complaint as we were part of the Force and they would not acknowledge our allegations, but the information would form part of any investigation into us. Our respective parents or relations were appalled at this stance. My father wrote to them as well, as did the relations of the other officers. Their answer to that was to say that because they were our relatives, it was as if we were making the complaint. So therefore they would not record it as a public complaint either. My dad then wrote to the Home Secretary, making it clear it was a public complaint. That didn't work either, he simply passed it across to Boles as head of discipline, and again we were 'stonewalled'.

Boles has left us with no option but to go public and also continue with our civil action. His choice, his lookout!

*

279

Detective Inspector Walker stood towards the end of the platform near the tunnel wall as he looked across at the silhouette tiles of Queen Victoria denoting that this was indeed the Victoria line at Victoria Underground Station. A heavy cold demanded his constant attention to blowing nose as he waited for the next northbound train to take him to Oxford Circus. He'd double dosed on his beta blockers from his doctor for his heart as well as two Lemsips to try and shake off the sensation of flu. His mind was racing through the problem he now had, created by that idiot Sutton who he thought he'd just done a favour for. He cursed his naivety over the purses and wallets, but worse still was the gun. In his contemporaneous note interview with Lyle and his sidekick Tate, he found out that it had been used in a couple of armed robberies in South London. Obviously what Sutton told him about it belonging to some old boy he was doing a favour for was was crap, pure and simple. He hated the fact he'd been had over, but the feeling of being 'fitted up' was overwhelming.

Delays on the service meant the platform was now heavily crowded. He could hear the rush of the train beyond the head wall as did the other intending passengers. A scream went up as the train emerged from the dark tunnel into the bright fluoresce lights. Walker had fallen forward on to the tracks in front of the train. Tumbling under the drivers carriage together with the blood spattered public seeing his fall, it was obvious he was going to be dead. Uniform Police were called and on scene within a couple of minutes. Their call for witnesses revealed a man in his twenties was close by Walker and ran off as he fell forward. The driver, in a state of shock had one more duty to perform: reversing the train back so the officers could gain access to the newly deceased. More officers appeared to provide a human screen as this down on the track carefully placed him in the body bags. An unenviable task, true, but not as unusual as one might think. On average two people each week fell or jumped in front of a train on the Underground system, most of which were suicides. So Walker was another statistic, the circumstances would require investigation, particularly given the man leaving the scene which may have been completely innocuous, or maybe not.

*

Bob was greeted by the guv'nor's secretary, and was offered a cup of filter coffee to take in with him which he gratefully accepted, which his mind meant the Commander was at least going to be friendly.

"Good morning sir," said Bob in a respectful tone as he occupied a chair to the side of the guv'nor's large conference table as his boss sat at the end of the table, leafing through a sheaf of papers in front of him.

"Now Bob, I'm speaking to you formally, as I've been requested to do so by Mr. Boles. The result of the enquiry into the alleged corruption of the squad has now been fully investigated and finalised. Before I go on, I can tell you that I have been instructed to speak to the other members of your squad who were like wise investigated, with, it appears, the same result. First of all I have to tell you that in future you must keep a precise and accountable pocket book register which you must submit to the Officer in Charge of the Police Station on a regular basis. I think probably monthly would be appropriate. There was comment that those investigating were not able to examine such a register when you were visited. Now say nothing until I've finished. Secondly you must keep your CID diary up to date — it's a daily requirement because it accurately records your duties, and should include everything you're engaged in during the course of your duty, such as the visit to Snow Hill Police Station to look at a prisoner arrested by Detective Constable Conroy. So you have now been given words of guidance by me, something which you know you cannot refuse to accept. It will of course be recorded on your personal file for a period of two years. So do you have anything you wish to ask or say to me?" He leant back, waiting, with a smirk on his face, he rated Bob, and hoped he'd have plenty to say and won't leave the matter to rest.

"Thank you sir. I think it's best if I deal with the points as you have raised them with me. The register — That was seized by Secrett at the time of the raid. I was not questioned about it or it's content, and I had been scrupulous in its completion because I fully appreciate how important that audit trail is. How strange they now choose to effectively deny its existence, perhaps because there was nothing wrong with the system. I'll accept their comment about officers having completed pocket books still in their property, but then they'd need them to give evidence in trials or appeals against sentence or conviction. Apparently they took issue in the use of Incident Report Books issued at Police stations. There is no reason why my officers shouldn't use them for making notes at the time, and in the absence of any Force directive, I'd rather they did that than leave it until later when their memory of an arrest is less clear."

"Secondly sir, I fully accept your guidance on the completion of my diary. All I'd say is that was I think a day out of date, no more, so I think that's a cheap shot by those investigating. As for the visit to the the City of London nick, I'd say how would I have known of the potential importance of looking through the wicket gate to see a sleeping thief who I didn't recognise and who never saw me? Can you help me, sir, with what prompted this extreme course of investigation in the first place? To that end can I ask formerly, for copies of statements of complaint made by Sutton and McMurray?"

Brown said, "I have been advised that I cannot do that because you were not complained about. Nobody impugned you, the only officer mentioned in any of the complaints and I'm not saying in each of them, was Detective Constable Conroy. So I'm afraid because you weren't complained against by name, you are not entitled to them. I cannot even tell you when those statements were made," with an air of resignation and disgust at how his best team of thief takers he'd known had been treated.

"Thank you guv. So this enquiry which has taken way over a year to reach this point, actually doesn't name any of us being involved specifically in corruption or any kind of conspiracy to pervert the course of justice. I'm obviously not taking issue with you, sir, you know that. In fact I feel if it hadn't been for you we would've been thrown to the lions. It looks like they've judged us by their own standards, I know why. They're bent, guv. We had this chat about Western before. Dennison was doing dips at the same time, and I believe Spooner was on that team as well. This has all occurred to cover their own bent activity. The statements were made after they'd done their raids and then they didn't come up to proof. That's why they've been desperate to find something on internal discipline to avoid their embarrassment."

"Bob, you say that and you might well be right and you also know I can't give you a definitive answer. I assume you're still pursuing an alternative course to resolve this to your satisfaction. Of course if I'm required to give evidence in court then I'd tell the truth, you realise that."

Bob stood believing the meeting to be over, and said, "Thank you guv, your support behind the scenes as well as upfront is deeply appreciated by all of the lads. It's not about getting money out of our action, you know that guv, it's the principle. If we don't make a stand against them, the job will never be rid of these bent bastards." Ed Brown nodded in agreement as Bob left.

So there we have it boys and girls, we've now gone full circle. You'll remember where we came in, with Boles efforts to kill off our allegations of corruption by dividing and ruling. I was summoned to see the chief as well, who also tried to put it to bed. I recorded him as well. It proved to be the right thing when he tried to lay off any responsibility to Boles! Lots of nothing to do with me, "I was upstairs collecting fares" but I'm sure there was something about corruption implied, although he couldn't be specific. The rats deserting a sinking ship it would seem. As for Spooner, Secrett and Dennison, that's their careers over hopefully, and Branch saw the writing on the wall with his early retirement.

As a matter of record I was sorry to learn of Walkers death. It's still being investigated as a suspicious death, and no we had nothing to do with it! Great temptation though! That said, had he not been so stupid in his dealings with Sutton or Jones or whatever, which led to him being raided, maybe he wouldn't have had the stress of the subsequent investigation. Who knows, maybe he'd still be alive today. Sorry, I weep no tears, he caused all this crap.

Our legal action? We won! Boles and the Force lawyers engaged in loads of sabre rattling, threatening to take us all the way to the Law Courts in the Strand. We stood firm, knowing we had a strong case despite their nuanced threats, and what I call corporate oppression. They folded at the steps to the court! We were each rewarded damages for unlawful arrest, false imprisonment and a percentage for malicious persecution and hurt. Their only stipulation is that we can never reveal this result or the amounts involved. I know you can keep a secret so fuck 'em.

It's nine thirty at night. I'm at Kings Cross waiting for my brief to turn up. She's coming with me up to Scotland on the night sleeper train while I get on with the American Express fraud. She wasn't keen on my suggestion the accommodation on the train is bunk beds. She's made it quite clear we shall be in the same bunk. Fine by me!

See you soon in the next adventure!

This book is printed on paper from sustainable sources managed under the Forest Stewardship Council (FSC) scheme.

It has been printed in the UK to reduce transportation miles and their impact upon the environment.

For every new title that Matador publishes, we plant a tree to offset CO_2, partnering with the More Trees scheme.

For more about how Matador offsets its environmental impact, see www.troubador.co.uk/about/